## "This is too spo

"It's like some mad... Hampleman to be my double. Or created me.... I feel like I'm losing my own identity...like she's becoming a part of me." Joanna began to tremble, her gaze locking with his.

Eric reached for her, drawing her to him, holding her gently, feeling her fear and, even more intensely, a longing that he sensed she felt, as well. "There are ways in which you're very different," he whispered reassuringly.

He kissed her softly. She shut her eyes, shutting out, at least for the moment, her mounting fears. And yet, even as she welcomed the warmth and passion of Eric's kiss, Joanna knew that this was a dangerous move, giving up even more of herself....

## ABOUT THE AUTHOR

Elise Title has long been fascinated by science, particularly new inventions and theories that have yet to be proven. When she started reading in the news about cold fusion, she decided to use her interest in new technology (and potential technology) as the backdrop for her next Intrigue. *The Face in the Mirror* also explores the fascinating duality of twins and Elise hopes her readers will enjoy this captivating combination. Elise lives in New Hampshire with her husband and children.

## Books by Elise Title

### HARLEQUIN INTRIGUE
97–CIRCLE OF DECEPTION
119–ALL THROUGH THE NIGHT

### HARLEQUIN TEMPTATION
203–LOVE LETTERS
223–BABY, IT'S YOU!
266–MACNAMARA AND HALL
282–TOO MANY HUSBANDS

### HARLEQUIN SUPERROMANCE
363–OUT OF THE BLUE

# The Face in the Mirror

## Elise Title

*Harlequin Books*

TORONTO • NEW YORK • LONDON
AMSTERDAM • PARIS • SYDNEY • HAMBURG
STOCKHOLM • ATHENS • TOKYO • MILAN

To Judy and Neal
with love.

Harlequin Intrigue edition published November 1990

ISBN 0-373-22149-5

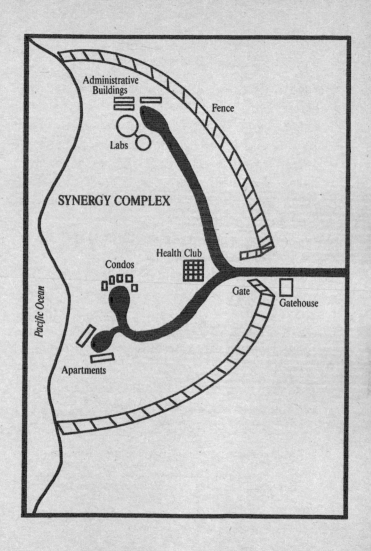

Administrative
Buildings

Fence

Labs

SYNERGY COMPLEX

Health Club

Condos

Pacific Ocean

Gate

Gatehouse

Apartments

# CAST OF CHARACTERS

*Joanna Clark*—She was confronting a side of herself she'd never dreamed of.

*Eric Logan*—Would his promise to protect both Joanna and Jennifer be impossible to keep?

*Marty Matthias*—His loyalty had never been questioned, until now.

*Hank Morgan*—Was the security chief guarding Joanna or her enemies?

*Lou Burton*—Did Hank's assistant have too many clues, or too few?

*Linda Matthias*—Joanna had cultivated her friendship, and her feelings ran deep.

*Toni Conners*—Was Jennifer's secretary the greatest threat to Joanna's masquerade?

*Gerta Hauser*—Had she changed sides once too often?

*Jennifer Hampleman*—Would Joanna have to pay the price her work demanded?

# Chapter One

Dusk mingled with a light drizzle over Manhattan, but it brought no relief from the late-July heat wave. As the raindrops hit the cement pavement, you could almost hear a little sizzle. Three young businessmen and one middle-aged woman loaded down with parcels vied for the yellow taxi that was pulling up to a luxurious East Side high-rise. The woman won, but not because of any uncharacteristic chivalry on the part of the businessmen. Their collective competitive drives had been displaced by the sight of the gorgeous, long, shapely legs of the woman exiting the cab.

Practically in unison, the three men stepped back to take in the rest of her as she set foot on the sidewalk. She was breezily dressed in a melon-colored T-shirt and a flouncy, peach-colored miniskirt. Judging from the mesmerized stares of her brand new fan club, the rest of the woman lived up to those Betty Grable legs and then some. Not one of the young men even noticed the victorious lady with all her shopping bags settle into the back seat of the big old cab and get whisked away.

With an air of abandon, the tall, trim, young woman paused on the sidewalk to sling her brown leather overnight bag over her left shoulder with a quick, expert twist that prevented her long butterscotch-colored hair from getting snared by the wide strap. Then she dug her hand into the small purse hanging from her right shoulder. She pulled out a clump of keys on a gold key chain and headed toward the doorman at the tall brass and glass door of her building. On some vague level, she was aware of being stared at by the trio of businessmen, but she was so used to that sort of thing she paid little attention.

Joanna Clark was one of New York's top photographic models. At twenty-seven, the beautiful blonde with the fascinating dark gray eyes fringed by sooty lashes had already appeared in all the leading American fashion magazines. Her career had really taken off, but her biggest coup ever had come earlier that week. While she'd been out on a week-long shoot in Taos, New Mexico, her agent had phoned to give her the great news. *Elle* wanted her for a major spread and a cover photo. The cover spot on that internationally acclaimed haute couture magazine would make Joanna's face world famous. The shoot was to start in Paris on September fourth. Her agent had already booked her flight and promised to keep her August schedule light so she'd be at her shining best when she landed in Paris.

Joanna had been so excited by the deal with *Elle*, she'd worked even harder than usual on her Taos shoot, finishing up a day ahead of schedule.

Only after picking up her mail in the lobby and stepping into the elevator did Joanna give in to her exhaustion. She'd held it carefully in check all through the grueling week of shooting under the desert sun. At this moment, leaning against the elevator wall, she longed for nothing more than a delicious bubble bath and a good night's sleep in her own bed.

Getting out on the fourteenth floor, Joanna gave her thick pile of mail a cursory check as she headed for her door. Realizing that she was too wilted and bleary-eyed to sort through the stack of bills, flyers and letters now, she decided to postpone it until the next morning.

She slid her apartment key into the lock and opened her door, switched on the hall light, dropped her pile of mail and her purse on the entry table and dipped her left shoulder so that her overnight bag thumped to the carpeted floor. The air-conditioned apartment was delightfully cool. Joanna slipped out of her sandals. Her stomach gave a little grumble, reminding her how little of her in-flight meal she'd eaten. She thought about making herself an omelet. But first things first—a warm, relaxing bath.

She was almost halfway across her living room on her way to her bedroom and adjoining bath when she stopped cold in her tracks, suddenly struck by something odd. Normally, when she set a pile of mail or a bag of groceries or any large package down on her front hall table she'd had to nudge aside her large crystal swan sculpture. Rose, Joanna's twice-weekly cleaning lady, had a thing about symmetry and was fanatical about setting it precisely in the center of the table.

So how come, this time she hadn't had to move the swan out of the way when she'd dumped everything on the table, Joanna wondered?

She swiveled around to check the sculpture, a puzzled frown marring her smooth forehead. It was off center, several inches to the left, just enough of a distance to have allowed her to dump her things there without disturbing it.

That's weird, she mused, certain she hadn't moved it herself before leaving for Taos. And she'd given Rose the past week off. No one else had a key except the janitor, who had to have a good reason, like a pipe bursting or a fire, for entering her apartment in her absence. And when he did enter, he always left a note on the front door. There'd been no note.

Joanna's frown deepened as an uneasy and downright eerie feeling started creeping up her spine. It was as if the apartment itself was telepathically sending her a message that all was not quite right. She turned her full attention to her living room, trying to discern if anything was missing or misplaced.

On casual inspection, she didn't spot anything. Her state-of-the-art stereo equipment, twenty-five-inch color TV and VCR were all in place in the antique pine wardrobe she used as an entertainment center. Her rather expensive pair of nineteenth-century English figurines were still on the mantel above the fireplace. Her few original paintings, some of them of modest value, hung on her ivory-painted walls.

She was about to shrug off her worry, telling herself she must have unknowingly moved the crystal swan herself before heading off for Taos, when her gaze was drawn to her glass-topped coffee table. Everything was there: a large gray and coral pottery bowl; a small green lacquered box where she kept her matches; her telephone; and a tidy pile of the latest fashion magazines.

Joanna dragged a breath deep into her lungs, trying to steady her mounting trepidation as she zeroed in on the pile of magazines. She was absolutely certain that when she'd left for her shoot, her latest *Glamour* magazine had been on top. Now a June *Mademoiselle* was on top. Someone had been here in her apartment. Joanna was certain of it now.

But who? And why? Certainly, she thought, any robber worth his salt would have stripped the place clean of valuables. And then an icy clutch of fear gripped her chest as a far more terrifying question popped into her mind. Could the tidy intruder still be in the apartment? Had she caught him in the act of surveying her belongs before selecting which items to steal?

Instinct more than common sense made her grab for her telephone on the coffee table to call for help.

Joanna's mind, temporarily numbed by fear, took several seconds to register that there was no dial tone; that nothing at all had happened when she pressed the buttons for 911. Reflexively she tapped down several times on the clicker built into the receiver. Nothing happened. The line was dead.

Dead. The word reverberated in her head.

Even as she held on to the useless receiver, her eyes were drawn to her bedroom door. It was ajar. Joanna was certain she'd shut it firmly before taking off for New Mexico. It was her habit to keep that door closed. While she kept the rest of her apartment neat and tidy, she was sometimes careless about her clothes, especially when she was hurrying off for a shoot. Since her bedroom opened onto the living room, she made it a point to keep that door shut unless Rose had just been in to tidy up, or when she was home alone.

Home alone...

Fear gripped her. Was she alone? Was the intruder, even at this very moment, standing just inside her bedroom, watching her through the crack in her bedroom door?

She had to get out of the apartment. Get out fast. Not take any chances. Certainly not take another step toward that bedroom door to confirm her increasingly growing belief that the intruder was, indeed, in there, watching her.

Her hand released its grip on the phone as if it were a venomous snake. Quickly, terror driving her, she broke into a run for the hall.

Even though a part of Joanna was already convinced that an intruder was lurking in the apartment, it in no way prepared her for the unfamiliar, deep masculine voice that ordered her to a halt. She had one foot in the hall, one foot still in the living room, but she froze mid-step, especially stunned as the intruder's order hadn't been simply, "Stop." It had been, "Stop, Joanna."

His calling her by her first name felt obscenely personal. It made her skin crawl. She didn't have a name plate on her front door and she was listed on the tenants' roster and mailbox as J. Clark downstairs. The intruder could only have learned her given name from riffling through her belongings.

She shuddered, all of her muscles contracting with fear and rubber-legged shock and, crazy as it was given her terror, a rush of outrage. How dare some thug come into her private domain, touch her personal possessions, cause her fear in a space she had always felt safe in?

"Please, don't be alarmed, Joanna," the man said to her stiff back. His voice was disquietingly pleasant.

She looked longingly at her front door, less than ten feet away. Could she make it? Could she reach the door, unlock it and get out before he reached her? She had to take the chance....

He must have been reading her mind. In a voice that sounded oddly sympathetic, he said, "I have to tell you I'm holding a gun. Please, Joanna. Come back into the living room and sit down. I just want to talk to you. I'm not going to hurt you."

Joanna's only move was a quick motion of her head in his direction to confirm the reality of the weapon. She didn't even turn far enough to see the man himself. All she saw was the gun. It was pointed right at her, the hand holding it rock steady.

Joanna's mind began to churn. What if the man wasn't a thief. Maybe all of her valuables were still in place because he never had any intention of stealing them. What if he were a madman—a rapist, a murderer, both? What if he'd been lying in wait for her, occupying himself with a study of her belongings until she came home....

If only she hadn't put in those extra hours on the shoot. If only she'd arrived home tomorrow as expected. Maybe he'd have grown weary of waiting for her. Maybe... maybe...

She deliberately kept her eyes off the man's face, afraid to discover he was wearing some hideous mask or stocking to camouflage his appearance. Or worse still, if he wasn't hiding behind a disguise, it might mean he wasn't concerned because he didn't intend to leave her in any condition to identify him....

Even as her eyes remained fixed on the yawning black hole of the gun barrel, she couldn't keep from imagining what he might look like. She had flashing visions of a hard, taunting face with leering grin, a trickle of saliva edging out of the corner of his mouth. She could picture his eyes. Blue, the kind of icy, vacant blue eyes that broadcast insanity, depravity...

*Do something. Say something,* she told herself, unable to tolerate her feeling of helplessness. Maybe he was just an ordinary armed burglar caught in the act, trying to calm her down and talk himself out of there.

In a voice heavy with desperation and breathless terror, she began to plead with the intruder.

"Look...take anything...everything you want." She made a wild sweeping gesture with her arm. "Just take it all and get out of here. I won't say...a word. I'm...insured. It's...no problem. I...I don't even know what you look like. I swear, I didn't see anything but the gun. I'll just close my eyes and pretend...I came home after...after you left. Some of these things are worth a lot of money. And...and there's cash in...in my purse. Almost three hundred dollars. All you have to do—" Her words were fumbling and tripping over themselves in a kind of babbling frenzy.

He cut her off, still maintaining that calming tone. "I'm not a burglar, Joanna. Honestly."

Was that bit of honesty meant to console her? If anything, it only confirmed her very worst fear. If he didn't want her stuff, he had to want...her.

Joanna felt faint. Only the terror of what he might do to her yielding, unconscious body kept her from collapsing in a heap on the spot. She had to keep her wits about her. She had to...what? Humor him? Submit to his commands? Scold him into submission? Hah! That would be like a woman about to be hanged demanding that the hangman remove the noose from around her neck this very instant. Fat chance!

"Look," he said, "it'll be a lot easier for us to talk if you come back into the living room and sit down. I swear to you, I have no intention of harming you in any way."

For all her terror, Joanna heard herself laugh disbelievingly. "If you don't want to harm me, why the gun?" Her throat was so dry her voice came across as a mere croak. She still had made no move to obey him. She felt suspended. Her body was still facing the front door, only her head turned in his direction, her dark eyes glued to the gun in his hand.

He followed her gaze. "I'll gladly put it away if you'll come and sit down and let me explain."

"Explain what?" A hint of outrage mingled with the panic in her voice.

"You weren't due home until tomorrow. I never expected we'd meet this way."

His remark about her arrival date completely threw her off guard. How did he know...? Without thinking, she glanced up at his face. The surprise and relief she felt were etched in her expression. There was no drool slipping out of the man's mouth. There was no leering grin. Instead a gentle, understanding smile curved his lips. And his eyes weren't cold blue, but hazel. Hazel eyes that looked bright, intelligent, as pleasant as his voice and smile. Indeed, he was attractive looking, if a bit roguish. He could have been a male model, posing for a detective picture. Only, she hastened to remind herself, he wasn't posing. And the gun in his hand didn't look like a prop.

"How did you know I wasn't due home until tomorrow? How did you get in here?" She lived on the fourteenth floor of a high-security building. She would have certainly noticed if her lock had been tampered with. How had he made it past the doorman? There was no way he could have come in through her sealed windows unless he were a combination of Superman and a ghost.

He smiled. Damn, but the man had an appealing smile. With his free hand he held up a key. "I used this."

A chill swept through her. "But...how did you get it? No one but the janitor..." Joanna stopped, going icy cold, fear overflowing, imagining the poor balding janitor, sprawled on his living room floor, blood and guts on the wall from the bullet hole this maniac must have made in his head, or his chest, before absconding with her key.

Was he some psycho who'd seen her photo in a magazine and tracked her down? If he knew she wasn't due home until tomorrow, why had he come today? Maybe he had been enacting some perverse fantasy of spending a day alone in her apartment, getting familiar with her belongings, sleeping in her bed....

"You look like you're going to pass out," he said softly. "Come on, Joanna. It's going to be okay. Maybe you want a drink? You're trembling. A drink would help settle your nerves."

*What would really help settle my nerves,* Joanna thought ruefully, *would be to figure out some way to escape.* But in order to escape she had to catch her intruder off guard. Not a very likely possibility. Unless...unless she was very clever. She struggled to think clearly.

Determinedly, she formulated a plan. A plan that just might work if she carried it out with cool, calm precision. She could do that, she told herself. She could do anything once she set her mind to it. That was part of her makeup. She hadn't made it this far on looks alone. She had brains, determination, perseverance. She had suffered adversity in the past. Okay, nothing as adverse as this—not by a long shot. Still, she did have a knack for chomping down on misfortune and turning it into something good.

"Okay," she said meekly. "I am a bit . . . shaky." As she pivoted fully round to the living room, facing him directly now, she shifted her gaze from the gun to the end table beside her couch. Then, on shaky legs—this was not part of her plan, but an unfortunate reality—she started toward her sofa.

"Okay . . . let's . . . talk," she said nervously, her hand going to her face, brushing her hair back off her forehead with an anxious gesture.

The man with the gun hesitated for a moment, studying her closely.

She was almost at the corner of the couch, reaching out a trembling hand for the end table, as if to steady herself. "Please . . . you said . . . if I cooperate . . . The gun . . ." She swallowed hard.

He nodded slowly and started toward her, but it wasn't until he was within arm's reach that he actually slipped the gun back into the inside pocket of his light blue linen jacket.

"Are you okay? Do you need help?" he asked solicitously as he watched her lean on the end table to keep herself upright.

She started to nod, meeting his concerned gaze with a dazed look. "I . . . I think . . . I'm going . . . to faint . . ." As she mumbled the words, she started to sway toward him, and he instinctively reached out for her. As he made the move that Joanna had anticipated, she made hers, reaching quickly for the brass lamp on the end table and swinging it at his head at the very moment she collapsed into his arms.

The brass base made direct contact with his left temple, and the intruder let out a sharp cry. For a moment his grip on her tightened, and Joanna feared all was lost. And then, a moment later, his hold on her loosened and, leaning heavily against her, he began to slip. Joanna pushed against his chest, his hands fell to his sides and he sank to the ivory carpet in a limp heap.

Joanna stared in horror at the blood oozing out of the gash in his temple, the gash she'd inflicted. His body was absolutely still, his eyes closed. She told herself she'd merely knocked him out. She tried to congratulate herself on having perfectly executed her plan of escape.

So why wasn't she racing for the door this very instant? Because an awful, dreadful thought assailed her—what if she hadn't merely knocked him out? What if . . . what if she had killed the man?

"Oh no, no," she said aloud, her words reverberating in the large, high-ceilinged room. She had to find out if his heart was still beating. She had to know if he was still alive.

Fighting fear and revulsion, she cautiously knelt down on one knee beside him. She couldn't get her hand to stop shaking as she slipped it inside his jacket to feel his chest.

It was beating. He wasn't dead. Her plan had worked perfectly. Now she could run to a neighbor's apartment, call the police . . .

Just as a sigh of relief was escaping her lips, just as she was about to rise to her feet and make good her escape, the man's large, strong hand suddenly shot out and gripped her wrist.

Joanna's mouth opened to let out a horrified scream, but before it escaped, the man clamped his free hand over her mouth.

Even as he winced in pain, he muttered, "That was a dirty trick."

Joanna struggled hard, trying to break free. He was surprisingly strong for a man who'd been knocked cold only moments ago. He managed not only to rise and get her to her feet, but he even maneuvered them both to the couch.

She mumbled pleadingly against his palm, which remained clamped on her mouth, as he held her in her seat.

"I'll take my hand away if you promise not to scream."

She gave a feeble nod, her large eyes wide with fear.

"Remember, I still have the gun."

Again she nodded.

He released her mouth and stuck his hand in the pocket where he'd slipped his gun. He moved his other hand from around her waist to his bloody temple, applying pressure to the wound.

He sighed wearily, his long legs stretched out in front of him so that his feet rested under the coffee table. "I certainly never expected any of this."

Joanna, shaken to the core by the series of twists and shocks that she'd faced since her arrival home, felt all of her energy drain away. "Neither did I," she said flatly, staring in front of her with a numb expression.

The intruder took his hand away from his wound, fumbling in his trouser pocket.

Joanna said nothing, but she did turn toward him and get in a quick glance at the gash before he pressed a white linen handkerchief against it. She could tell it wasn't all that bad, but the man certainly had to be in pain. Surprisingly, he caught her eye and smiled, the smile holding a certain degree of admiration.

"I never saw it coming," he admitted. "You're a quick thinker, Joanna. And you certainly have lightning-fast reflexes."

"Not fast enough," she muttered, ruing her overdeveloped conscience.

His smile deepened. "Now, will you give me a chance to explain everything?"

She shrugged in defeat, her arms crossed over her chest. "I guess I've run out of other options."

"Well, that's a relief anyway," he said, laughing wryly as he reached into his inside jacket pocket.

As he started to pull his hand out of his pocket, Joanna stiffened.

"Relax," he said.

Instead of the gun which Joanna fully expected to be facing once again, she was surprised to see a thin, black leather billfold in his hand.

He tossed it into her lap.

She gave him a wary, sideways glance.

"Go on, open it," he said, watching her closely, his expression one of anticipation.

She hesitated for a moment before reaching for it. Then, picking it up she realized it wasn't designed to hold money at all. On the inside right flap was a head shot of the man who was sitting beside her. Synergy Labs was embossed across the bottom half, Code Red printed below. The man was actually more attractive in person, but not everyone was photogenic. On the left flap was an ID card. She examined it for such a long time that the look of anticipation on the man's face turned to puzzlement.

Joanna let the leather ID case drop to the couch as if to avoid contaminating contact. Then she looked sideways at the man beside her, her dark, arresting eyes still reflecting fear and distrust. "Dr. Eric Logan? A chemist?" Was that supposed to explain anything? Was that supposed to calm her down, make her less afraid of him? Her head started to throb, and she gave an involuntary shudder. Dr. Jekyll had been a chemist, too.

## Chapter Two

Dr. Eric Logan smiled at Joanna's skeptical glare and took back the ID. "It's legit. I am a chemist. Got my doctorate from Cal. Tech. I'll show you my degree. It's hanging on a wall in my office at Synergy Labs out in Los Verdes, California." He flipped the ID open again and held it in her direction. "Granted, I don't take a great picture, but I'm sure you can tell it's me. And, since Synergy Labs is a government-run nuclear energy research center, I had to go through a rigorous security check to get a Code Red clearance. See, it's written right under the photo...."

Joanna's fear was diverted by a rush of bitter anger. "And that gives you the right to do heaven-only-knows-what to my poor janitor so you could steal a key to my apartment? That gives you the right to snoop through all my personal belongings, hold a gun on me, cut my phone line, assault me...?"

"Whoa, firstly I didn't do anything to your phone. It wasn't working when I got here, which was annoying because I needed to make a call. Maybe you forgot to pay your bill."

Joanna opened her mouth in indignation, but the man went right on. "And as for assault," he said, holding out his bloody handkerchief for inspection. "You're the only one who did any assaulting."

Her dark eyes gleamed with fury. "What did you expect me to do? Stand around and let you . . . ?" She couldn't finish the sentence. All the possibilities were too dreadful to verbalize.

"I keep telling you I'm not a robber." He paused, comprehension showing on his face. "Oh . . . you thought I was going to . . . attack you . . . rape you?"

"I wouldn't put that question in the past tense," she admitted without stopping to think.

To her surprise, he gave her a slightly roguish smile. "You are very tantalizing, Joanna—even more beautiful in person than in those magazines." He motioned to the pile on the table, confirming what she already knew, that he'd gone through them. There were spreads of her in each one. "But I'm not that kind of guy. When I'm interested in an intimate relationship with a woman, I usually manage to win her over with my charm and reasonably okay looks."

Okay looks? The man was too good-looking by far. Which was part and parcel of her continuing distrust and fear. While it was true that he didn't resemble her stereotype of a perverted rapist, it was just as true that he didn't look like a typical scientist, either. For all she knew the ID was a complete phony. Or maybe he'd stolen it from the real Dr. Eric Logan and simply exchanged photos.

For a sickening moment she had an image of the poor chemist lying dead in his Los Verdes office in a pool of blood. . . .

She stared at the bloody handkerchief still in the man's hand, then she stared back at the gash in his temple. It was starting to bleed again. And her mind was starting to function once more. Maybe all was not lost.

"Your head . . . it looks pretty bad. I've got a first-aid kit in the bathroom."

"How are you at administering first aid?"

She wasn't foolish enough to think he'd actually leave her here in the living room while he went off to tend to his wound alone in the bathroom. "Not bad."

He smiled. "I bet you're good at everything you do."

She barely heard his remark, nodding distractedly. Meanwhile, her mind was racing, trying to sort through her next plan of attack. All she had to do was catch him off guard just one more time, snatch up her hair dryer in the bathroom—not as heavy as the brass lamp, but this time she'd swing harder and not wait around to check on his heartbeat. She'd let the police do that. Let them clarify his credentials. Let them find out what he was doing in her apartment and how he'd gotten in.

He rose to his feet. "Lead the way."

She stood up, saying caustically, "Why? Don't you already know your way around the place?"

He scratched at his jaw and actually gave her a sheepish smile. Joanna thought she'd scored a point.

But she hadn't.

His gun reappeared in his hand, and she understood fully why he wanted her in front of him. He didn't trust her.

Any more than she trusted him.

Unfortunately, Joanna thought despairingly, he had a definite advantage in the trust department, at least as long as he had that gun in his possession. So much for the great hair dryer plan. He could squeeze off a shot long before that dryer made it to his skull.

He saw her stare wanly at the gun. "I'm sorry, Joanna. It's just, right now, I can't take the chance of you having another...fainting spell. You get dizzy and I pass out."

Joanna didn't find his attempt at humor at all amusing. Did scientists have a sense of humor? Did rapists? Murderers?

"If it eases your mind any, I never met your janitor," he said as he followed her across the living room to her bedroom.

Joanna came to an abrupt stop and swung around. If she hadn't jumped back a step the gun in "Logan's" hand would have stuck right into her rib cage.

"If you never met the janitor, how did you get a key to my apartment?"

"I'll explain all that. Later." He motioned her to turn around and continue walking. His free hand was once again pressing his handkerchief against his bleeding temple.

Joanna hesitated at the door. She was more than a little reluctant to enter her bedroom with him.

"I promise, Joanna, I'm not a rapist," he said, guessing again at what she was thinking. "Scout's honor."

Joanna had no choice, since he had the gun, but she did move very quickly through her bedroom, giving a little shiver as she thought about Dr. Eric Logan, or whoever he really was, going through her lingerie drawers, the personal papers in her desk....

"I was a devoted Boy Scout for years. Troup 84 in San Diego, California," he went on conversationally. "That's where I grew up. You should have seen all the merit badges I won. It made my Scout leader real proud."

"And just what would your Scout leader think of you now?" she asked acerbically, stepping into the bathroom, her "Boy Scout" right behind her, gun in hand.

He grinned. "It would take some explaining but he'd understand."

"Terrific. He must have been one heck of a role model," she muttered, reaching under the sink for her first-aid kit, wistfully eyeing the hair dryer beside it.

She was not exactly gentle in ministering to his wound, but she was quick and efficient as she cleaned and bandaged it. Being confined with the man in the small bathroom was even more nerve-racking than being with him in the living room where, at least, she had a little breathing space. She wanted out of there as soon as possible.

When she exited, he was right behind her.

"How about that drink?" he suggested.

Wanting to stay clearheaded and stave off the exhaustion that was closing in on her, she suggested coffee.

"Sounds good," he said amiably.

Her kitchen was down the hall from the living room. Once again, she was "coaxed" into leading the way.

The kitchen, compact and modern, with a breakfast nook under a bay window at the end, looked undisturbed at first glance, but Joanna observed that the row of canisters on the butcher-block counter was closer to the stove than usual. So, he'd had time to search through this room, too. What in the world was he looking for? What could he hope to find in her white formica cabinets, in her utensil drawers? Maybe he'd been waiting a long time and simply gotten bored...or hungry. Maybe he just wanted to know whatever he could find out about his "prey."

Joanna shivered. Nothing about this mysterious man made any sense to her. None of his behavior, manner, remarks, helped her sort out the puzzle of his presence or his intentions in any way.

"Cozy," he said politely.

"Yeah, make yourself right at home." The snide remark slipped out. She was amazed that she could actually be cynical given the precariousness of her situation. She eyed her toaster. Could she fling it at him fast enough...? Never.

"How about if I put the gun away again? Will that help?"

"It's a start," she said, surprised by his accommodation.

She watched him slip the gun back into the inside pocket of his jacket. But as he made that move, he also made a move closer to her. She could see they were going to be making that pot of coffee together.

"Okay," she said, after they'd completed the task of putting the coffee up to brew, "anytime you want to explain, go ahead. You can start with how you got the key to my apartment."

He was leaning against the counter, observing her contemplatively. "I think I should start by telling you that I came to New York to obtain your help. Vital help."

Joanna gave him a double take. Of all the possible explanations he might have given, that one had never occurred to her. And to think there'd been a moment or two back there when she'd actually started thinking maybe the man was sane. What a fool she'd been. Next he was probably going to tell her he needed her to help him fight little green people from Mars.

He continued watching her. "This isn't exactly the way I planned to go about it."

"How exactly did you plan it?"

"I had every intention of our first meeting being much more conventional. I was going to call you tomorrow..." He paused. "There, another reason why I wouldn't have tampered with your phone. Anyway, I was going to ask you to lunch..."

"What makes you think I would have accepted a lunch date with a total stranger?"

He didn't answer immediately. Instead, he reached for mugs from a cupboard—of course, he knew where she kept them—poured two cups of coffee and motioned for her to join him at the kitchen table.

When they were both seated he leveled his gaze on hers. "I planned to tell you I was *Elle*'s American representative and needed to go over some details with you for your September shoot. I have a feeling you'd have accepted my invitation. It was going to be at one of Manhattan's four-star restaurants." He sighed. "Too bad. I've got to level with you. The food in Los Verdes isn't exactly the four-star variety. But you probably don't eat much anyway. I mean, models don't, do they?''

Joanna was listening to him in a daze. "How did you know about *Elle*? My agent?"

He took another swallow of coffee. Then, skipping over her question, he merely continued on. "Once we'd had our lunch, I was going to explain that I'd actually misled you a bit."

"A bit?"

"I was hoping, after a good meal, you'd be more understanding...."

"I don't understand anything. Like what you are doing here in my apartment if you planned on a luncheon 'date'?"

"Well, I was just doing a...security check."

"A security check? Why?"

He gave a quirky smile. "I had to make sure you weren't into drugs, or heavy into alcohol, or anything unsavory...or too kinky."

Joanna was unaware that her mouth was hanging open as she stared at this madman in utter disbelief. "Kinky?"

"You check out A-okay."

"Oh, well, that's a relief," she said, her voice dripping sarcasm.

"As a matter of fact, I was just finishing up when you walked in. You put quite a scare into me." He grinned. "I thought you were a thief until you stepped into the living room and I got a glimpse of you. Man, was I relieved."

All Joanna could do was stare at him in utter confusion.

"I don't understand a word you're saying. I still don't know why you were doing a so-called security check."

"Before I met you and...got you involved in the...project, I had to be sure about you, that's all. It's strictly routine."

"Are you telling me you came here to recruit me for a job at your company? Well, I hate to disappoint you, but I'm perfectly content with my present occupation, and furthermore the last time I had anything to do with chemistry or physics was in high school.''

''I know that.''

Her eyes narrowed. ''Is there anything about me you don't know?''

''I don't know what it's going to take to win your cooperation,'' he said, smiling again.

''Well, let's just say you aren't off to a winning start.''

His smile broadened to a grin. ''I know that, too.''

''Look mister, cut to the chase.''

''You can call me Eric.''

Joanna glared at him.

He exhaled a full breath. ''Okay. The chase is, we need you at Synergy Labs for a special assignment.''

''Gee, my schedule is pretty well booked. Anyway, why would a nuclear lab need the help of a model?''

''Not any model, Joanna. It had to be you,'' he said emphatically.

She did not like the way he said that. There was something very final, very uncompromising in his tone.

''We're quite willing to pay you for your services. Perhaps not as much as your hourly modeling rate, but . . .''

''What services?''

He stuck his hand inside his jacket.

*Oh no,* she thought, her panic returning in a flood, *not the gun again.*

But it wasn't the gun. It was the ID again. This time he opened it and turned it toward her.

She didn't look at it. ''You showed me that already. It didn't fill me with confidence before and it doesn't now.''

He smiled at her. ''You're tough, Joanna. That's good.''

*Good for what?* she wondered despairingly.

''This isn't my ID. It's the ID of one of the physicists at Synergy Labs. Have a look.''

Joanna looked. The physicist was female, Dr. Jennifer Hampleman. Also with Code Red clearance. The photo showed a youngish woman with horn-rimmed glasses that Ralph Lauren would have cringed at, mousy brown hair severely pulled back from her face, and a dour, mug-shot expression.

"At least she looks like a scientist," Joanna muttered.

"And I don't?"

"Somehow I just can't picture you spending your days and nights hovering over a Bunsen burner or whatever it is chemists hover over."

"Well, it just goes to show you that you stereotype scientists as much as I used to stereotype models. I say 'used to' because after spending this fascinating time with you, Joanna, my view of models has altered. You're not only beautiful, you're smart, nervy—"

"Look, it's not that I don't appreciate the compliments...and maybe you have a point about stereotypes, but—"

"Okay, I guess I should play it absolutely straight with you if I want to win you over." He gave her one of those charming "win the ladies over" smiles of his.

Joanna, however, wasn't about to be won over. Not by a long shot. She kept her gaze wary, her mouth compressed in a tight line.

"The straight scoop is..." He stopped, sighing deeply.

Okay, she thought, here comes the little green men story.

"I've got to tell you, Joanna, you've thrown me a little. I had this great speech all worked out...for tomorrow."

"If you drag this out much longer, it'll be tomorrow," she said dryly.

He laughed. "First, look at the photo of Jennifer again. Inspect it very closely. Really study it."

Reluctantly Joanna did as he asked. She took the ID and scrutinized the photo. As she did, she developed an odd sensation in the pit of her stomach. Take away the unflattering glasses, imagine the mousy brown hair several shades lighter, falling loosely from the physicist's shoulders instead of pulled back from her face, put a smile on those serious lips...

"It's hard to tell from the photo," Logan said softly, "but her eyes are the same dark, smoky gray as yours, with the same thick, black lashes."

Joanna kept staring at the photo. She opened her mouth to speak, but she found herself speechless.

"Yes," he said, "the similarities are remarkable. In person, even more so."

"Well, I admit there's a little..."

"Wait." He retrieved a folded-up magazine page from his pocket and passed it over to her. She regarded him skeptically, then unfolded it. It was a perfume ad layout, from *Harper's Bazaar*'s May issue, featuring Joanna as a doctor. She was fitted with stylish horn-rimmed glasses, wearing a white lab coat, and while her hair wasn't done in the physicist's severe style, it was pulled back off her face to give her a more crisp, professional look.

Joanna stared at the layout and then at the photo of Hampleman, then at the layout again, her head reeling.

"How did you come across this ad?" Joanna's voice quivered. The similarity of the face in that ad and the photo of Dr. Jennifer Hampleman was more than striking. If Joanna hadn't been certain she was an only child...?

"I know. Its probably a little shocking to discover there's someone out there that looks so much like you. But," he added, trying for a lighthearted note, "you don't have to worry about any competition. Jen is devoted to her work. She's one of the most brilliant people in our field."

Her eyes clicked up at him. "Who are you, really? What do you want?"

"I want you to impersonate Jen over at Synergy Labs. Just for a few weeks."

"You're crazy. You really are crazy."

"Nothing crazy about it, Joanna. You'll be perfect. Oh, we'll need to make a few adjustments...."

"A few adjustments? Come on, Logan. Okay, granted there are certain similarities. I have to admit it's amazing what a good beautician and an expert touch of makeup will do for a person. When you get back to your lab you ought to tell her...."

"I'm not going to see her when I get back to the lab. And anyway, Jen would never go for it. Actually, I think she's gone out of her way to appear...as unattractive as possible. Beautiful women are often not taken seriously."

"Where is she?"

"She's not at the labs at the moment. That's why we need you."

Joanna could feel all the color drain from her face. What if he'd murdered this poor Hampleman woman and wanted her to fill in so suspicions wouldn't be raised? He'd said he needed her for two or three weeks. Maybe it was all part of an escape plan he'd hatched to get away with the murder.

"No," she said, unaware that she had spoken aloud.

"No?"

She gave him a look of sheer revulsion. "I won't do it. I won't have any part of it."

"You don't have the full picture yet."

"Oh, but I do. And you'll never get away with it."

Logan looked puzzled for a second and then he laughed. "It will be a cinch, Joanna. Especially now that I know you..."

"I won't be involved in your sick plan. You won't get away with it. Even if you kidnap me, get me to that research center, you can't watch me twenty-four hours a day...."

"Oh, but I will watch you, Joanna. Day and night. See, Jen and I sort of live together."

"Live together?" She stared back at Hampleman's photo. It was hard to imagine the two of them . . .

"We aren't lovers, Joanna, if that's what you're thinking. We're housemates."

"So where is she . . . living now?"

"I'm afraid I can't tell you that. It's classified."

"Classified?" Her tone was arch. "I bet it's classified."

He scowled. "You think I did something to Jen? Hurt her? Killed her? Boy, Joanna, you certainly seem to go from one low opinion of me to even lower ones. Robber. Assaulter. Madman. Rapist. Murderer."

"Can you prove to me she's alive?"

"In time."

"That won't cut it."

"Look, Jen is working on some very sensitive, highly classified work. To ensure the secrecy of her work, she's had to leave the lab and go into seclusion. She's close to finishing her project. Two to three weeks more, that's all it will take. But if word got out that she had suddenly left the labs for an extended time, suspicions would be raised and security would be compromised. Right now, the story is she's just gone on a long weekend break and she'll be back on Monday morning. So you see, if she doesn't show up on Monday, someone might go looking for her, might get lucky and track her down. Her work could fall into the wrong hands. Her life could be in real danger. And it would put us in terrible jeopardy, too."

"Us?"

"Us. All of us. You, me . . . everyone in the free world."

"Don't forget Mars and all the other planets," Joanna couldn't stop herself from adding, not believing a word of his cloak-and-dagger story.

"Everything I'm telling you is true, Joanna."

"Who are these people who are after Hampleman and her work?"

"Not someone from another planet," he said with a wry smile. "I know it may cause you some disillusionment about our own government, Joanna, but for all the security checks that are run on the employees of Synergy Labs, it appears somebody at the lab has been...turned."

"Turned?"

"You know...someone who decides to switch loyalties. Someone who gives, or more often sells, secrets to the bad guys."

"This is really incredible," Joanna muttered.

Logan merely sighed. "Not as incredible as the average citizen may think. Anyway, as it stands, everyone at Synergy has been led to believe Jen's come up against a dead end in her research and has given it up. They think that she was so depressed about it she had to get away for a couple of days, before going on to other projects. Obviously if she did really come back, she would have to steer clear of her work. And the research she's involved in, Joanna, is extremely important, crucial, in fact."

He leaned back in his chair. "You'd not only be paid quite well for the impersonation, Joanna, you'd be doing your country a vital service."

"My country and the whole free world."

"You still don't believe a word I'm saying, do you?"

She eyed him with suspicion. "Okay, how about if I put in a call to Synergy Labs and check out a few things."

"Like?"

"Like that there really is a Dr. Eric Logan and a Dr. Jennifer Hampleman employed at the lab. Like a description of Dr. Logan. Like confirmation that you were sent here to...hire me to impersonate Hampleman."

"I'm afraid you can't do that."

"I see," Joanna said in a low, mocking voice. "First, you say I can't speak to Jennifer Hampleman because she's in seclusion. Now you tell me I can't even speak to the person at Synergy who authorized your little trip east. Why can't I do that? Let's hear your answer for that one, Dr. Eric Logan," she said, turning a pair of dark, brightly suspicious eyes on him.

He met her wary gaze with a sheepish smile. "Well, you see, Joanna, the people at Synergy aren't exactly the ones who sent me to enlist your assistance."

# Chapter Three

"Drink your coffee, Joanna, before it gets cold." Eric Logan's eyes reflected sympathy.

But Joanna didn't want sympathy. She wanted answers. "Who sent you? What do you really want with me? How did you get in here? How did you know about *Elle*?"

Logan folded his hands on the table and gave her a long, scrutinizing look. "I'm not just a chemist, Joanna."

It was such an absurd understatement that Joanna laughed dryly.

"And I'm not an emissary from another planet," he added with a beguiling smile. "I do work for Synergy Labs as a nuclear chemist, but I'm not only there to spend long hours over Bunsen burners. I'm there to ensure that Dr. Hampleman's work is kept out of the wrong hands."

"Are you telling me you're some sort of secret agent?"

He shrugged. "Nah. That's putting too glossy a sheen on it. Makes it all too cloak and dagger."

Joanna's eyes narrowed. Logan's denial made her start thinking that this was precisely what it was about, after all. *Cloak and dagger.* If he was a secret agent, how did she know whose government he actually worked for? Now she, too, folded her hands on the table. "You have authority from someone to be here, Dr. Logan. You were given a key. You must have shown my doorman some official ID to gain access to the building. You've offered me money to impersonate this Dr. Hampleman. Which agency is it, Logan? CIA? FBI? DEA?''

Logan grinned. "I bet you were a whiz at the alphabet when you were a tot."

Her mouth pulled in a tight line. Logan observed her thoughtfully. Joanna didn't know it, but it was a carbon copy of Hampleman's expression when she was running out of patience.

"Okay, Joanna. I do have connections with a government agency." Before she could ask which one, he said, "None of the above."

Joanna's folded hands tensed. "KGB?"

He laughed. "My, oh my, so now I've gone from the rock bottom status of murdering rapist to glamorous double agent."

Joanna was getting close to the end of her fuse. "Damn it, Logan. Stop playing games with me. You said you wanted my cooperation. Well, hell is going to freeze over before—"

He raised a hand in apology. "Sorry. Really, I am sorry." He took a moment to compose himself, his expression turning serious. "The agency I work for doesn't have any initials you'd be familiar with. It's a small bureau of specially trained scientists who happen to be, despite our cynical times, highly patriotic."

Joanna eyed him closely. She couldn't tell if he was being serious or pulling her leg. "I want to speak to your superior. Give me his number..."

"Your phone is out of order, remember?"

"So that's why you cut the line."

"I didn't cut the line." He sighed. "But I couldn't let you make that call even if the phone was working." He leaned a little closer to her. "I'm afraid I'm your only contact. That's how the bureau operates. That's how it keeps from getting popular initials.''

"I don't believe a word you're telling me, Logan."

He drew back, tipped his chair a little, lowered his jaw and regarded her in silence for a few moments. "This *Elle* assignment means a lot to you."

Joanna stiffened, but she didn't respond.

Logan didn't seem to mind. "You've got a flight booked to Paris in four weeks' time."

"If you're trying to tell me that I'd have plenty of time to take your . . . assignment . . . forget it."

"I'm trying to tell you, Joanna, that unless you take the assignment, I'm afraid you might have to cancel that trip to Paris."

Joanna forced herself to remain coolly detached. "And why is that, Mr. Logan?"

He took a sip of his now lukewarm coffee. Joanna had yet to touch hers. "I'm sorry to tell you this, but your passport has been put on temporary hold. How temporary . . . ?" He shrugged, not bothering to complete the sentence.

"You're crazy. My passport is in perfect order. I just used it last month to do a shoot in Guatemala."

"Some question of diamond smuggling," Logan went on blithely.

"You *are* crazy."

"Probably just some dumb foul-up, but who knows how long it will take to sort out. A real pity if it doesn't get straightened out before you have to be in Paris for that major shoot."

"I don't believe you. I would have received some kind of notice, some . . ."

"Have you checked your mail since you came home?"

Automatically Joanna's eyes shot to the hallway.

"Go ahead. Check through it now."

She stared at Logan. Then slowly she rose.

Logan went with her, of course. They stood together in the entryway as Joanna picked up the large stack of mail on the hall table.

The notification was there. On official U.S. Immigration stationery, Joanna was informed that her passport had been temporarily revoked during which time she would be unable to travel outside of the United States.

"If you want to find a phone that's working, you can call to verify..."

She glared at him with furious indignation. "You did this? You arranged all this?"

"Well, not me personally, Joanna. But, maybe now you'll realize just how important your cooperation is to us."

"Cooperation? Cooperation? You call this getting my cooperation," she screamed, throwing the letter at him. "Well, let me tell you something, Dr. Logan, Mr. Secret Agent, whoever you are, whoever you work for, I wouldn't cooperate with you if you...if you...took my passport for good. I'll get a lawyer. I'll fight you. I'll make this precious secret agency of yours a household word by the time I'm done with you."

Logan put a calming hand on her shoulder. She shoved it off. "Don't touch me."

"Take it easy. The passport business isn't the point here, Joanna. We don't want to use coercion."

"I won't do it. Do you hear me? I won't."

"Joanna..."

"Wouldn't the public just love to know that an ordinary, upstanding citizen is being harassed—"

He cut her off. "You don't read a lot of spy books, Joanna. It happens all the time." He continued smiling, much to Joanna's fury. "Anyway, you don't want to start a public outcry. Those things get ugly. And do you really want the notoriety, all that publicity? Diamond smuggling?" He shook his head. "An ordinary, upstanding citizen? Well, maybe the public won't see it that way, Joanna. Maybe your agency, your friends, your...family...won't see it that way. You wouldn't want to upset all of them.''

Joanna went cold. *Family*. There was something about the way Logan had said the word, the pause just before and just after, the look in his eyes. What did he know about her family? Or more precisely, her mother, since her mother was all the family she had?

Logan saw the effect his words had on her. And he knew what she was worrying about—exactly what he'd intended her to be worrying about. Damn, but there were days he really hated this work.

''You're not going to make a federal case out of this, Joanna,'' Logan announced with a world-weary sigh. ''Your mother is a very fragile woman. According to her doctor—''

Joanna gasped in horror. ''You've talked to her doctors? You've been down in Palm Springs? To the sanitarium?''

''Your mother knows nothing,'' Logan assured her. ''And the psychiatrist who's been treating her merely thinks he was filling out a routine insurance form.'' He placed his hands together in front of him. ''She'd be distraught if she thought you were in some sort of trouble. It would be impossible for you to keep the news from her. And I don't think you want to do anything to...tip her over the edge.''

''I hate you,'' Joanna said with icy calm.

Logan nodded grimly. ''Yeah. Well, you don't have to be fond of me, Joanna. What you have to do is...cooperate with me. For everyone's sake.''

''And what would happen to my mother's state of mind if something were to...happen to me...in Los Verdes?''

''Nothing is going to happen to you, Joanna. You can trust me, even if you do hate me.''

She stared at him, her face expressionless. He'd won. Dr. Eric Logan held the trump card. She might risk her career, her reputation, her own state of mind, but never would she put her mother at risk. After the death of her father six years ago, her mother, a high-strung, nervous and fearful woman at the best of times, had a complete breakdown. She'd tried to take her own life. Joanna had been the one who found her, sprawled out on the floor of her bedroom, an empty vial of sleeping pills at her side. That awful vision of her mother was indelibly printed in Joanna's mind.

After a week's stay on the psychiatric ward of a general hospital, Alice Clark had remained in a severely depressed state. Joanna had arranged for her admission to a posh, private sanitarium in Palm Springs. Her parents had always spent their vacations down there and Alice Clark loved the area. Joanna had hoped a few months rest and psychiatric care would do the trick. But, while her mother's depression did lift with medication, she continued to regress. Finally Joanna resigned herself to the fact that her mother would never be able to manage independently, that she would never be able to leave the sanitarium.

Joanna thought about her confiscated passport. She'd been so high and mighty, telling Logan she could care less. But the truth was she not only needed that *Elle* assignment because of the boost it would give her modeling career, she needed the money it would bring in. While her father, a well-established obstetrician, had left a sizable insurance policy, Alice Clark's on-going medical costs had eaten away most of the inheritance he'd left. For the past couple of years, her mother's bills had rested squarely in Joanna's lap.

Finally Joanna met Logan's gaze evenly. "I don't trust you any more than I like you. And if my mother's health is in any way jeopardized, Logan, I swear I'll make you pay. Whatever I have to do, I'll make you pay."

Logan nodded, his expression tinged with admiration. "I believe you, Joanna."

"I've got a busy calendar of local shoots lined up for the next three weeks. What do I tell my agent?" she asked in a dull monotone.

"You can mail her a note. Say your mother's ill and you're going down to Florida to be with her."

Joanna flinched.

"You can also tell her that you'll definitely be on that plane for Paris next month," he added softly.

An awful abyss of helplessness confronted her. "Okay, Logan. You win. I guess I better go pack a few things." She gave him an acquiescing shrug, but Joanna was still far from convinced about Logan's credentials. What if he really was a double agent? What if he'd gotten hold of official U.S. Immigration Department stationery and typed that letter about her passport himself? And now he thought he had won. He'd guessed correctly that she'd do anything to cooperate in order to protect her mother. But for all she knew, he could have been bluffing about that. The gun, however, was no trick. Logan's determination to get her to Los Verdes was no bluff.

She'd have to bide her time, look for a place to make another move. If Logan was on the level, than he'd have to come up with more concrete proof before Joanna stopped looking for a way out. Camouflaging her refusal to give up hope, she sighed wearily.

Logan reached out a hand to her, but when he saw her cringe he immediately dropped his hand to his side. "I know you couldn't care less, Joanna, but I feel really lousy that it had to come to this. Maybe, some time down the road, you'll feel . . . differently."

She didn't say a word. Instead she walked past him, heading for her bedroom.

"Wait," he called out.

She stopped, but she didn't turn around. "What is it now?"

"Don't bother packing."

She spun around, the color instantly flowing back into her face, expectation written on her features. Had he changed his mind? Had she actually gotten to him? Was he really feeling lousy enough to cut her loose?

He saw the look, interpreted it correctly, and felt like an even bigger heel. "Jen wouldn't wear your clothes." His eyes flicked down her body, taking in the melon T-shirt and the very short, very sexy ruffled skirt which revealed Joanna's long and shapely legs.

Joanna's arms instinctively crossed over her chest, as if Logan were undressing her with his eyes.

Logan walked over to her. "I came here straight from the airport. I've got a few of Jen's things packed in my suitcase. I took them from her closet. My bag's in your bedroom."

"You've thought of everything, haven't you?" Joanna's features were hard, her voice tight.

"It goes with the job."

Ten minutes later, Joanna stepped out of the bathroom. Logan, sitting on her bed, scrutinized her closely. The drab navy shirtwaist dress fit her well. She and Hampleman were just about the same size.

"How are the shoes?" he asked.

Joanna stared down at the low-heeled black maidenly pumps. "Very chic," she said sarcastically.

"Do they fit?"

She glared at him. "Didn't my dossier give my shoe size? What about my bra size? Do I wear Hampleman's bras and undies, too?"

He smiled faintly. "Actually, yes. Just in case anyone thinks of checking Jen's laundry. We wouldn't want to raise any suspicions. Unfortunately I didn't bring any of her undergarments, but once we get to Synergy you can switch underwear and get rid of your stuff." He continued his scrutiny of her. "I know it will disappoint you, Joanna, but your dossier didn't go into every intimate detail. My guess is, though, Jen's build is similar enough to yours for you to make do with *all* of her clothes."

Joanna sneered at him. "Your guess? Don't make me laugh. You can't expect me to buy that roommates nonsense."

He smiled. "It's true. Scout's honor. My relationship with Jen is purely . . . professional. Don't get me wrong. I think she's a terrific person. Inspiringly dedicated to her work, gutsy, determined, a woman who doesn't back down easily." His smile deepened. "A lot like you, actually."

She ignored the compliment and stepped in front of her full-length mirror. After reflecting on her image for a few moments, she focused in on Logan. "It'll never work." She drew her hair away from her face, now washed clean of all makeup, per Logan's orders.

"Wait." He dug his hand into his gray leather suitcase and plucked out a brown wig already done up in the hairstyle Hampleman had worn in the ID photo. He tossed the wig to Joanna and then walked over with a pair of utilitarian horn-rimmed glasses. They were an exact duplicate of the physicist's, fitted with plain glass.

Joanna adjusted the wig on her head and then slipped on the glasses. As soon as the disguise was complete Joanna once again studied her reflection in the mirror.

She fought back a gasp, prickles of shock playing up and down her arms. It was uncanny. She swayed a little, Logan catching her by the shoulders. She was too stunned by her remarkable transformation into Dr. Jennifer Hampleman, a woman who was a perfect stranger, to balk at Logan's touch.

He, too, was studying her reflection, but instead of shock, disappointment played on his face as he examined her critically, impersonally. "No," he muttered, turning her to him.

"No. The wig won't do. It's too risky. Someone might spot it. Or you might lose it in a good breeze. I wasn't really counting on the wig. No. We'll have to do something about your hair."

Joanna stared at him in horror. "No. No, I won't."

"A quick dye job, a few snips here and there, a professional styling..."

"Styling? You call this..." she pointed to the wig, "a *style*?"

He laughed softly. "Look, personally I like your style better, but I'm not here to make personal decisions."

She backed up, bumping into the mirror. "Logan, listen to me. You swore that if I cooperated, I'd be able to get to Paris on time for the *Elle* shoot."

"I did. I'll promise you again."

"Well, I can't show up with chopped-off brown hair...."

"It'll grow. And you can dye it back to your natural shade. That is your natural shade?"

"Yes, it's my natural shade," she bit back. "And do you have any idea what my hair's going to look like, how impossible it's going to look, after two dye jobs in a matter of weeks?" She pulled off the wig, shaking out her luxuriously thick butterscotch hair. "My hair is my fortune, Logan," she hissed.

He fought back a smile. "I understand."

Forgetting all about the gun in his pocket, forgetting her earlier fear of the man, she shoved him hard in the chest. "You don't understand a thing. You think my concerns are... are dumb, superficial, inconsequential, compared to your supposedly lofty interests. What's hair texture compared to a threat to the free world, right?"

"Joanna, I'm not going to demean your concerns. You make your living by being beautiful. and I can see why you've come so far. I do understand. And I sympathize with you. You feel trapped, abused, manipulated, helpless..."

Tears sprang into Joanna's eyes as Logan gave such accurate voice to all of her feelings. She tried to blink the tears away, refusing to let Logan see that he had gotten to her, refusing to admit it even to herself.

Joanna took great pride in being able to keep her emotions in check. She was forever guarding against her emotions for fear they might get out of hand, afraid she was more her mother's child than she could admit.

Not, she always told herself, that she would become as constricted and emotionally guarded as her father. Dr. Donald Clark had taken that control of feelings to its extremes. He was a private, aloof man, strong willed, kindly but never intimate. Joanna had never seen him cry. She'd never even seen him lose his temper. She loved him, but she'd always felt intimidated by him. He'd kept everyone at a distance, everyone except his wife. With Alice, Donald Clark had been uncharacteristically solicitous. Joanna felt that her father, for all his tenderness toward her mother, was also very manipulative and overbearing. She secretly believed that her mother was a little afraid of him, too, although Alice Clark was unendingly ingratiating, and seemed to believe her husband could do no wrong. It had always upset Joanna that her mother was so dependent on her father. Joanna was terrified that if she gave up control of herself to someone else, she would be swallowed whole . . . just like her mother had been.

"Joanna."

For a moment she'd almost forgotten about Logan. Absently her hand went to her cheek. She felt the wetness. Distressed, both hands covered her face.

"Joanna," he repeated gently. "It's going to be all right. I'm sorry. I'm truly sorry."

When his arms moved around her and he drew her against him, she felt too numb and drained to protest the supportive embrace. For a few moments, she let her head drop so that her damp cheek fell against his shoulder. She was superficially aware of the tangy scent of his after-shave mixed with the impersonal odor of starch from his freshly laundered shirt. Her consciousness was focused on an inner ringing in her head. A warning?

She pushed away and Logan immediately let her go. When their eyes met she was taken aback to see a hint of disquiet in his expression. He quickly eradicated it with another of his quirky smiles. "It's a shame, Joanna, but we've got to take care of your hair."

Caught up in a maelstrom of emotions, Joanna had forgotten about her hair. "Oh please, Logan. We can manage with the wig."

"The wig won't do." He took on a crisp, almost officious air now as he glanced at his watch. "Actually, your showing up a day early works out all the better. I'll have an extra day to introduce you to your new surroundings at Synergy before you have to be at the labs." He stuffed the wig back into his suitcase, snapped it shut and lifted it by the handle. "Come on. Let's go."

"Where?"

"There's a beauty parlor just down the street." He took her by the arm, but Joanna pulled away.

"La Mirage? Oh no."

"What's the matter?"

"I'm not subjecting my hair to those butchers. If I have to do this, at least let me go to my regular hairdresser. It's just over on Madison. Madison and Sixty-eighth Street." *Yes, her own hairdresser. That was it. Vanessa. Why hadn't she thought of it before? She could get a message to Vanessa that she was being taken against her will to Synergy Labs in Los Verdes, California, by a man who was claiming to be a secret government agent. Vanessa would contact the FBI. They could get to the bottom of this. If Logan was an enemy agent or simply a madman, the authorities would*

*come after him. Hopefully in time to rescue her. Vanessa.*
*Vanessa was her last hope.*

"Sorry, Joanna. La Mirage will have to do. We can't waste time..."

"You can't just show up there without an appointment. We might end up waiting hours..."

"I don't think so. I'll offer a big tip."

"They...they know my hair...at my place, Logan. They won't do a botch job..."

His quirky smile returned. "Come on now, Joanna. I do think you are getting a little carried away about your 'fortune.'"

Anger overrode caution and she swung out her hand, intent on socking him. But Logan's reflexes had improved. He ducked the shot and grabbed her wrist, none too lightly.

"Don't get physical, Joanna. We'll both make out better in the long run."

He let her wrist go and she quickly straightened up. "I'm sorry," she muttered. "I just don't think it's asking all that much, damn it, just to let me have my hair done by my regular beautician."

He smiled at her, one of his pleasant, understanding smiles. For a moment Joanna thought he'd relent.

"Look at it this way, Joanna. Maybe you'll discover there's someone at this local beauty parlor who's just as good as your regular beautician. Maybe better. Think of how much more convenient it'll be for you to have someone just down the street."

She felt her final hope of rescue going down the drain. Had he guessed what she'd had in mind? Was it pure cunning that made him so emphatic about refusing her request?

As they left the apartment and started down the hallway to the elevator, Joanna decided she could still outfox Logan. She would somehow convince whatever hairdresser he chose for her that she was in danger and needed help. Maybe the beautician would think she was a kook, but if she was convincing, the hairdresser would probably report the message to the authorities. Joanna would have to time it right. While she was having her hair washed... Yes, that would be the best opportunity. With the water running, she couldn't be overheard.

Just the thought that there was still hope for a way out of her predicament made Joanna's step more buoyant. And, she thought, there was still the doorman. She could make eye contact with the doorman; show through her glance that she was afraid, that she was in danger. A person could convey so much with a look. And she was a professional at it.

As they stepped into the elevator and Logan pressed the button, Joanna had to scratch the doorman idea. Logan had pressed B for basement. He was taking her out through the service exit so they'd avoid having to pass the doorman at all. He gave her a quick, knowing look.

When they exited the elevator at the basement level, Joanna saw one of her neighbors coming out of the laundry room. Logan saw her, too, and immediately gripped Joanna's arm. "Don't do anything dumb," he warned in a low breath.

The neighbor, a middle-aged woman whose arms were loaded with laundry, called out, "Oh, hold that elevator for me like a dear, Joanna."

Logan's free hand held open the door. "Here you go," he said cheerily as she hurried over.

"Oh, what a day. What a day. First the phones fail, now the dryers aren't working right...."

"The phones?" Joanna gave her neighbor a surprised look.

"Don't tell me your phone is working?"

"No."

"No, of course not. The phones are out along the whole street. I had to go clear over to MacKenzie's Market on Fifty-second to use the pay phone to call the telephone repair service. And they inform me it's a problem with their computers, and then they have the nerve to tell me it could take two, maybe three days before service is restored. I tell you, Joanna, what with the muggings, the break-ins, the crazies roaming the streets, and the lousy services in this city, we should all pack up and move someplace else."

"Yes," Joanna said a little breathlessly. "Get out of the city. Now there's a thought. Someplace like—"

"Oops, sorry," Logan broke in, having deliberately let the elevator door start to close. He stuck his hand out again and got it open. "There you go. Have a nice day. And maybe you'll be lucky and they'll get the phone service restored by tomorrow." As he spoke, Joanna's neighbor stepped inside the elevator and by the time he'd finished, the door had shut.

Joanna gave him an icy look. "I was going to say, someplace like Florida."

He grinned. "Hey, think of the positive side. Now you know I didn't mess with your phone. Tell me, aren't you just a teensy bit more convinced I'm on the level?"

"I didn't say I wasn't convinced," she retorted.

He still had a firm grip on her arm. "Your mouth says yes, yes, but your eyes, Joanna...there's no, no, no in your eyes."

Fifteen minutes later Joanna was having her hair shampooed by Gwen, a small, trim brunette with a Betty Boop mouth. Logan was at the front of the shop using the telephone. This was Joanna's chance.

Hardly moving her lips, she began. "Please, you've got to help me. That man I came in with...he's kidnapping me. He's taking me to Synergy Labs in Los Verdes, California.'' She repeated the destination as the beautician scrubbed her scalp.

"Look, I..."

"No," Joanna hissed. "Don't say anything. I don't want him to spot us talking. Just listen. As soon as I leave, call the FBI. My name is Joanna Clark. The man with me says his name is Eric Logan. Dr. Eric Logan. As soon as we leave here we're heading for the airport. Most likely Kennedy. Tell the FBI the man claims to be a secret agent."

"Hey..."

"Please, I swear I'm telling you the truth. You've got to call the FBI. Just tell them everything I told you. Please."

The beautician merely nodded, giving nothing away in her expression. Joanna took it as a good sign. *Yes. Perfect. Play it cool. Neither of us can afford to give away our hand.*

Joanna spent the next half hour silently, glumly allowing her hair to be dyed a mousy brown, trimmed a good three inches, and pulled back into a severe chignon.

Logan, with narrowed, assessing eyes, oversaw the finishing touches. He was pleased. It was as good as he dared hope. Of course, Joanna had an innate sense of style that came through even with the dreary hairstyle and the drab clothes. But chances were no one at Synergy would spot it unless they were looking for it. And no one who knew Dr. Jennifer Hampleman would look for it.

Gwen removed the plastic drape from Joanna's shoulders. She caught Logan's glance in the mirror. "What do you think?"

He nodded. "Another masterpiece, Gwenny. I knew I could count on you. Good thing you got yourself set up here a day early."

The pretty brunette with the Betty Boop mouth gave Joanna an ingratiating smile. "I tried to tell ya, honey, but you didn't let me get a word in."

As Joanna's heart sank to the pit of her stomach, Gwenny's smile brightened. "Hey, you got nothing to worry about. Eric here will take good care of you."

Joanna found no comfort at all in that Betty Boop smile or in the verbal reassurances of Logan's accomplice. Nor did she find any comfort in the thought that whoever was behind this plot to substitute her for Dr. Jennifer Hampleman had covered all the bases to ensure that there would be no slipup.

As promised, Logan made a show of handing Gwenny a big tip, pointing out to Joanna that she really hadn't done a bad job of it at all.

# Chapter Four

They didn't go to Kennedy Airport. Instead, a nondescript black sedan picked up Logan and Joanna outside of La Mirage and drove straight to a private airstrip out past the potato fields on Long Island.

"Your secret agency certainly has a lot of clout," Joanna muttered acerbically, as the car pulled up in front of a small private jet. "Your own hair dressers, chauffeurs, planes. Everything so neatly arranged, so very organized. I gather your group never doubted my 'cooperation' for a minute."

He shot her a wry smile. "You might enjoy yourself, you know. Synergy is a very exclusive little compound. Besides state-of-the-art labs, we have luxury condos, a full-service health club, swimming pool, tennis. Why not think of it as a nice holiday?"

It was nearly 11:00 p.m. The rain was still coming down and the late-night air was only slightly cooler than it had been at mid-afternoon. Logan took Joanna's arm, motioning with his free hand to the driver.

The sound of the departing car filled Joanna with a sense of doom. *No turning back now.*

The gaping door of the jet beckoned and Joanna walked stiffly toward it. She stumbled on the first metal step up to the plane, then shrugged off Logan's grip and made her way smoothly up the rest of the steps.

"Is this a Synergy jet?" she asked, looking around at the sleek, classy appointments inside. Every comfort for the weary CEO.

"No. Synergy wouldn't spring for transportation like this for a mere chemist."

"Ah. The agency, then, with the mystery initials."

"What do initials matter?" he said, smiling.

The pilot, an attractive blond-haired young woman in a blue designer uniform, came back from the cockpit and greeted her two passengers with a friendly, "Hello. All set whenever you two are."

"Give us a minute to buckle up and we can take off, Danielle," Eric Logan answered cheerily. Then, addressing Joanna, he said, "Once we're airborne, we can have a bite to eat and something to drink. I bet you're starving."

Joanna vaguely recalled having been hungry when she'd first arrived home. And there was that nice, relaxing bubble bath she'd so looked forward to. A peaceful evening at home, early to bed...

And now, here she was, in the middle of the night, wearing some other woman's clothes, her hair in ruin, alone in this plane with a perfect stranger, being dragged off on some insane adventure that she didn't even vaguely understand. All she understood was that she had every reason to be scared out of her mind. She couldn't think straight. One thing was certain, though. In her wildest dreams she would never have been able to concoct a scenario like this. Would anyone ever believe it? And then the terrifying thought assailed her, Would she live to tell about it?

"I'm not hungry," she said weakly as Logan guided her to a seat.

"I suppose you'll want to strap yourself in without any help."

She did up the seat belt without so much as a glance at him.

Logan took the executive-style leather airline seat beside her and buckled up as well.

Minutes later they were soaring through black skies. Logan unclicked his belt, rose and went to a built-in bar and poured them both glasses of milk. In the refrigerator were two plates of food.

"Roast beef or turkey," he asked her.

"I told you, I'm not . . ."

"I'll split up the sandwiches then. Half roast beef, half turkey." He approached her, smiling. "See. Compromise. I give a little, you give a little."

He set her food on the fold-down tray in front of her. Joanna hesitated then took up the roast beef half. Maybe if she ate something she'd ease the gnawing pain in her gut. Even though she knew the distressing sensation had nothing to do with hunger.

Eric Logan looked pleased. He ate with gusto. Sandwich, potato salad, cole slaw and the pickle. He washed it all down with the milk and then leaned back in his seat, stretched his legs out in front of him and sighed contentedly.

Joanna glared at his self-satisfied pose and settled down into eating her food.

Logan said, "If you want to rest, the seat reclines all the way."

"I'm not tired," she said, attacking the turkey half of her sandwich.

"It's a long flight. We'll get into Los Verdes around 5:00 a.m., have some breakfast and spend a few hours in town going over some notes before we head out to Synergy."

"Notes?"

He smiled slyly. "Dossiers. On the staff. You have to be able to act as though you know them all. Hampleman's been there for sixteen months."

"This is never going to work, Logan. I'll never be able…"

"Don't worry. Hampleman was rather reclusive. Except for me, she never socialized or chit-chatted with the others. She's a very private, self-contained young woman. All work and no play." He gave her a meaningful glance.

"And what if they start asking me questions about my work?"

"That's absolutely not done. Everyone at Synergy is very protective of their projects. Whatever is known is revealed through professional papers and reports that are highly classified and may never see the light of day. No one will make inquiries about her prior work, especially the last project. It was very hush hush, right from the start. Only a handful of people even knew what she was working on and none of them were supposed to be privy to the details. Last week Hampleman made a general statement to the top echelon at Synergy, reporting that her research had not panned out and that she would henceforth be dropping all research in that area. She answered some general broad-based questions and then made it clear that the topic would no longer be open for discussion. She did a great job of convincing everyone that she was embarrassed and humiliated by her failure to produce results and wanted only to put the disaster behind her. No one will even broach the topic with you. It would be tasteless. And our friends at Synergy pride themselves on taste," he tacked on with a wry smile.

"I still say it's too risky, Logan."

"Eric, Jen. You call me Eric and I call you Jen. Starting now."

"And if I goof? If I get found out? What happens then, *Eric*?"

He leveled his warm hazel-eyed gaze on her. "You won't goof, Jen. And you won't be found out. That's why I'll be at your side. To look after you."

"To keep me in line," she said acidly.

"Don't take that attitude, Jen."

*Jen.* A perfect stranger had coerced her into a mysterious charade and was now complacently sitting here calling her Jen as though he'd been calling her that for years.

"How long have you known Hampleman?"

"I've known you for sixteen months," he said with a smile.

"How well?"

"I thought we already established that we aren't lovers, Jen."

"Then why are we living together?"

"We've deliberately led the folk at Synergy into believing we were lovers. That way we could live together and I could take care of you."

"Take care, huh? Don't you mean that Hampleman was in danger and you had to protect her."

"I mean that I was there to make sure there would be no danger."

"You really must think models are dumb, Logan."

"Come on, Joanna . . ."

"Jen. Remember?"

He swiveled in his seat to face her. "There was some reason for caution while . . . you . . . were working on your special project. Now that you're off it, there's no reason for any concern."

"If everyone's really bought that story."

"They have bought it."

"If this whole tale you've been spouting has even a word of truth to it."

"You still have doubts about me."

She laughed sharply. "Oh, Logan, you are a master of understatement."

"I'm on your side, Joanna."

"Jen."

He reached out and took hold of her hands even though she struggled against his touch. "I'm on your side, Joanna. How can I get you to trust me?"

"Give me proof of even one word of your story," she challenged. "Let me meet Hampleman. If she backs your story, I'll be more...trusting."

He sighed. "I can't do that. For your own protection I can't divulge Jen's location."

"My protection?"

He was still holding on to her hands. "I'm just trying to be very careful about covering all bases. It's a precaution, but precautions are always wise, to prevent screwups down the road."

Joanna tried to pull her hands away, but Logan held them firmly. "You mean," she said with a tight voice, "if this supposed person at Synergy who wants to sell Hampleman's secret research to our enemies decides I'm not Hampleman, he might torture me into revealing where the true Hampleman can be found. And if I don't know, he can torture me till...death. And Hampleman and her work stay safe and sound."

"Joanna, I said precaution. If there's any sign of suspicion, if I have even an inkling that your cover is not secure, I'll pull you out." He released her hands and pressed his palm to her cheek. "Long before the torture till death."

She shoved his hand away. "Then verify your credentials, Logan. Prove to me that you're on the side of truth, justice and the American way."

He studied her thoughtfully. "Joanna, listen to me. I don't think all models are dumb. As for you personally, I think you're very bright. But no matter what I show you, no matter who I let you phone, no matter how I verify my loyalty to this country, you would legitimately have your doubts anyway. If I was an enemy agent, or a demonic alien from outer space for that matter, I could phony up documents, cover my tracks. Trust is a funny thing, Joanna. It doesn't really come from outside. It comes from in here." He gave his chest a thump. "You've got to feel it, Joanna. Like a sixth sense. My sixth sense tells me you trust me more than you think you do."

Joanna scowled. "That doesn't say much for your sixth sense, Logan. You're right about one thing though. I am smart. Too smart to buy anything without knowing exactly what it is I'm buying. One way or another, I'll find out what's really going on. And if you're tricking me into abetting a felon or a double agent, Logan, you won't get away with it."

He grinned. "Hey, someday the president himself might be pinning a commendation on your chest."

"Mine or Hampleman's?"

"Maybe both of you."

"What is this mysterious project she's working on, Logan? Just what would warrant all this subterfuge?"

Logan didn't answer.

Joanna laughed dryly. "Oh, right. I forgot, keeping mum is for my own protection. Not that I'd be tortured into giving anything away. It's merely a precaution. Isn't that right?"

He closed his eyes. "Get some sleep, Jen."

"Talking about sleep, Logan . . ."

"Eric," he corrected opening one eye for a brief moment.

"Talking about sleep, *Eric*, exactly what is our sleeping arrangement at the condo?"

"We each have our own bedroom."

"Do the doors have locks?"

He opened his eyes and regarded her with a wry smile. "There are locks. But, given your suspicious nature, Jen, you'll probably worry that I have a key."

"I probably will."

His smile deepened, a seductive glint in his warm, hazel eyes. "And I'm sure there'll be times over the next few weeks when I'll wish I did have a key."

AS THE PLANE DESCENDED Joanna had a panicky sensation of falling from space, plunging into an abyss. As she debarked, she again found herself on a desolate, private airstrip. It had to be close to a hundred degrees in this flat, Southern California desert region. The heat seemed to clamp down over her like a glass dome. She could see everything quite clearly, and yet she felt constricted, caged.

"There's a small office just ahead," Logan said.

The office was a shabby wooden shack. The door was locked. Logan opened it with a key, ushered her inside and flicked on a fan. The sudden breeze made Joanna shiver. With bleary eyes, thanks to having gotten only a couple of hours of fitful sleep on the plane, she looked around the barren room. There were a couple of chairs, an old wooden desk, a file cabinet and a pint-sized refrigerator. The room's one small window was covered with a dingy graying curtain. She heard the bolt in the door click shut and she swung around to face Logan, her chest tightening with a now familiar anxiety.

Eric Logan did his best to give her a reassuring smile. "A bit of a comedown from the private jet, but we'll only be here for a couple of hours."

Logan crossed the room, opened the fridge door and called out, "Oranges, papayas and melon. Fresh orange juice. What'll it be, Jen?" He turned around to face Joanna when she didn't answer. "I really wish you'd stop looking at me like I was the creature from the Black Lagoon.''

"How should I look at you, *Eric*?" she asked, her voice flat and low in the leaden silence of the musky room.

He crossed over to her. "Like a friend," he answered softly. "That's what I'd like." He smiled, his eyes lingering on her face. For all the effort put into disguising her allure, she remained distractingly appealing. Logan had to remind himself sharply that he was carrying out an assignment, which meant he'd better start restraining his libido.

"Juice," she said blandly, maintaining eye contact, but deliberately keeping her expression blank.

She had to repeat the request. Logan was having trouble concentrating.

"Right. Juice." Still, it took him a moment to pull his gaze away.

Joanna sat down in one of the two wooden chairs, and Logan brought a glass of orange juice over to her. Then he started some coffee in an automatic coffee maker on top of the file cabinet. While it was dripping, he opened the top drawer and retrieved a small stack of files.

"These are the most important people at the compound, and the ones you'll have the most dealings with," he explained, bringing the files over and setting them on the desk.

He opened the top file, revealing an eight by eleven glossy color photo of a distinguished-looking man. His well-cut dark hair was going gray at the temples, his features very regular and even except for a hawkish nose. Joanna stared at the picture then lifted it up to see the single typewritten sheet behind it. As she sipped her juice and scanned the page, Logan said, "That's Martin Matthias. He's the administrative head of the labs. He came on board about four months before Hampleman and I got to Synergy. Before he came to Los Verdes he headed a private scientific think tank in Maryland. He's in his late forties. Very straight-arrow, lots of family dough, a strong supporter of the current administration, comes from a long line of distinguished public servants.''

Joanna looked up from the sheet of paper which gave a brief biographical sketch. "And his wife?"

Logan pulled out another file and flipped it open. "Linda Benson Matthias."

Joanna observed the glossy photo of a young, fine-boned woman with short, curly sandy-colored hair and blue eyes. Pretty, a sweet smile tinged with some camera shyness. Joanna looked up at Logan.

"Yeah, she is a bit younger than Martin," Logan said, pouring coffee into two mugs.

"Like...twenty, thirty years?"

Logan grinned, setting a steaming mug in front of Joanna. "Twenty-two years to be exact. A very sweet girl. Not overly bright, but well-intentioned. Feels a bit out of her element at the Synergy compound, but she tries very hard to be the perfect hostess, the perfect wife. Martin fawns over her, and from all appearances she's completely wild about Marty."

"It doesn't sound like you are," Joanna observed.

Logan gave her a sly glance over the rim of her coffee mug. "He's not my type."

"Is she?" Joanna raised a brow.

"Linda?" He laughed. "No. Personally, I like women with a little more oomph."

"Oomph?"

"Oomph," he repeated without further explanation, hurrying on to the next file. "Hank Morgan. He's head of security at Synergy. During the Vietnam War he was a Green Beret. When he got back he went through some tough reentry changes, then did a stint with the CIA. He soured on the job after his partner was killed down in Mexico. They were good buddies. Morgan's a hard-nosed, tough guy who doesn't say much, but has a way of getting his point across." Logan paused. "Women go for him. He's quite popular, especially with some of the lab techs and secretaries at Synergy."

He pulled out another file. "Like our secretary, Toni Conners."

Joanna studied the photo of *her* secretary. Toni was a plain-looking woman in her mid-thirties with fading red hair, clever gray eyes and a benignly melancholy smile.

Joanna sat forward, chin resting on the palm of her hand, as she reexamined Morgan's photo. He was attractive in a bulldog sort of way: broad-faced; pronounced, jutting jaw; blue eyes that were a bit chilly and placed a little too close to a flat nose; blond hair, clipped military short. Nothing subtle in his sex appeal—rippling with muscles, but no character. She could guess what Toni saw in Morgan, but not what Morgan saw in the secretary. Then again, maybe he saw nothing, and it was a case of unrequited attraction on Toni's part.

"Morgan's not your type though?" Logan queried.

Now it was Joanna's turn to give Logan a sly look. "I'm trying not to typecast."

Logan smiled. "That's good, Jen. Admirable."

She found his playful, provocative look disturbing and grabbed for the next file.

Inside was a photo of a dark-haired woman with sizzling black eyes, a willful smile, and flawless, alabaster skin. Joanna's eyes shot up to Logan.

"That's Dr. Gerta Hauser, a nuclear physicist who defected from Poland a couple of years ago."

"Poland?" Her expression took on a wary cast. Poland. The Eastern Bloc. Who was a better candidate for selling secrets...?

"You're not typecasting, remember?"

Joanna lifted the photo and read the brief bio. Thirty-seven years old, born in Krakow, Poland, married to a Polish physician for seven years, no children, divorced just before her defection to the States. Again, Joanna studied the photo. "I have a feeling it's going to be tough to pull any wool over her shrewd eyes," she said in a low voice.

Logan smiled. "Don't worry. You won't have much in the way of dealings with her. Hampleman and Hauser don't get along. They've both been working in the same field and there's been an unspoken competition between them from the word go. Just play it like Jen does, cool and uninterested."

"How do you play it with Gerta, Eric?"

He laughed. "I do admit Gerta has oomph. But she's a bit overbearing and intense."

Joanna studied Logan in silence for several moments, then let her eyes drop again to Gerta's photo. "Are you sure Hauser's only in competition with Hampleman over work?"

"What else?"

"What about matters of the heart?"

Logan tipped back on his chair and rubbed his jaw. "You mean did Gerta ever come on to me?" His lips puckered. "Gerta has had her flirtatious moments. I don't think she likes losing out to the competition in work or play," he admitted, confirming Joanna's guess. "But she's convinced at this point that I'm already taken. It'll be helpful if you would keep her convinced."

"Or you might get distracted from the task at hand?"

He gave her a long, lingering look. "I've been at risk of that for the past ten hours." With a thud, he let the front legs of his chair bang back down on the floor. "We better wrap this up," he said, his voice a little raspy, a faint flush on his cheeks.

Joanna found herself touched by Logan's surprising show of vulnerability. But it didn't last very long. He launched into a concise run-down on the other key members at Synergy: Dr. Andrew MacIntyre, the compound's resident physician, Barry Lester, Matthias's administrative assistant, and two other scientists—physicist, Roland Ivers, and chemist, Andre Hoffman. Hoffman, Logan explained, was a reclusive man who rarely left his lab. He often worked round the clock and slept on a cot in the lab. She wouldn't have much of anything to do with him. As for Ivers, he was at a convention in London at the moment and wasn't due back for at least two weeks, so she wouldn't have to worry about him for now. There were three other scientists working at the compound, but they were all on summer holidays or sabbaticals so Eric didn't bother with any details on them. When he wrapped it up, he asked Joanna if she wanted a second run-through.

Joanna shook her head. For the first time since this whole mad adventure had begun, some of her anxiety and fear had bled away. It was probably just sheer exhaustion taking center stage. "I've got the picture."

Joanna's calm seemed to trigger a counterresponse in Logan. He felt suddenly cautious, edgy. "Are you sure?" he asked nervously.

"You can test me later. Let's get out of here." She got up and started for the door.

Logan checked his watch. It was just a little past 6:00 a.m. He'd figured on at least two hours, but he saw now that Joanna was a quick study. He pulled back his chair and rose.

"How far is it to Synergy?" she asked.

"About forty-five minutes."

Joanna reached for the bolt on the door.

"Hold it," he ordered sharply, hurrying over.

He drew her away from the door, unbolted it himself, cautiously cracked the door open a few inches and looked out.

So much for her newly won calm.

"Logan? Eric? What's out there?"

"Just a precaution." He glanced over his shoulder and smiled, but there was tension in that smile. For a moment there, he'd thought he'd heard a car driving off. Since this air-strip had been closed for several years and the road did not lead beyond it, any car in the vicinity would have had this spot as its destination. *Had someone managed to tail him out here when he'd taken off for New York and stuck around to monitor his return? He thought he'd been so careful. Maybe there was no being careful enough. Then again, maybe he'd only imagined that car.*

He opened the door wide, but Joanna hesitated. "How do we get to Synergy?"

"I've got a car parked over at the hangar."

The hangar was a good hundred yards from the shack. A hundred yards of flat, open space.

"Who did you think might be out there?" she asked nervously, refusing to budge.

"I told you. Just—"

"I know, a precaution."

He closed the door again and turned fully around to face her. "Look, we know that someone at Synergy was eager to get their hands on Jen's work and sell it to an Eastern Block contact. If Jen's research is bust there can be no deal. But, maybe that someone isn't fully convinced yet. We just have to keep our guard up and play it safe." He paused, his gaze unwavering on hers. "That means not trusting anyone at Synergy."

Joanna stared back at him with a cool air of defiance. "Don't worry about that, Logan. I have no intention of trusting anyone but myself."

But as Eric Logan smiled disarmingly at her, Joanna felt an unbidden flurry of attraction, causing a whole new worry to spring into her mind. Could she trust herself?

JOANNA AWOKE with a start.

"We're almost home, Sleeping Beauty."

She sat up stiffly in the tight confines of Logan's silver hatchback, only now aware that she'd been sleeping with her head resting on his shoulder. She looked nervously out the window at the brown, sun-baked desert grass and dry, rocky landscape.

He slowed and glanced over at her. "You better put your glasses back on, Jen."

*Glasses. Jen.* She shut her eyes, a resurgence of panic biting at the back of her throat. "I . . . I can't do this, Logan."

He reached out a hand and smoothed down a wayward strand of her hair. Brown hair. Dyed brown hair. Hampleman's hair. She shivered.

"Take it easy. We'll go straight to the apartment and you can lie down for a few hours." He squeezed her shoulder. "We're coming to the gate."

Her hands trembled as she slipped on the horn-rimmed glasses and stared at the heavy steel gate attached on either side to a twenty-foot-high, white concrete wall. Trimming the top of the wall was a network of barbed wire. Just outside the gate and to the left was a surprisingly green grassy patch of lawn and an attractive, single-story, cedar-shingled guard house.

As Logan drove up to the gate, he rolled down his window, displaying both his and Hampleman's IDs. A gray-haired man, uniformed in khaki slacks and a short-sleeved blue shirt with a gold and white Synergy emblem on the chest pocket, came out of the guard house and stepped over to the car. He bent over a little to look inside, resting his fleshy palms on the windowsill.

"Dr. Logan. Dr. Hampleman. Have a nice weekend?"

"Great time, Lou," Logan said with a grin, slipping his ID in his jacket pocket and handing Hampleman's to Joanna. "Right, Jen?"

Joanna managed a small smile. "Right. Right, Lou. Great time."

Lou gave her a steady look. "You feeling okay, Dr. Hampleman?"

"Fine," she said weakly, cringing inside as the guard continued his scrutinizing gaze. Could he see right through her disguise? Well, if she couldn't even fool this Lou, maybe Logan would come to his senses and realize his whole plan was a bust. And he'd let her go home and she could try to forget this madness had ever taken place.

Lou was frowning as he gave her an even closer scrutiny. "I don't know, Dr. Hampleman. Your eyes still look a little watery. These summer colds can really hang on. Like I told you when you and Dr. Logan took off on Friday, you really gotta watch out or you'll end up with pneumonia."

*Or a nervous breakdown,* Joanna thought miserably.

Lou went back inside to open the electronic gate and Logan gave her a bright smile. "See. A piece of cake, Jen."

# Chapter Five

"Insurance." The statement lacked force. There was a slight quiver in the voice.

A snort followed by a tight grimace appeared on a pale, overtaxed face. "That's it? Insurance? We don't want insurance, you idiot. We want Hampleman's papers, her data, her experimentation."

"With the two of them out of the way, I thought we..."

"Your job is not to think. How many times have we been over that?"

"I thought you'd be pleased."

"Exactly. You *thought*. Fortunately your actions are as incompetent as your thoughts. They just arrived at Synergy."

"But..."

"Timing. Timing is everything. Now, let me make myself perfectly clear. You are to do nothing but keep a close watch until..."

"Until?" A heightened note of expectation hung in the air.

"You hate her, don't you."

A sharp laugh.

"And what about Logan? Do you hate him as well?"

A low whisper. "Even more."

"Hate has its place. But it can also drive us to act impulsively. We haven't come this far to let our emotions destroy our chances for untold wealth, economic and political superiority, the rightful return of power. When it comes time to act, we will do so with cool, calculated control of our emotions. Is that understood?"

A moment of hesitation. "What if we're wrong? What if she really did reach a dead end in her experiment?"

"Then why their secret little weekend trip? And what would the two of them need to discuss in that shack before returning to Synergy? Strategy. How to proceed with caution." A dry laugh. "There's no dead end. She was too close. Too sure of herself. You said it yourself. It was in her eyes. Conquest. Victory."

"Yes, I could smell it on her. And if she'd nailed it down completely, the government would never have had her return to Los Verdes. She must still have some finishing touches to do."

A sardonic grin curved the hard mouth. "For once, you're thinking on your feet."

"Thanks."

"Don't let it go to your head."

As Logan drove past the gates, a gasp of surprise escaped Joanna's lips. A minute ago they'd been in a brown barren desert and now they had entered a lush green paradise. Rolling fields of grass, a tree-lined road, even a small babbling brook filled the landscape. This government-run high-security laboratory, which, according to Logan, drew the cream of the crop in the scientific community, had been designed to please esthetic sensibilities as well as stir creative juices.

"That's the clubhouse," Eric said, pointing to a modern, low-slung, white-washed adobe building with red tile roof. "There's exercise equipment and a lap pool inside and a purely recreational pool out back."

The clubhouse was of modest size but then, Logan had told her there were only twenty people housed on the compound. That included the scientists, the small administrative staff and a handful of technicians. Maintenance staff lived off the compound and had only limited access to the buildings.

"What's that?" Joanna asked, gesturing to a sprawling complex of interconnected, windowless white structures that most resembled oversized igloos.

"The labs. There are a dozen self-contained units which are connected by restricted-access passageways. Each of the scientists, along with their chosen assistants and lab techs, has his or her own private, secure, climate-controlled space in which to work. Behind the labs, and connected by another network of hallways, are the administrative offices."

Joanna stared grimly at the labs. "A little like solitary confinement. No windows, no connection with the outside world. A kind of... purgatory."

Eric smiled. "You won't hear the scientists complaining. We're a rather idiosyncratic lot. We live more in the inner world of our imaginations than in the one that exists outside our minds."

Joanna shot him a curious look. "I still can't picture you as one of them."

He grinned. "It does get a bit... schizophrenic at times. But, for the next three weeks, *Jen*, I am only one of them," he emphasized.

Slowly Joanna nodded her head. *Yes, he was one of them.* The Synergy guard had confirmed his identity as Dr. Eric Logan, chemist. And the guard had also confirmed that Hampleman was alive and well as of two days ago. *She leaves, I come back. No one is any the wiser. Or so Logan hopes.*

"The condos are just around the bend. They're actually detached town houses. Which is nice since it makes for more privacy."

Joanna was only half listening, so that when they rounded the bend her eyes widened in surprise. A small but quaint grouping of colonial-style town houses stood in a curved row on well-manicured lawns. It looked for all the world like Main Street, U.S.A.

"For a group of scientists who live in such an interior world, the government has certainly gone to great lengths to make their exterior world quite charming," Joanna observed.

"There's some private funding as well. And those groups like to see something concrete for their investment." There was a touch of cynicism in Eric's voice.

"Haven't there been any major scientific breakthroughs coming out of Synergy?"

There was a brief pause. "Not yet."

Logan maneuvered the car into the driveway of the second town house on the left. "Less than half the houses and labs are occupied right now. Synergy has expansion plans but at the moment it's still a small operation." He came to a stop beside a pair of mopeds. "We use those to get around on the compound. Everyone does. It's easier and more efficient."

Joanna had only ridden a moped once, down in Bermuda on a shoot a couple of years back. But she'd found it fun and not at all difficult to maneuver. She turned her attention to the town houses on either side of theirs. "Are those occupied or vacant?"

Logan gestured to the right. "Gerta Hauser lives in that one. She's not home now, though. She had a convention in San Diego this week-end. The house on the other side is empty."

"So Gerta and I are next-door neighbors," Joanna reflected uneasily.

"Don't worry," he said with a smile as he opened his car door. "She's not going to be dropping by for a coffee klatch or to borrow a cup of sugar."

"Does Jen use sugar, by the way?"

Logan was halfway out the car door. He glanced back at Joanna. "No. Actually she doesn't."

"That's . . . good. I don't, either."

His eyes were still on her. "I don't think you'll have much trouble fitting into her shoes," he said softly. "I'll give you some pointers and go over some of Jen's quirks and habits after you've had a little sleep."

Joanna glanced down at the black leather pumps on her feet and then looked back over at Logan. "I wonder what must have gone through your head, Eric, when you came across that layout of me in *Harper's Bazaar*. You must have been . . . stunned by the similarities between us." Just as she'd been when she'd really looked at Jennifer Hampleman's ID photo.

"It was . . . a very lucky break, as things turned out."

"Yes. Very lucky," she echoed.

"Shall we go inside?"

Joanna experienced a strong reluctance to leave the car. Or, perhaps it was actually entering the house that provoked the reluctance. Hampleman's house. The home of her remarkable look-alike. She felt as if she were entering *The Twilight Zone*.

Logan got out of the car. He crossed round to Joanna's side and opened her door, his hand extended to help her out. This time Joanna took his hand.

They walked together up the front path. The closer they got to the front door of Hampleman's town house, the more anxious Joanna became.

"It's good to be home, Jen. I like the way you've decorated the house," Eric said with feigned nonchalance, slipping his free hand in his trouser pocket and pulling out a key. "For a science type, you've got a nice way with design and color."

Joanna fixed her eyes nervously on the door as Eric unlocked it and swung it open. A cool blast of air-conditioned air rushed out to greet them. Eric gestured for her to enter, but she hung back, feeling rooted to the spot.

Logan went in first, switching off what looked to be an alarm system on the wall just inside the door.

"It's perfectly safe inside," he said, drawing her in and shutting the door. He tapped the alarm. "An anti-bugging device. It's built into the general security system for the entire compound. After all, Jen and I are working on high-level and often top-secret projects." He tapped a glass dot on the box. "If you ever see this red light lit, be careful of what you say until we can track down the bug."

She nodded.

"Still, we should maintain the charade at home as much as possible. It'll keep you from slipping up around the others."

Joanna didn't answer. Instead her eyes fixed on the small entry table in the hallway, a strangled gasp escaping her lips. On the table sat a small glass sculpture. *A blown glass swan.* It was smaller than hers, and the swan's position was different, but still, seeing one here was eerie.

Logan's eyes followed Joanna's. He, too, remembered the glass swan in her apartment. It had given him a bit of a start when he'd seen it. "I bought that for Jen, actually. Last Christmas." He didn't tell Joanna that Jen had admired it first in a shop window and told him that she had a special fondness for swans.

Joanna's legs felt rubbery and she put one hand out to the wall for support.

"It's just coincidence," Eric said softly. "Come on. I'll show you around."

She pulled her eyes from the glass swan and tried to calm down. *Coincidence.*

He led her into the living room. Joanna breathed a sigh of relief. It was pleasant, cozy even, but not her taste at all. Well, the French Provincial decor wasn't her taste, but Jennifer Hampleman did seem to be partial to a rose shade in the draperies and upholstery that Joanna also happened to favor. But plenty of people liked that shade of rose. It was quite a popular color in decorating these days.

Eric was pleased to see a bit of color return to Joanna's face. He watched her in silence as she crossed the room and stood by the oak mantel over the fireplace where a couple of framed photos were displayed. One was a posed portrait of a middle-aged couple. The woman was regally seated in a brown leather armchair, studded at the seams with gold upholstery rivets. It was the sort of chair found in the libraries of distinguished homes. Standing just to the side of her was a tall, pleasant-looking man with thinning dark hair, a tanned, ruddy complexion, blue eyes and a slightly pug nose. He was dapperly dressed in a gray silk smoking jacket and well-tailored charcoal slacks. One of his hands curved around the bulb of the pipe in his mouth. The other rested comfortably, affectionately, on the woman's shoulder.

"Mom and Dad," Eric said lightly. "Rhonda and Elmer Hampleman. Elmer's retired from the plumbing business. Rhonda still does her good works. Right now they're off sailing on their yacht in the Caribbean."

"Dad's plumbing business did well, then?"

"You've never wanted for anything, Jen. A fine home in Teaneck, New Jersey, the best private schools, European vacations."

"Teaneck, New Jersey. That's so close to Manhattan. I . . . I grew up on Sutton Place. Jen must have come into

Manhattan sometimes when she was a kid. What would it have been like, I wonder, if we'd ever met?''

It was harder than he'd expected to call Joanna, Jen, especially while talking about Jen's past. Logan decided to go along with Joanna's need to put things into perspective. ''Maybe you did and neither of you ever looked close enough to notice the similarities. Jen told me she always played down her looks even as a teenager.''

Joanna gave him a sharp look. ''And you assume I always used mine to advantage?''

''Whoa. I thought I was handing out a compliment there, not a rebuke.''

''I was very shy as a girl, Logan. I didn't think I was pretty. I was too skinny. Too tall, Gawky. I always thought it was so unfair that I took after my father rather than my mother. She's small and delicate. Her features are so dainty. The only similarity between us is our hair. Even there, my mother's is a paler blond, more ash.''

She looked at the other photo. It was of a teenage boy. A candid shot, it looked as if it had been snapped at a summer camp. The boy was sitting on a step outside a cabin. He was dressed in a T-shirt and jeans. He was a nice-looking boy with dark brown hair that was in need of a trim.

''Jen's brother, Marc,'' Logan edified. ''That was taken about five years ago. He's at Harvard now.''

''He doesn't look anything like Jen,'' Joanna remarked.

''No, not in the picture anyway. Looks more like his dad.''

''I always wished I had a brother or a sister,'' Joanna reflected. ''But my mother couldn't have any more children after me. I used to think, when I was little, that my father ought to have been able to do something about it. He was an obstetrician. He specialized in infertility and difficult births.''

''Was yours a difficult birth?''

"Yes. My mother almost died delivering me." A shadow fell across her features. "Her health was...poor... afterward. Not just...physically," she added in a low voice.

Eric, standing just behind Joanna, placed his hands lightly on her shoulders. "You don't blame yourself for that?"

Joanna didn't respond. Instead her eyes fell again on the photo of the Hamplemans. "They look like nice people. Nice, warm, caring parents."

"Jen says they are."

Joanna crossed her arms over her chest. Without thinking she let herself lean a little against Eric. She closed her eyes for a moment. It felt good to lean on someone for a change.

It was a feeling she couldn't afford to give in to for very long. With a quick intake of breath she righted herself. "I guess it's time for 'Jen' to check out the rest of the place."

Eric let his hands drop to his sides. He followed her into the kitchen.

Idly Joanna ran her hands along the scrubbed white Formica counter tops. Other than a stainless steel toaster and a set of stainless steel cannisters, the surface was bare.

"Neither of us cooks very much, do we?" she reflected.

Eric's eyes held a glint of amusement, wondering whether she meant herself and Jen or Jen and him when she said "us." He decided to assume the latter. "I'm good with steaks. You're a whizz with omelets. Neither of us goes in for elaborate meals."

"Where do we go for groceries?"

"There's a pretty decent supermarket a couple of miles from the compound. We passed it on the way in, but you were sleeping."

Joanna opened the drawer next to the refrigerator. Inside were boxes of tin foil, plastic wrap and waxed paper. She stared at the contents.

She opened a few more drawers, a little unsettled to find that Hampleman's kitchen organizing was a fairly close duplicate of her own. But then, probably lots of households had a similar methodical organization.

She went through the door to the dining room. It was a modest-sized square space which comfortably held a round oak table, four chairs and a matching sideboard. The centerpiece on the table was a silk flower arrangement. Joanna was surprised at how relieved she felt to remember she, herself, never cared for silk flowers.

Before they went upstairs, Eric pointed out the small bathroom off the hallway. "There's only one bathroom upstairs for the two bedrooms. If you prefer, I'll use this one."

"I prefer," Joanna stated without equivocation.

Eric smiled and led the way up the stairs. He stopped at his bedroom first. It was done up as a combination office den. The decorating was minimal and strictly functional: a sofa; desk; reading chair with standing reading lamp; bookcases on one wall; two Da Vinci anatomical prints on the opposite wall.

"The sofa opens into a bed." He gave her a sly smile. "Of course, being lovers, we only have the sleep sofa for guests."

"And do we have guests?" she asked stiffly, not at all amused by his quip.

"Not very often."

"Who've we entertained?" she persisted.

"Marc spent a few days during his spring break."

"Marc?"

"Your brother."

"Oh. Right." She eyed him narrowly. "And where did you sleep while my brother was staying with us?"

He smiled at her. "On the couch in the living room. If you want to verify that, you can always write to Marc."

She knew he was teasing her, but still she said, "Wouldn't my brother think I was awfully weird not to remember a detail like that?"

He laughed. "Scientists are known to be absentminded about anything other than their work."

"Is Jen?"

"No," he said quite seriously. "Jen is a very together woman. You might fit her into the scientist stereotype at first glance, but once you got to know her..." His lips curved up. "You'd like her." And then before she could respond he said, "Come on. I'll show you your room."

But Joanna made no move to leave the den. "Who else has visited us besides Marc?"

Eric hesitated. "Some acquaintances of mine. From Washington." He chose his words carefully. But then he added, almost flippantly, "A couple of old college buddies. You didn't like them."

"I didn't?"

"No, you thought they were crude and rambunctious." He made no attempt to hide his amusement.

"Were those my exact words?"

He laughed. "A direct quote."

"I don't use those words." She paused. "But I don't care for crude, rambunctious men."

He studied her with amusement, making her uneasy. She turned away from his distracting smile and walked over to the door leading back into the upstairs hallway. "I can find my bedroom myself. I think I'll go lie down."

"Good idea," he agreed, following her out to the hall. "I think I'll take a little stroll over to the clubhouse. Take a swim."

"Fine." She started for the opposite bedroom door.

"Jen."

Would she ever get used to being called Jen? After a moment's pause, she answered, "What is it?"

"If you should need to reach me, you can ring the club-house by dialing extension 311."

"I'm sure that won't be necessary," Joanna said firmly.

He watched her closely. "You will stay put?"

Their eyes met and held. "And if I don't . . . ?"

"It wouldn't be in your best interest." He didn't like having to say that, not one bit. But that was not to say he didn't mean it.

Joanna believed he meant it, as well. She thought about her mother, her Paris shoot, a possible tangle with the government over a trumped up charge of diamond smuggling. Logan could definitely make life miserable for her. She glared contemptuously at him. "Isn't it comforting to know we both have my best interests at heart, dear Eric?"

The glint in his eyes told her that her facetiousness had been noticed, but his smile was oddly tender and affectionate. "Yes, it is comforting, dear Jen."


SHE WAS IN HER BEDROOM—Jennifer Hampleman's bedroom, that is—when she heard the front door click shut. Finally alone, she stood in the center of the room surveying it. It was larger and airier than the spare bedroom, and more effort had gone into decorating it. A bright, cheerful floral wallpaper, again with the accent on rose, an upholstered chaise coordinated to the paper, a thick mauve carpet, and a matching set of mahogany bedroom furniture gave the room a cosy, tasteful and decidedly feminine appearance. Hampleman might play down her femininity in her appearance, but as far as her decorating tastes went, she definitely allowed that part of her nature more freedom.

Joanna eyed the bed. But, as exhausted as she was, she felt too restless and tense to lie down. Her eyes flitted past the closet, the bureau drawers, a small desk over by the window. She wanted to snoop around the room, to learn more about Jen, but curiosity vied with repugnance. And perhaps something more, an inexplicable fear. It was more than a little disconcerting to know that someone existed who looked so much like you, who even shared some of your likes, even put her waxed paper in the same kitchen drawer...

Joanna crossed to the five-drawer bureau, giving a little start as she saw her reflection in the mirror above it. Staring back at her was Jennifer Hampleman. The resemblance was uncanny, downright eerie.

Joanna flattened her palms on the top of the bureau to steady herself. Her shoulders were knotted with tension, her mouth was dry, the room starting to spin before her eyes. She forced down several deep, reviving breaths, pulling her gaze from the mirror.

Her hands moved to the knobs of the top drawer. She would have to survey Jen's belongings. Because they would be her belongings now. Every item of clothing she'd be putting on for the next three weeks would be Jennifer Hampleman's. Jen's dresses, skirts, blouses, slacks. Jen's nightgowns, her underwear...

Neatly folded in the top drawer were bras, panties and a tidy pile of panty hose. Nothing frivolous, but not entirely utilitarian either. Still, the thought of wearing another woman's undergarments...

Logan wouldn't understand. Logan operated strictly from expedience. *Cover all bases for security reasons.* Right down to the underwear.

But as she looked closer, she saw that the top items in the drawer, while exact duplicates of the ones beneath, were actually brand new. She checked the sizes. Perfect. Had Jen bought them? Or had Logan actually been thoughtful enough, sensitive enough, to realize how she'd feel?

She opened each drawer in turn. Nightgowns in the second drawer, also some of them brand new. And then in the other drawers there were shirts, tank tops, running shorts, exercise wear.

Joanna went to the closet. Jen was definitely not a clothes horse. Simple cotton day dresses, a few pairs of slacks, several print and solid-colored blouses, a rose-colored cotton robe. On the floor of the closet were a half dozen pairs of shoes on a shoe rack.

Joanna bent down. The running sneakers were brand new. So were a pair of white leather sandals. Her size. Hampleman, she noted, wore a half size larger. So it wasn't Jen who'd done the shopping.

Joanna walked over to the window, pulled the drapes fully open and stared out. The view faced the bedroom window on the second level of the unoccupied house next door. There was a drawn venetian blind on the window so that she couldn't see inside. Joanna was glad her window didn't face Gerta Hauser's bedroom window. From the little Logan had told her so far, Joanna felt very uneasy and distrustful of the Polish defector. Maybe it was typecasting, but Gerta Hauser certainly did look like a modern-day Mata Hari.

Leaving her drapes open to let in some sunlight, Joanna went and locked her bedroom door, undressed and donned Hampleman's rose-colored robe. Leaving the white chenille spread on the bed, she lay down on top of it. There seemed nothing to do now but try to get some much needed sleep.

The silence of the house, broken only by the soft whir of the air-conditioning vents in the ceiling, worked on Joanna's nerves, making it impossible to doze. A strange bed, she told herself. But as a model who traveled the globe, she was used to sleeping in strange beds.

She switched on the clock radio on the end table beside the bed. It was tuned to a jazz music station. She didn't find the music soothing or diverting. She switched off the radio, stared up at the ceiling.

She closed her eyes. *Maybe if I go to sleep I'll wake up and discover this was all some bizarre nightmare.*

The events of the last fifteen hours unwound in her mind like a film, and the film kept winding back to one persistent image: Eric Logan.

She was his virtual captive here in this strange, unsettling desert compound, thousands of miles from home. She railed against what he had done to her, wanted to hate him for the threats he held over her, even if they really were being done in the name of truth and justice. And yet there was something disturbingly compelling about Dr. Eric Logan for all that. Her flurries of attraction to him distressed and alarmed her. Wasn't her present situation precarious and unsettling enough without her deliberately complicating it?

She finally managed to doze off, but she awoke in a sweat an hour or so later. The sun had shifted so that its rays were falling directly on her bed. Groggily, she rose to close the drapes, hoping to cool the room down so she could go back to sleep.

As she reached to pull the drape closed, her gaze focused on the bedroom window in the vacant town house across the way. When she'd gone to lie down the venetian blind on that window had been drawn fully closed. Joanna was certain of it.

But now the slats of the blind were at an angle. Not enough for Joanna to see into the room, but enough for someone to see out. Someone was in that room watching her. Maybe even at this very moment.

With a sharp jerk of her hand, Joanna pulled the drapes shut. She wanted to rush out, to find Eric, and she had even started moving toward the door when another thought struck her. It was more than likely that Eric already knew about the watcher—it was pretty likely that he was doing the watching himself.

## Chapter Six

"You're up already." There was a mix of surprise and relief in Eric's voice. He crossed the living room and took a seat beside Joanna on the sofa. He studied her more closely. "Did you get any rest at all?"

"A little," she said tightly.

"I met Matthias down at the pool. He invited us over for cocktails this evening."

Joanna didn't respond.

"Don't be nervous about it. Marty takes care of the conversation for everyone." He gave a little laugh. "He definitely likes to hear himself talk, and since we want to stay in his good graces, we all pretend we do, too." He paused, concerned about the distant glint in her eyes. He decided he probably shouldn't have left her alone just yet. It had given her a chance to sit around and fuss over her predicament.

"You're going to make yourself ill," he said softly. "Maybe you should ask the doc for some sleeping pills."

She shot him a hard look. "So now you want to drug me as well."

"Joanna..."

"Jen, remember? You don't want to mess up now, Eric. Not with all the trouble you're going to."

He took firm hold of her shoulders, forcing her to face him. "Look, get it all out of your system now. The rage, the feeling of helplessness. Sock me, scream at me, just let it all out so that it doesn't build up inside of you until you go off like a time bomb."

"Get your hands off me, Logan," she said bitingly.

"No."

"You're the most despicable, insidious man I've ever met."

His smile barely faltered. "Good. Go on."

She struggled to break free of him, but his grip was like steel. She punched him hard in the chest, regarding him with a furious gaze. "I hate you."

"You've got plenty of reason," he said sympathetically.

She hated his sympathy, hated his touch, hated the miasma of emotions he was putting her through. "And you talk about trust," she screamed. "'You've got to feel it in here, Joanna,'" she mimicked him broadly, with yet another thump on his chest. "But that's a one-way street in your mind, isn't it Logan. Sure, I'm supposed to trust you, but you aren't taking any chances, are you, Logan? Are you?" Tears sprang from her eyes. Her voice was low and strained. All the color had drained from her face. "I will not..." A wracking sob broke from her and she couldn't complete the sentence.

"Joanna, don't. Don't cry," he said uncomfortably. Fury was one thing, but Logan never could stand a woman's tears. "I know it's rough for you. I'm trying to make it as easy as I can."

"Is that why you have me watched when you take off? Are you worried that your blackmail alone isn't enough to keep me in line?"

She gave him a fierce glare.

Logan slowly eased his grip, but he still didn't release her. "What are you talking about?"

She dropped her head to her hands. "I saw...I saw the blinds open..."

He took hold of her hands, drawing them away from her face. "What blinds?"

"Next...door." She tried to swipe at her wet cheeks, but was thwarted by Eric's grip on her hands. "The upstairs bedroom."

He released her hands and reached up to wipe the tears from her cheeks. "Gerta's place?" he asked softly. His gaze was unwavering on her face.

Joanna tried to avert her eyes, but Logan seemed to draw her like a magnet, his steady look too compelling and intense to ignore. "The...house you said was vacant."

He held her gaze. "And you thought I'd put someone in there to keep a watch on you?"

She didn't answer.

"Joanna," he whispered huskily. "I didn't." A shadow of worry crossed his features and he looked away.

Joanna stared at Logan. For some inexplicable reason she believed him. His comment should have increased her fear but, oddly enough, it didn't. "Then someone's already doubting my identity," she whispered.

Slowly, Eric shook his head. "No, not likely. You haven't even met any of them face to face yet."

"The guard. Lou. What if he...?"

Eric rose from the couch. "I told you before. Whoever it is that wanted to get their hands on Jen's research may not be fully convinced that she's stopped work on the project. So he's watching. Waiting." He looked down at her. "That's all he'll do though. Watch. As long as we're convincing, we've got no problems."

Joanna didn't respond.

He felt sorry for her. It wasn't an easy thing to know your every move was being watched. What worried him was that he was feeling more than sympathy.

She leaned back wearily on the sofa and shut her eyes. Eric's gaze roamed her face. She did look incredibly like

Jen. A carbon copy on the surface. But there was an illusive and yet compelling aura that emanated from Joanna that was all hers. If he noticed it, would the others?

No, he thought. Not as long as they didn't get too close to her. But how was he going to keep from getting too close, himself?

Joanna's eyelids fluttered open. Their gazes met and held. She could feel her pulse beating. It seemed to match the sudden pulsating tension in the room.

This time it was Eric who backed away, physically and emotionally. "I have to go out. I'll be back soon. You'd better get dressed for cocktails over at Marty's. Oh, and I...uh...made up a brief rundown of some of Jen's quirks and habits." He pulled two sheets from his trouser pocket. "You should go over them before we leave and then burn the papers in the fireplace."

She stood up and took the papers from him, but her eyes didn't leave his face. "You're going next door."

He didn't answer.

"What if he's . . . still there?"

A hint of a smile curved his lips. "You sound worried. Does that mean you don't hate me any more?"

Maybe she didn't hate him any more, at least not quite as much. But admitting that would give him an edge. Joanna had little enough control right now. She wasn't going to voluntarily hand over Logan any more advantage. "If something were to happen to you, where would that leave me?"

He smiled reassuringly. "Ah, I see. Yes, that would put you in an awkward position."

"I suppose...someone else...would rush in to take your place. A new 'chemist.'"

Eric's smile deepened, became more provocative than reassuring. "Not to be immodest, but not all chemists are blessed with charm, sophistication, decent looks and a good sense of humor. You could have it worse, *Jen*."

She laughed dryly. "Not to be rude, Logan, but immodesty is the least of your problems."

He chuckled. "You're probably right. But I'll work on it." He hesitated as if about to say something more, then he turned and headed for the hallway.

"Eric," she called out.

He stopped, glanced back at her.

"Be...careful."

He was touched by her concern and his expression showed it. Perhaps they were moving to a new accord. A part of him felt a rush of pleasure at the thought. But another part saw caution signs flashing.

WHILE ERIC WAS GONE, Joanna tried to fix her attention on the notes about Jen. She read the two sheets through a few times then went back to review the highlights.

"Quiet, reserved, rarely initiates a conversation. Never drinks hard liquor or beer. Prefers white wine over red. Red sometimes gives her a headache."

Joanna paused. She tended to avoid red wine herself. It didn't give her headaches, but it did sometimes upset her stomach.

"When nervous, smooths back imaginary strands of hair from her face. When angry, she takes off her glasses. Doesn't openly lose temper though. Eyes just get icy. Voice drops. As for voice, yours is slightly lower pitched than Jen's. We'll use lingering cold as excuse."

Eric's final note was—"Act natural. Trust your instincts. You'll do great."

She heard the door open and rushed out to the hall.

"Nothing," Eric said immediately. "The blinds were drawn shut on every window."

"I wasn't imagining it," Joanna insisted.

"You didn't change your clothes yet."

"Eric..."

"I didn't say you were imagining it."

He didn't have to say it. She could see it in his eyes.

"There's nothing wrong with my vision, Eric. Or my mind. Not yet, anyway."

He smiled. A noncommittal smile. "How about that pink print dress, Jen? You look great in that."

"Damn you, Logan."

"Remember, Jen. If you get angry in front of the others, take off your glasses."

She stormed past him and went up the stairs, slamming the door to her room. She locked it, too.

A half hour later, showered and dressed, she found Eric waiting downstairs in the kitchen.

He grinned as he took in the plain lilac shirtwaist she was wearing. "I still like the pink one better, but you look nice, Jen."

"I look awful," she snapped, crossing to the refrigerator to get a cold drink. "Doesn't she even let her hair down for cocktails?"

Eric gave her a teasing grin. "Not for cocktails."

She eyed him narrowly. "Just what was it like being her roommate for sixteen months?"

"We didn't move in together right away. We had to let the relationship develop. Jen isn't the sort of woman to jump into something so...intimate...without careful consideration. Anyway, my living here only became...imperative...about three months ago. Until then, we had no reason for concern."

"Three months is a long time. How did she feel having you around for three months, day in and day out, Logan?"

"We both managed to keep it amiable," he said flatly, almost flippantly. But Joanna sensed something more. And she was surprised by how curious she suddenly felt about the relationship between Eric and Jen. If their being lovers had all been for show, had it been a choice or an order? And if it had been choice, whose choice had it been? Jen's or Eric's? There were moments when Joanna had caught him looking at her with something more than professional interest. Was that because he was unable to mask feelings that he had for Jennifer Hampleman? Feelings that her remarkable resemblance to the scientist provoked?

"We've got to be there by five," Eric said. There was a roughness to his voice. There were times when Joanna Clark made him frustratingly uneasy. Like right now. She had a way of looking at him ...

Joanna looked away. Whatever Eric's relationship was with Jen, it really had nothing to do with her. She was just filling in. Temporarily. A long shoot. A quirky assignment. Do it. Do it well. Wrap it up and go on to the next one. Keep Paris in mind. Paris was only four weeks away. Once she was in Paris this would be nothing but a bizarre dream.

"Where do the Matthiases live? In one of the townhouses?" Joanna deliberately made her voice light and conversational.

"No. Matthias needs a bigger place. He and Linda do a lot of entertaining. And when visiting dignitaries come to tour Synergy, the Matthiases put them up. They have a whole wing that's strictly for guest quarters. It's quite a place. You'll like it." He smiled. "More in keeping with your taste."

Joanna arched a brow. "Oh? And do the Matthiases have a glass swan sculpture in their entryway as well?"

Eric grinned. "Now that would be taking coincidence too far."

THE MATTHIAS HOME was a graceful, two-story, stucco house with a single-story wing off to the right that Joanna took to be the guest quarters. Special care had gone into the landscaping. A skillful blend of wild desert cacti and exotic flowering shrubs bordered the residence.

They had ridden the mopeds over. Eric had alighted first and offered Joanna a hand. But her hands remained wrapped around the handles, panic gripping her heart and immobilizing her.

Eric smoothed back some wayward strands of her hair and slid her glasses higher on the bridge of her nose. "All you have to do is sit around for an hour or so, have a glass of wine, and act as though your cold is bothering you."

"White," she muttered.

"Huh?"

"White wine."

He smiled. "See, a..."

"A piece of cake. I know." She unwrapped her fingers from the moped and looked over at the house. "I'm not doing this with wholehearted enthusiasm," she said sarcastically.

"No problem. Jen isn't the wholeheartedly enthusiastic type when it comes to social situations," he said, leaning close to her. "However she is enthusiastic about my affectionate attentiveness."

"You mean she *acts* that way in public," Joanna bit back. As she got off the moped she glared at him to let him know that regardless of her blackmail-prompted cooperation in this charade, whatever happened from this point on was very much his full responsibility.

Martin Matthias greeted him at the door. "Hi. Come on in. Linda will be down in a minute." He stepped aside to let them enter.

The hallway, a spacious area with a marble floor, curved mahogany staircase and a finely polished cherrywood sideboard, was well lit by a skylight thirty feet overhead.

Matthias led them across the hall to a large and beautifully appointed living room, decorated in a smart, contemporary fashion. In the center of the room two white leather sofas faced each other, close enough for conversation or combat, depending on the mood of the inhabitants. A scattering of tables, mostly marble or glass topped, were tastefully and functionally placed around the room. One pair served to frame a love seat under a large picture window, a couple of others stood beside brandy-colored upholstered arm chairs, two more flanked the stone fireplace. One whole wall of the room held a built-in display and entertainment center. On the other walls, painted a pale canteloupe color, hung some very expensive-looking modern oil paintings.

Matthias encouraged them to go over to the couches. Joanna and Eric sat on one, Eric moving to sit closer to Joanna than she liked. Marty Matthias sat directly across from them.

"So, how was your trip east? Catch any shows? I hear that the new musical...what's the name of it again...? Well, Linda will know."

"We thought about going to a show, but Jen wasn't feeling great," Eric explained. "Actually, we ended up staying in our hotel room most of the time."

Matthias gave a snorting laugh. "Well, that's not such a bad way to spend your little holiday." He immediately looked over at Joanna with a sheepish smile. "Sorry Jen, I know you don't like it when I tease. How are you feeling now, my dear?"

"Not...great," Joanna said hoarsely. Her voice only vaguely reminded her of her own.

Marty gave her a narrowed gaze which in no way eased her mounting anxiety.

"You don't look yourself, Jen. To be perfectly frank, my dear, I've seen better coloring on a corpse."

"Marty," a high, feminine voice called out from the entry hall. "What a thing to say."

All three of the living room occupants looked over to watch Linda Matthias enter the room. Joanna noted that although Linda had spoken out about her husband's altogether crude remark, she wore a self-effacing smile as she joined them. She had a trim, lovely figure, but she moved with her shoulders hunched slightly forward, like a teenager who felt gangly.

But there was nothing gangly about Linda Matthias. She was prettier in person than in the photo in her file. She wore her sandy hair a bit longer, in a more stylish cut. With greater self-confidence, she could have been a model, Joanna thought, noting how well Mrs. Matthias looked in her flared, pin-striped gray slacks and stretchy cuff-necked navy and white blouse.

Linda smiled at her, a warm, accepting smile. And Joanna took an instant liking to the young woman who, indeed, seemed more out of her element than Joanna felt.

"I think you look fine, Jen," Linda said sweetly, taking a seat beside her husband. "Just a bit peaked, that's all."

Marty stood up. "So, what would you all like to drink?"

"I'll have a Scotch." Eric turned to Joanna. "White wine, hon?" He smiled affectionately at her, his arm going around her shoulder.

Joanna nodded, surreptitiously casting Eric a narrow look.

Her look got her a playful kiss on the cheek.

Linda watched with a bright smile. "You make such a nice couple," she said softly.

Was there a touch of wistfulness in her voice? Joanna wondered. She watched Marty place his palm lightly on his wife's shoulder. "Club soda with a twist for you, darling."

It wasn't a question but a statement. Did Marty simply know what his wife wanted or did he decide what she wanted? Joanna put her bet on the latter after she saw Linda's faint flush.

"You know Jen, since you're starting on a new project anyway, you might want to take a few extra days to rest up and kick that cold," Marty said, heading for the bar. "Besides, for all your stiff upper lip, we all know how hard it is to get so close to success only to see it evaporate before your eyes."

Joanna could feel Eric watching her out of the corner of his eye. He still had his arm around her and she felt the slightly increased pressure of his hand. Inwardly her nerves were as tight as a coiled spring, but she did her best to present a cool facade. "Every scientist must be willing to face defeat, Marty. How else can we ever get close to success?" She held her breath. Had she said too much? Was her remark out of keeping with what Jen might have said? *Oh, this whole farce was crazy.*

But Marty chuckled as he handed her a crystal wine-glass. "I could have bet you'd say something like that, Jen."

She felt a surge of relief and took a swallow of the white wine.

Linda sipped daintily at her club soda, her eyes on Joanna. "You haven't said anything about my new purchase yet, Jen."

Joanna froze. *A new purchase?*

Eric quickly jumped in. "Oh, right. The new—"

"No, no, Eric," Linda cut him off, wagging a finger at him. "No fair. You were over here when it arrived. I want to see if Jen notices."

Joanna could feel beads of sweat form and trickle down her back. Her eyes nervously scanned the room. "Well, I...I'm so bad at this, Linda." She shot Eric a quick look hoping for a clue, but his eyes were downcast.

"Linda, you're putting Jen on the spot, here. She probably doesn't like it and so she's pretending not to even notice," Marty said jocularly.

"No. No, it isn't that," Joanna said hurriedly. "I...I think you have wonderful taste, Linda. It's just...well, it all blends together so nicely, you just...I just..." In the midst of her stammering explanation, Eric crossed his legs, accidently bumping her arm. Some of the wine from her glass spilled. "Oh," Joanna exclaimed, "your rug. I'm..."

"See," Eric cut her off. "Jen's more observant than you gave her credit for, Linda." He looked over at Marty and winked. "And don't jump to conclusions that she doesn't like the new rug just because she accidentally spilled a few drops of wine on it." He smiled at Joanna. "You do like the new rug, don't you, hon?"

"Oh...oh, yes. It's...great. Lovely. It goes perfectly with...everything. Navaho, isn't it, Linda?"

"Why, yes." Linda's voice held a note of surprise. "That's very good."

Joanna realized she was pushing it. "A lucky guess."

"It's museum quality," Marty said proudly, coming round to blot the wet spots on the rug. "Actually, I found it at a gallery in town and told Linda it was just the thing for the room. I never did care for that woven rug she had here. If you're going to buy something, buy quality. I'm always telling her that."

Joanna caught the twitch of embarrassment in Linda's eyes and felt sorry for her. But Linda was quick to recoup. "This rug was so expensive. I would just never think of buying something this costly on my own. But...it is beautiful. Marty has such exquisite taste. Really, this house would never have turned out so well without his input."

Marty gave her a solicitous smile. "Don't be modest, darling. You've been a very good student. I'm quite proud of how much you've accomplished." He leaned forward a little, eyeing Joanna, "You'd never guess she was the same girl I met four years ago in Los Angeles."

"How did the two of you meet?" Eric asked. "I don't recall you ever mentioning."

"Why, we met at a very posh cocktail party," Marty said, giving Linda a sly smile.

Linda smiled sweetly back, but Joanna got the distinct impression this was not a story Marty's wife enjoyed having told. To make matters worse, Marty said, "Go on, darling. You tell them. It's a very amusing story."

Linda's gaze slid toward the living room entry as though to assess the possibility of escape.

"Maybe Linda doesn't feel like reminiscing at the moment," Joanna said in an effort to help her out.

Marty laughed. "It's not that. She just hates for people to know that she used to be a waitress for a catering service. She was at the party passing around the canapés." He gave his wife's knee a little squeeze. "A godawful liver pâté. I told you so there and then, didn't I, darling?"

"Yes," Linda said tightly. "Yes, you did."

"And what else did I tell you that evening?"

Linda gave her husband a pleading look. "Please, Marty..."

"I told you that I'd never tasted a worse pâté and I'd never met a more beautiful woman." He touched Linda's flushed cheek. "And I meant it. I always say what I mean."

"Yes, you always do," Linda whispered, her eyes downcast.

Matthias folded his wife's hand in his and brought it to his lips. "And you're even more beautiful now, darling."

Joanna and Eric shared an uncomfortable glance. There was something almost obsessive in Matthias's affection toward his wife. Matthias either picked up on their discomfort or simply liked to fill in any silences. For the next half hour he kept up what was mostly a lively monologue on everything from art to the latest news events around the world.

"Would you like another Scotch, Eric?" Linda asked when Marty finally paused to catch his breath.

Marty shot up. "Here, let me." He took Eric's glass. "How about you, Jen? Top off your wine?"

"No. No thanks." She fought back a yawn.

Eric put his arm around her again. "On second thought, maybe I'd better skip that refill, Marty. Jen here is exhausted. Her cold has been interfering with her sleep and I promised to tuck her in early."

"Sure, sure. I understand," Marty said amiably. "I want our Jen nice and rested. I still expect grand things from you, my dear."

Joanna smiled. "I'll try not to disappoint you, Marty," she said, rising. Eric and Linda followed suit.

"I'm sorry to hear you're having trouble sleeping, Jen," Linda said, setting down her barely touched club soda on the glass coffee table.

They all started walking toward the entryway.

"Yes," Joanna said off-handedly. "I even tried to take a nap this afternoon, but I just couldn't doze off." There was a brief pause. They were almost at the front door. "Oh, funny thing. I just happened to be looking out my bedroom window and I noticed that someone was in the vacant townhouse next door. Has someone new arrived at Synergy?"

Joanna saw Linda pale and Marty's eyes narrow. She shot Eric a quick look. He didn't look altogether pleased at her inquiry. Did he think she was stepping on his toes? Still, he was obviously watching the Matthiases' reactions.

"What's up, Marty?" Eric asked.

"Damn," was Matthias's response.

Linda blinked rapidly. "Yesterday afternoon, while Marty and I were at the pool house, someone broke into Marty's office in the house and rifled through all his drawers."

"But . . . the alarm system," Joanna said.

"Cleverly circumvented," Marty mumbled. "I wasn't going to broadcast it." He gave Linda a clearly disapproving look. "Morgan and Lou found one of my pearl cuff links in the room of one of the security guards. Fired him on the spot. I didn't want to press charges. You know how Washington gets. I figured, boot him out and our troubles are over."

Linda clasped her hands together. "But if Jen saw someone prowling around in a vacant town house, then our troubles aren't over at all," she said worriedly.

Marty scowled, but then suddenly he slapped the side of his head with his palm. "What am I thinking? I know who must have been next door. Your secretary."

"Toni?" Eric said incredulously. "What would she be doing over there?"

Marty gave a relieved laugh. "Her air-conditioning unit went on the fritz and Morgan told her she could stay over at one of the empty units temporarily. I remember now. Morgan did say he'd given her the key so she could check out the unit next door to yours. We just had that one painted, thinking Menkin was coming over from Berlin to do some work, remember?"

Eric nodded slowly.

Marty gave Joanna's shoulder a reassuring squeeze. "No need to worry about peeping Toms or anything, Jen. I'm sure that by the time you get home, Toni will have settled in next door. You have nothing to worry about."

*No, nothing to worry about except Hampleman's secretary, Toni Conners,* Joanna thought.

When they were alone at their mopeds, Joanna turned to Eric. "Could Toni be the one?"

Eric shrugged. "Anyone could be the one. But finding out who it is, is not your problem," he said firmly, seeing the glint of curiosity in Joanna's eyes. *Great,* he thought with a rueful grimace. *First she refuses to cooperate without coercion. And now she's not only getting into playing Hampleman, she's ready to play amateur secret agent as well.*

Joanna caught Eric's scowl. "I did okay in there, didn't I, Eric?"

His scowl slowly faded as he swung his leg over his moped. "Yeah. You did okay. But, just remember, I was there to catch you when you stumbled."

She raised an eyebrow. "Well, I guess at this point, if I fall flat on my face, we're all in trouble, aren't we?" She climbed onto her moped. "You, me, and the whole free world."

## Chapter Seven

The watcher saw a silhouetted figure cross behind the drawn curtains. "Something's up. I sense it."

There was an assessing pause. "Yes? And what do you suggest?"

A sneering smile. "I thought that was your department."

For a few moments the drone of the air conditioner was the only sound in the room. And then a begrudging admission. "That little trip of theirs this weekend does worry me."

"Maybe it's time to stop watching and take action. I tell you, she's nervous. He's better at concealing it, but he's nervous, too."

A cigarette was snuffed against the crystal edge of the ashtray. "Perhaps we should make them more nervous."

"I don't understand."

"Nervous people get sloppy. So far this pair has been far too neat and tidy."

"I don't think . . ."

"I do think. And that's what counts. We'll play them along for a while."

"And then?" The question was heavy with expectation.

Another cigarette was lit, jets of smoke shooting toward the ceiling. "In the end, we'll get what we want. I've never found a problem that a bit of the proper persuasion at the proper time couldn't put right.''

One eyebrow was cocked in feigned dismay. "You can be ruthless, can't you?"

A sharp laugh. "Of course, and we're two of a kind."

As SHE ENTERED the house, Joanna experienced another tremor as her eyes flickered over the swan sculpture on Hampleman's entry table.

"I'll make us some dinner," Eric said, closing the front door.

Joanna turned to him, her hands clasped together in front of her. "Did you see that the lights were on at both houses?"

"Gerta's back and Toni must have settled in for the night."

"If it is Toni?"

Eric nodded. "That was her car in the driveway."

"Did you believe Matthias's story?" she asked suspiciously.

"What do you mean?"

"That Morgan just happened to pick out the place next door for Toni because it had just been spruced up?"

"It makes sense," Eric said quietly, walking into the kitchen.

Joanna followed him. "Or did Toni specifically ask for that house so that she could keep watch on me?"

Eric was at the open fridge. "There's some leftover stew from Friday or cold chicken..."

"Either." She crossed her arms over her chest. "I hate this. I feel like they're all watching me. Matthias, Toni, Gerta..."

"I wouldn't put Marty on the top of your list." He pulled out the wrapped plate of cold chicken.

"Why not?"

"Because next to Jen herself, Matthias, as head of Synergy, gets all the glory if her research pans out. And our Marty likes glory."

"Wouldn't he get that glory if he sold Jen out to the competition?"

"There's nothing in his background or activities to suggest he isn't true-blue. Quite the contrary. He's as close as anyone I know to being beyond reproach."

"I don't like him."

Eric laughed. "That's not exactly reason to hang the man."

"I don't like the way he treats his wife." There was a brief pause. "She's pretty. Prettier than her photo. It's clear she feels intimidated by him."

"You think she could have done better?"

"Don't you?" Joanna asked.

"I don't know," Eric said thoughtfully. "For all Marty's pomposity I think he really loves Linda. For some women, that's what counts."

"He's more than pompous," Joanna persisted. "He's controlling, manipulative, demanding..."

"Whoa. You saw all that over one glass of wine?"

Joanna's lips compressed. "I've known men like him."

Eric stood silent, staring at her. Did she always make snap judgments about men? She'd certainly made more than a few about him. Once she formed an opinion, how likely was she to change her mind?

Could he get her to change her mind about him? And just what kind of an opinion of him did he want her to have? Eric busied himself making up plates of cold chicken and salad. As he sliced tomatoes he went over a silent litany in his head. *She's off limits, man. Don't go getting any dumb ideas.* From their first encounter he'd had an unnerving reaction to Joanna Clark. He'd felt immediately drawn to her. Why not? She was astonishingly beautiful with that butterscotch hair; alluring dark gray eyes made all the more exotic by those thick, sooty lashes; a mouth that was at once delicate and determined. But it wasn't only her looks that he found compelling; it was her disarming manner, her sharp intelligence, an indomitable curiosity even under the most trying of conditions. Of course her curiosity was something he'd have to worry about, he realized. And, the way things were going, he had plenty enough to worry about already.

Joanna walked over to the kitchen window, which faced the Hauser townhouse. The shades were drawn, upstairs and down, but Joanna could make out a light in the kitchen and another in the dining room. "How long has she been back, I wonder?"

Eric stopped working on the salad and came up to stand behind her. "Whoever's watching, there's nothing for them to see. Relax."

"I can't. Not in this house. I feel...strange." She turned to face Eric. There was desperation in her look. "I feel *her* here. We're...so much alike. I'm not just talking about appearance."

"In some ways, you are alike," Eric said softly. "Not in others."

Joanna's palms moved to her cheeks. "When I was in her bathroom earlier, I realized my...my skin was dry. I've got...sensitive skin. I have to use special hypo-allergenic creams and moisturizers or...I get a rash." There was a marked quiver in her voice. "So does she. Her skin...Jen's skin is sensitive, too. She even uses...the same brand of moisturizer I use. It was...in her medicine cabinet."

Eric gently drew her hands from her face and smiled. "Hey, millions of women have sensitive skin. Why do you think companies produce the stuff?"

But Joanna wasn't listening. "Her shampoo...it's for dry hair. I have dry hair, too. And other things, the things you wrote down about her habits. I can't drink red wine, either. And...and when I get angry I do exactly what she does. I withdraw. People have said...they've said my eyes get like ice when I'm angry.

"This is too spooky, Eric. It's as though we were twins. But...but that can't be. And that makes it even weirder. It's as if Jennifer Hampleman were...my clone. Like some mad scientist created her to be my double. Or...or created me. I feel like we're blending together, that I'm losing some of my own identity. I...feel...like she's creeping inside of me, becoming a part of me." She began to tremble, her gaze locking with his. She could feel her control slipping away, all of her thoughts dissolving into an incoherent jumble.

He reached for her, drawing her to him, holding her gently, feeling her fear and, even more intensely, feeling a longing that he sensed she felt as well.

"There are ways in which you're very different," he whispered reassuringly, running his fingers along her forearms. Her skin was smooth and cool. Joanna's trembling increased. She couldn't have moved away from him if she wanted to—and she didn't want to. All she could focus on was the intimate way his fingertips were caressing the sensitive skin of her inner arm.

Then his arms were around her. He kissed her softly at first. Joanna's lips parted. She shut her eyes, shutting out, at least for the moment, her mounting fears, allowing herself an instant of weakness. And yet, even as she welcomed the warmth and passion of Eric's kiss, Joanna knew that this was a dangerous move, that she was giving up even more of herself. He'd said she was different. But he was holding and kissing a woman who could be Jennifer Hampleman for all the similarities. And his hands were moving down the back of Jen's dress...

"No," she gasped, pushing him away.

He drew back immediately. "Jen, I'm sorry." His voice was raw and husky.

A rage washed over her. "Joanna. Not Jen, Joanna." And then she fled from the room.

Minutes after she had sought the refuge of Jen's bedroom and locked the door, she heard Eric's soft knock.

"Please, Joanna, open the door. I brought your dinner. Some cold chicken, salad..." He knocked again, rattling the knob this time. "Joanna, let's talk. We're both tense. It's only natural. Don't shut me out, Joanna. We need each other."

She leaned wearily against her side of the locked door. "You've got the wrong idea, Logan. I don't need you."

"Okay. Okay, I need you. I shouldn't have...kissed you before, Joanna."

"Were you kissing me, Logan?"

"Joanna..."

"Are you in love with her?"

"I told you..."

"You told me you two aren't lovers. That's not the same thing."

"It isn't what you think." Again he knocked. "This is no way to talk."

Exhaustion made her slide down to sit on the carpeted floor. "How am I different, Logan? Am I weaker than Jen? Did I give in more easily?"

"Joanna, stop it."

"Do I kiss differently, Logan? Does my body feel any different to you?"

There was a long pause. "I've set your tray of food out here on the floor, Joanna. I'm going to turn in for the night. Eat something and then get some sleep. Maybe tomorrow...we can start fresh."

She heard his footsteps fading, the door across the hall closing. Did he lock his door? She hadn't heard a bolt click.

She sat on the floor, feeling drained, shaken. She flung off her glasses, pulled the pins from her chignon so that her hair fell free to her shoulders. Then she dropped her head into her hands and began to cry softly, angry at herself because she wasn't even sure what she was really crying about.

Whatever the reasons, the crying didn't help. She dragged herself to her feet and stared around the room. Jen's room. Yes, she could feel her in here. Joanna's gaze fell on the bed. A double bed. Did Jen sleep in that bed alone? Had Eric lied to her about not having had an intimate relationship with Jen?

She walked over to the bed and sat down. And how did Jen feel about Eric? Did Eric make Jen's pulse race the way her own pulse raced? Did Jen tremble in his arms the way she trembled? Had Jen been drawn unerringly into Eric's web, as, even now at this very instant, she was being drawn? Did Jen realize the danger and the potential pain of falling for a man like Eric? Joanna had but to breathe to feel the danger, fear the pain.

Idly, she pulled open the top drawer of the table beside the bed. Inside was a small notepad, a leather-bound address book and a framed photo turned upside down. She stared at the back of the photo for a moment, then reached for the notepad. There was nothing written on it. For telephone messages, probably. Joanna kept one beside her own bed at home. Next she flipped through the address book. Unfamiliar names, except for Jen's parents and brother, addresses, phone numbers. She closed the book, her gaze falling again on the framed photo, still facedown in the drawer. For some inexplicable reason, she felt a mixture of anticipation and trepidation about looking at it. Very slowly, she took hold of the silver frame and drew the photo out of the drawer. Still, she hesitated before finally turning it over.

As she stared down at the photo resting squarely on her lap, a dry, cackling voice seemed to whisper through her. *Jen and Eric*. Strictly a professional relationship, Eric had said. But there was nothing professional about this eight by ten glossy. Jen and Eric on the beach, arms around each other, laughing. Jen in profile, looking up at Eric. She wasn't wearing her glasses. Her dark gray eyes were shining. Shining with adoration. And Eric, eyes ahead, winking at the camera, cocky, bold, king of the walk.

Was she reading more into that photo than there was? Was this evidence? She stared at Jen. This picture of the physicist spooked her even more than Jen's ID photo. The similarities were even more striking in this candid shot. It was like seeing a twin she never knew she had. And her *twin* was gazing up at Eric Logan with a look that Joanna imagined she, herself, had worn on her face, just minutes ago when they'd kissed.

Jen's in love with Eric. She knew one photo wasn't a lot to base her conclusion on. But Joanna knew. That was all. She knew.

And Eric? Had it been her resemblance to Jen that had aroused him, drawn him to her? There was no denying the attraction there. On both their parts, she admitted to herself. A chilling thought swept through her. Was she so much like Jen Hampleman that she was compelled to be attracted to the very same man?

Tears spilled from her eyes. She swiped at them angrily, then shoved the framed photo back in the drawer—face-down. Then she shut the drawer.

*What do I care? What is their relationship to me? What is he to me? Nothing. Nothing. I've been attracted to plenty of men in my life. I never made a fool of myself over one.*

Anyway, it was probably a purely psychological phenomenon. She'd read about this happening to people in captivity: a prisoner falling in love with her captor. Well,

Eric was her captor. Oh, he didn't use force or violence to hold her. And even the blackmail business hadn't turned out to be his true ace in the hole. It was Eric himself. Eric, flashing his charm and sensuality, disarming her with glimpses of his vulnerability, making her believe his motives were honorable. A man with ideals. Brave, intrepid, loyal, tender, true to his values. Was he all that he seemed? And, most troubling of all, just how powerful would his hold over her prove to be?

Her eyes fell on the closed drawer. What was she trying to hide from herself, trying to avoid? With a resolute grimace, she pulled the drawer back open. Without hesitation this time, she removed the framed photo and set it on the bedside table, angled toward the bed. She stared at it, nodded. *Eric and Jen. Keep that in mind.*

THE DARKNESS is like a tomb. It's hard to breathe with a throat drier than sandpaper. A door. There must be a door. She can't think. If only her head would clear. That wine she'd drunk...had it been doctored? Matthias. She can picture him bringing her the glass. White wine. Jen never drinks red wine. No, no. Not Jen. She's the one. She never drinks red wine.

Light filters in. *You don't look bad.* Linda Matthias is smiling. Pretty Linda. But...but wait. Not Linda. Jen. Jen smiling. *You don't look bad.* Jen presses her hand to her mouth and giggles.

*This is no laughing matter, Jen. It's not your life that's coming apart at the seams,* she scolds Jen soundly. *What kind of a twin are you, anyway, to put me in such a precarious situation? Just because you look like me...*

*Relax.* Eric is speaking to her, his hands cupping her face. *You're different, Joanna.* She moves against his hands as he strokes her. He kisses her mouth. Oh yes, her pulse is racing. She is trembling. Her eyes are shining with love. Her eyes. Jen's eyes . . .

The curtain is open. The room is bright now. She runs to the window. There, across the way, in the vacant house . . . eyes. Eyes watching her. Gerta, Toni, Linda, Marty. Wait. Wait. Eric is there, too. And Jen. Watching her. Jen watching herself.

She feels dizzy. Her head throbs. Drugged. Yes, that's it. The wine. Can't breathe . . .

*Help.* The word slides into the air and disappears. Panic bubbles like club soda in her throat. Her hand lurches out. The shattering of glass . . .

JOANNA WOKE with a jolt, her body trembling. She sat up in bed, her hand pressed to her racing heart. Her night-gown was damp, her skin clammy. A dream. A bad dream. She rubbed her eyes, then saw the photo of Eric and Jen on the floor in a pool of shattered glass. She must have knocked it over in her sleep. The glass couldn't have been shattered by hitting the soft carpet. It must have hit the corner of the bedside table first.

She still felt groggy. Like in the dream. And even now, awake, she realized she was having difficulty breathing. There was a funny smell in the room. Cloying. Nauseating. She swung her legs out of bed. Dizzy. So dizzy. Like in her dream, she wondered if she'd been drugged. But now, it's that awful smell that's making it so hard to breathe.

*Got to get help.*

She stood up, but her legs were shaky. It was pitch black in the room. The door. Where was the door? Swaying on her feet as she walked, she groped her way across the room, banging into furniture. Tomorrow she'd have black and blue marks. Tomorrow . . .

At last her fingers touched the cold metal door knob. Weak and so very dizzy, she dropped to her knees, reached up to unlock the door and pulled it open.

She'd prayed the smell wouldn't be so bad once she'd escaped the room, but it was worse, thicker, out here in the hall.

Gas. Yes, that was it. Gas. There was a gas stove in the kitchen. She remembered now. She had electric at home. She'd always worried about gas leaks. Oh God, that was it. A gas leak. The fumes were suffocating her.

*Eric. Got to get to Eric. Save him.* She didn't have the strength to get up on her feet again. She half crawled, half dragged herself across the hall.

It felt like miles, her gaze was fixed on his closed door the whole time. Oh no, she thought in a panic. What if he had locked his door? He'd suffocate. He'd die.

Her breath erupted from her chest in great heaving gasps. She was afraid she wouldn't even make it to his door to find out . . .

But then she was there. It took a lot of effort to lift her arm so that her hand could reach the knob. *Don't be locked. Please, please don't let the door be locked.*

She let out a rasping sigh of relief as the door gave way.

"Eric. Eric." She tried to shout; she wanted to shout; but her throat was raw from breathing the fumes. "Eric, please. Gas. We . . . have . . . to get . . . out."

Eric's room was dark. The darkness seemed to seize her voice, making it echo back at her. "Eric . . ."

She was crawling again, her fear that Eric had already succumbed to the noxious fumes egging her on. She had to get to his bed. Maybe he'd only passed out. Get to the bed, shake him, force him awake. Then, together, they had to get out of the house. Fast.

She couldn't find the sofa that made up into a bed. The bed for guests. Strictly for guests. She was disoriented.

*Think. Picture the room in your mind.* Yes, yes, she remembered now. To the left. The sofa sat against the wall all the way over to the left. In the corner of the room. This room had seemed so small to her this morning. And now, now as she crawled along the cool wood parquet floor, it seemed enormous, without end.

Her hand hit the leg of the sofa. *Oh, thank God.* "Eric," she croaked. "Wake up."

She pulled herself up, her fingers cloying at the light cover. She tugged on it. "Eric. Please..."

Silence.

She reached out, found his arm. It hung limply off the edge of the sofa. She shook it. "Eric. Eric...wake up."

Her heart leaped into her throat, hammering, pounding, lodging there.

Eric didn't move.

Joanna's head was ringing, her brain pleading for oxygen.

"Eric...please..." She could hear the desperation in her voice, the terror. And then she heard a faint sound...a low moan. "Oh Eric, Eric, you're alive..."

"Joanna...?"

"JOANNA."

The whispered sound of her name fluttered against the edges of her mind. She tried to reach out for the sound, grab it, but she couldn't.

"Joanna. Can you open your eyes?"

"Mmm," she said groggily. But she didn't heed the order.

"There was a gas leak, Joanna. You passed out. You're okay now. You're fine."

"Eric?" Her eyelids fluttered open. He was looking down at her, concern etched on his features. And tenderness.

"How do you feel?"

She wasn't sure. She wasn't even sure where she was until she looked around the room. Jen's bedroom. She was in Jen's bed.

"How did I get back here?"

"I carried you."

Slowly her head was beginning to clear. She took in a deep breath, relieved to smell cool, pure air. "Gas..."

"A leak. There's a buried propane tank just outside the kitchen. It feeds the stove. The valve must be defective. I'll call in a repair man in the morning. An accident."

Her gaze was fixed on him now. "An accident?"

"Yes."

"We could have...died."

"You woke me just before you passed out. I got all the windows open, and brought you back in here. How do you feel now?"

Instead of answering him, Joanna gave him a wary look. "An accident. How convenient."

"Joanna."

"Is that how you got rid of her, too?" There was an edge of hysteria in her voice.

He exhaled wearily. "We're not back on that track again."

"It all fits. You lure me here with threats, tell me it's all in the name of patriotism. You have my passport confiscated. Oh yes, I checked to confirm it. You obviously weren't taking any chances. Meanwhile, you've done away with a leading physicist. No, that's not it. You didn't...kill her. You had her kidnapped. Then you brought me in. Everyone believes Hampleman is safe and sound. And then a freak accident. Poor Hampleman. She died in her bed of suffocation from gas fumes. A faulty valve in the gas tank. How awful. How tragic. But everyone would stop looking for her."

"Joanna, think. You didn't die. If I'd wanted to do away with you, I would have left you to die, wouldn't I?" His eyes flicked to the photo beside the bed. "Jen hasn't been murdered or kidnapped. She's safe. And she's grateful to you for helping her."

"You saw her? Tonight?"

"I spoke to her."

Emotions curled through Joanna's eyes like smoke as she stared at him. He returned her look with a tender smile.

"You're going to be fine, Joanna."

"Am I?"

"Yes," he said softly. But torturous images flashed through his mind: the panic when he'd come to and smelled the fumes; fear slamming against his chest; his voice trembling as he'd watched her pass out. If anything had happened to her he would never have forgiven himself. And the agency would have had his head. But that wasn't what he'd thought when he'd seen her, when the terror had overtaken him. He wasn't as tough as he'd thought. The cool, invincible Eric Logan. It stunned him how quickly she'd gotten to him.

"You don't really believe it was an accident," she said challengingly.

Her voice cut through his thoughts. "What?"

"I don't think you believe, any more than I do, that the leak was due to a faulty valve...a faulty anything. It was...deliberate, wasn't it?"

Eric was picking up the glass shards from the carpet, placing them carefully on top of the photo. He stopped and stared up at her. He sensed that if he tried to deceive her now, even for her own good, he would never win her trust. "Yes," he said quietly.

She didn't say anything.

He left his task and sat on the edge of her bed. Gently, he cupped the side of her face and touched his thumb to her dry lips. "Someone must have been watching the house; waited until we'd gone to sleep and gotten to one of the feeder valves outside the kitchen. It was shut off and not leaking when I went out to check on it, and the papers in your desk and mine have been gone through."

"Did this crazy person really think that we'd keep top-secret experimental data in the house?"

Eric gave an inward sigh of relief. At least she wasn't still accusing him of being the villain. For the moment, anyway. "No, not actual documents. But some scribbled notes, maybe. Anything to indicate whether you were still involved in the research that was supposed to be abandoned."

Joanna looked away. "But if they'd killed me, what would have become of the completed research they apparently want so badly?"

Eric hesitated. "I don't think they meant to kill you. Just put us both out so they could search the house. They almost succeeded, too. I expect we weren't even supposed to know they'd been snooping. And my traps didn't catch them either."

"You laid traps? You thought this would happen?" She stared at him in horror.

"Not...the gas. I just figured our stuff might be checked over. That's all. Some time when we were both out. I never thought they'd go and do something this stupid."

"Why did they?" Joanna sat up fully in bed, curiosity pushing her fears and outrage aside for the moment. She stared at Eric. "Why didn't they make their move when we were at the Matthiases'?"

Eric had to admire her. For all she'd been through, Joanna's mind was ticking away like a finely crafted Swiss watch.

"Matthias," she whispered. "If it was Marty..."

"Or Linda," he cut in.

Joanna's eyes narrowed. "Or Gerta, for that matter. She could have arrived back just minutes before we came home from the Matthiases'. She could have watched from her window and then decided to make her move."

"We can go right down the list, Joanna. Toni's as prime a candidate as the others. And then there's..."

"How'd the bastard get into the house? What about the security system? Why didn't it go off?"

Eric frowned. "Whoever broke in obviously knew how to circumvent the system."

"Who'd know enough? Matthias? Gerta? Morgan?"

"Yes, any one of them. But you wouldn't have to be a Ph. D. scientist or top level security person to figure out how to beat the system if you had access to the original schematic drawings."

Joanna's pulse quickened. "The break-in at the Matthiases' yesterday. Maybe it wasn't just cuff links that were stolen."

"I'll speak to Marty first thing tomorrow. We'll have to have the security locks reworked and make sure the new schematics aren't obtainable."

"But if Marty's the one..."

"Just to be on the safe side, I'll arrange to have the system here at the house done by one of my people," Eric said soberly.

Joanna shut her eyes, recognition of what had nearly happened to her hitting her full force. Someone had been in Eric's den, rifling through the papers in his desk as she and Eric slept. She opened her eyes again and met Eric's intense gaze. "What we have here," she whispered emotionally, "is a callous, ruthless, despicable traitor." Fresh tears seeped into her eyes.

"Don't cry, Joanna." He could see her pulse beating visibly in the hollow of her throat. Her dark gray eyes were wet and luminous. He could feel his heart pounding against the wall of his chest. He wanted to take her in his arms more than he wanted to take his next breath. But he didn't dare, because he knew he'd never be able to stop there.

# *Chapter Eight*

Eric had a white-knuckled grip on the phone. "I don't like it, I tell you. This isn't the way—"

"Calm down, son. We have to view these events without letting our emotions carry us away," came the solemn voice on the other end of the line.

"You don't mean *our* emotions. You mean my emotions. So, say it."

"You're doing it for me."

"She doesn't deserve this. Any of it. That's what's got me riled."

"Is it?"

"Sometimes this business we're in gets too ugly even for me."

"Maybe that's what makes you so good."

"I thought you objected to my emotions."

"No, no. That's not what I said, Eric. I just don't want your emotions to interfere with your objectives. A certain degree of feeling will keep you on your toes. And we can't afford to get sloppy here. Too much is resting on our success."

"When is that success going to come?"

"Soon. You know that."

"I still say we should be straight with her."

"No. It's working just fine this way."

"You call this working fine?"

"There was bound to be some . . . activity after the weekend."

"Activity? Damn it, she could have died."

"I admit it was risky, but I have no doubt they were looking after her, in their own way. Dead, she's of no use to them. Alive, she's of value, if only for what they believe she still might accomplish. And later, possibly, as a bargaining chip. They don't want her permanently harmed any more than we do."

"Not as long as they think they're looking after Jen. But, if they find out the truth, Joanna's life won't be worth a plugged nickel. And she doesn't even know what she's risking her life for."

"For heaven's sake, Eric. She's a model. How much thought does a woman like that give to the environment, to the vital need to conserve energy . . . ?"

"You know damn well that's not what I'm talking about. But you're wrong, anyway. You don't know her. You sit there behind your big desk sticking people into little boxes. Models go in the same box as dumb blondes, is that it? Models are vain, vapid . . ."

"You *are* riled up, Eric. She must be something."

"Yeah . . . she's something. But, don't worry, chief. I know my place."

"I just hope you remember your priorities."

Eric frowned. "If these *activities* persist, my priorities might change."

"Oh?"

"There's one thing I didn't and won't lie to Joanna about—her safety. When I convinced her to impersonate Jen, I promised her that she'd be perfectly safe. Maybe I was being too optimistic to believe our ploy would fool the opposition."

"It is working, Eric."

"No, not the way I see it."

"Look, they have to take some steps to be sure Jen's truly given up the research. And once they are . . ."

"What if, in the process, they discover our little ruse?"

"It's your job to see that they don't. I thought that was understood. You seemed confident enough back in New York when you phoned me from that beauty parlor. And again, after your little get-together with Matthias and his wife. You said she was perfect. And clever. Another thing— you were wrong before, son. I never for a moment considered Joanna Clark to be vapid. Indeed, I would have been quite shocked if she were. I'm as sure as you are that she'll be just fine."

"And if I'm not so sure anymore?"

"Is that your perception speaking or your emotions?"

"You didn't see the look in her eyes when she came to. She's badly shaken. It could affect . . ."

"I'll tell you what. Have her stay home for a few days, until things settle down. We can use that cold story. Spread the word that it's gotten worse, she needs some quiet, some bed rest. The less time she spends at the labs the better. Even though I have no doubt that you can carry her along, even there."

Eric laughed dryly. "Well, I'm glad one of us has no doubts."

AT FIRST it was easy enough to keep Joanna housebound. Physical and emotional exhaustion compounded by the inhalation of gas fumes had done a thorough number on her. She slept most of Monday, and on Tuesday she was just beginning to get her bearings again. By Wednesday, however, she was not only rested but edgy.

"I'm not staying home another day." *Home.* This wasn't her home. This was Jen's home. Joanna felt the need to get out. That need seemed to be growing more intense with each minute she spent among her alter ego's personal possessions. Maybe the labs would provide a more *sterile* and impersonal atmosphere. "I mean it, Eric. I don't want to stay in this house for another whole day."

"If you're still scared, I'll stay with you." He'd remained home with her for the past two days, but he'd said it would look odd if he didn't show his face at the labs for at least a few hours today.

"Should I be scared? Do you think they'll be back?"

"No. No, I don't. The place has already gotten a thorough going over. There's no reason for them to come back."

"If I stay here for much longer, it might raise suspicions."

"Just give it another day or two. You're still pale..."

"Jen's always pale. That's what comes from spending all her time in the labs." She hesitated, thinking about that photo of Jen and Eric. "Well, maybe not all her time. She did manage to get to the beach on occasion, didn't she?"

"Not very often," he muttered.

Joanna stared at him. Jealousy. She'd been telling herself for days it was a dumb emotion, a wasted emotion, a ridiculous emotion for her to be experiencing. Almost as ridiculous as her escalating attraction to this man who remained an absolute enigma to her. Drawn as if by some mysterious force to Logan, Joanna remained angry and wary of him. He was too secretive by far. Yet, was it only her imagination when she sensed that those secrets were beginning to weigh heavily on him?

"What happened to that photo, Eric?"

"Photo?"

"The one of you and Jen."

He rose from the kitchen chair and started cleaning the breakfast dishes off the table. "The glass broke. I...stuck the picture in a drawer until I could get it framed properly again."

"A drawer in your room?"

"What's the big deal about the picture?"

"I want it back."

The cups clanked in the sink. "It isn't *your* picture, Joanna."

"It's Jen's. She kept it in her room." Joanna walked over to Eric at the sink. "She didn't keep it facedown in her bedside table drawer. She kept it on the table, facing her bed. So she could look at it. You were the one who stuck it away."

"Since when did you become a mind reader?"

Joanna felt a ribbon of tension shoot down her spine. "Since... you brought me here to *her* house. Before that, even. When I saw that ID photo of her, really saw it... It's as though I can feel... what she's feeling. I can picture her in my mind, getting up each morning, her eyes falling on that photo..." Joanna's voice faltered. "I can...see...the look in her eyes." The tip of her tongue darted out, moistening her dry lips as a wave of desire fanned out across her skin. "Why did you stick the photo in the drawer, Eric?"

His gaze was riveted on hers. "She asked me to," he said simply.

Joanna wasn't sure what made the lump well in her throat just then. Maybe it was the combination of the tension and everything else that had happened to her since Eric had come into her life. Or maybe it was the plaintive look in his eyes, the ties of attraction tightening between them, making their mutual struggle to keep their distance nearly impossible.

There had never been anyone who aroused Joanna like Eric did. She'd spent her life deliberately avoiding men like him, men who threatened to obliterate her self-control, her ability to think clearly, rationally, her desperate grip on independence.

But now she realized she wasn't safe, from him or from her own intensifying desire. Joanna knew that if she didn't pull away now, Eric would take her into dangerous uncharted regions. But, suddenly those regions held an irresistible allure.

She moved swiftly into his arms.

THEY LAY TOGETHER on the thick living room carpet, their heads resting on pillows pulled down from the couch. Eric had known instinctively not to take Joanna up to Jen's bedroom. While there was no *neutral* territory in the house, this room held the least of Jen's spirit and the most of his. He knew it was vital for Joanna to keep Jen's spirit at bay.

He leaned over her, kissing her lips, her throat. His tongue slid around a nipple, Joanna emitted a soft, low sound like a hum, her arms locking around his waist.

His hands roamed over her body. Everywhere he touched—her breasts, her spine, her buttocks, the curve of skin behind her knee—she came alive. She moved her body against the pressure of his hands. They rolled. She rose up over him, her gray eyes luminescent with desire. And something more. Boldness. She'd never been bold before. Before today she'd had no idea that making love could actually empower her.

Eric wasn't taking away anything. He was giving. And, even more important, he encouraged her to give. Eric made her bold, awakened her to her own hunger and yearning, pushed aside her fears and questions, at least for the moment. In his arms, her naked body pressing down on him, her hand guiding him so that he slipped inside of her with ease, she shed the boundaries of her anxieties, felt Eric shedding his. She could barely breathe as he kept the rhythm of their lovemaking slow and deliberate.

"You're driving me crazy," she gasped.

"It's only fair, Joanna." He breathed the words into her.

Her heart raced. *Yes. Joanna. Joanna. It's me, Eric. Joanna. Not Jen.*

Over and over, he whispered her name as if to still any doubts. "Joanna, Joanna, oh yes, Joanna."

Together, they melded into something wonderful, until nothing remained for them but the incendiary flood of sensation and the whispered sounds of pleasure.

Even after they were both spent, their hands caressed each other's bodies. Neither of them wanted to sever the connection.

Eric drew her close. "Joanna, there's something I want you to know."

His somber tone made her tense. "About Jen?"

He sat up a little. "About her research."

"Her research?" She didn't hide the disappointment in her voice. Oh, certainly she remained curious about her look-alike's secret research. But, over the past few days, her curiosity about Jen's work had taken a back seat to her curiosity about the woman herself. And about this woman's relationship to the man she had just made love with.

Joanna sat up, reaching for her clothes. Eric followed suit. They dressed quickly. The silence was suddenly tense and awkward.

"I thought you couldn't tell me about her research."

"I don't always follow orders. There are times when other...priorities kick in."

Joanna sat down on the sofa. Eric sat down beside her. "You think you owe me something...now."

He smiled. "I owe you a lot, Joanna. But I want to tell you about Jen's work because I believe that you have a right to know what you're risking yourself for. I know you didn't choose it, but we are in this together. And...I want you to know that what you're doing...matters greatly."

It had already gone beyond that for Joanna, but she waited quietly.

"Did you ever hear the term . . . cold fusion?" he asked.

Joanna had to think for a moment. "I remember reading something about it in the papers a while back. Some sort of scientific hoax, wasn't it?"

"A couple of scientists announced they'd used a simple electrode to create atomic fusion in a flask at room temperature. If it were true, do you have any idea what it would mean?"

"We could do away with dangerous nuclear energy plants?"

He smiled approvingly. "And we'd have a virtually inexhaustible source of energy. Cheap, safe, unlimited."

"And that's what Jen is working on?"

"Yes. Those two scientists you read about in the papers had actually laid some of the groundwork. But they couldn't take it far enough. They couldn't reproduce their results. Neither could anyone else. Jen's close to doing it. With certain modifications, which she's now working on, she's very likely to achieve success. Jen's work was going great when we discovered that security at Synergy had been breached and that someone here had either been bought, or was even possibly a mole for the Eastern bloc. We knew we had to move quickly. Our safest bet was to convince this agent that Jen had hit a dead end."

"How did you find out about this agent?"

"An effort was made to recruit Jen."

"Who did the recruiting?"

"It was all done through untraceable written communications."

"And when Jen refused?"

He hesitated. "There were threats."

Joanna blanched, cold fear trickling down her spine.

Eric reached out for her, but she drew away. "So if they don't believe I've stopped working on the project . . ." She grimaced, unable to go on. *No, not me. Jen. They have to believe Jen's stopped. But I'm Jen. Those threats to her have become threats to me.*

He'd said too much. He knew it. He'd frightened her and that would make things riskier for both of them. And yet there was even more....

"I'm going to the lab," Joanna said, springing up from the couch, her mouth set in a determined line.

He grabbed for her. "No, not like this. You're too upset. Take another day..."

"The only way I can be safe...and protect Jen and her research for that matter...is if I convince this bastard that I'm above suspicion. The only way to do that is to face my unknown enemy. He is mine now, Eric, isn't he? And it all boils down to this. I'm only as safe as my ability to carry off this charade makes me. I have to convince my enemy that I'm hard at work on a new project." She couldn't quite meet his gaze. The gaze of her lover. The gaze of a man who was in so many ways no less a mystery to her now than he had been before. "Let's get to work, Dr. Logan," she said, avoiding his eyes.

A faint smile played on his lips. "Did anyone ever tell you you're a very stubborn woman, Joanna?"

She met his gaze then, one eyebrow raised. "Did anyone ever tell Jen?"

Eric's smile disappeared at the thought.

TONI CONNERS was standing by the file cabinet and Hank Morgan was perched on the corner of her desk when Joanna and Eric walked into their secretary's office.

"You saved me a phone call." Morgan slid off the desk, eyeing them both in turn.

"I...I called Hank first," Toni piped in nervously. "I mean...I thought he'd..."

Morgan cut her off. "Someone broke into your files." He gave Toni a little nod. "You ought to get yourself a cup of coffee, honey. Settle your nerves."

Toni gave Hank Morgan a smile that was both nervous and grateful. Then she looked over at Eric, giving Joanna the most cursory of glances. "If it's all right with you..."

Eric produced an easy smile. "Sure. Just one thing, Toni. Was anything taken?"

"No. I...wouldn't have even noticed the files had been touched, except a couple of them were out of order. And you know, Dr. Logan, how fanatic I am about my filing."

His smile broadened. "We both know that, right Jen?"

Joanna's eyes flickered over Toni. "Yes, of course. And most fortunate, too."

There was a tense moment of silence.

"Well, I think I will get that coffee," Toni said finally. "Can I bring anything back for anyone?"

All three declined. Toni started for the door.

"Oh, Toni, by the way," Joanna called out. "How are you managing in your new digs?"

A brilliant flush of pink burst out in perfect circles on Toni's cheeks. "Why...fine...just fine."

Joanna caught the silent exchange between the secretary and Morgan before Toni made her fast exit.

Unlike Toni, who seemed to have eyes only for the males in the room, Morgan, the ex-Green Beret, seemed particularly interested in the female contingent. First Toni, now her.

"Are you okay, Doc?" His voice had a husky, nasal quality.

Eric gave her shoulder a little squeeze and was the one to respond to Morgan's question. "Not particularly soothing to return to work after nursing a rotten cold for days only to discover your files have been rifled," he said with just an edge of cynicism.

Morgan nodded in Eric's direction, but his eyes remained fixed on Joanna as he stroked his chin reflectively. "Yeah, and then there was that gas leak. You better be careful, Doc. They say bad luck comes in threes."

Joanna could feel all the muscles in her body tighten. Was Morgan's comment meant to be a warning, or a threat? She yearned to check out Eric's reaction to the security chief's remark, but a voice inside her head told her Jen wouldn't do that. *What would Jen do?*

"Good thing I'm not a superstitious woman, Hank." She adjusted her glasses higher on the bridge of her nose, the same way a stereotyped absentminded scientist would.

Hank emitted an easy laugh. "Yeah, good thing, Doc."

"Well," she said rubbing her palms together. "No use crying over spilt milk. I've got to get going on this new project of mine, and you, Hank, better figure out some way to beef up security around here."

She could see that he didn't like being rebuked, especially by a woman. But she also sensed that he wasn't surprised to hear it coming from Hampleman.

"I'll check for prints, but I won't find any," Morgan muttered sullenly.

Joanna smiled pleasantly. "Well, do your best, Hank. That's all we can ask."

Eric stuck his hand into the slot next to the locked lab door at the far end of Toni's office. His fingerprints were recorded and a buzzer went off, acknowledging his legitimate right to enter. He opened the door and motioned to Joanna. "Work calls." She'd done great. Better than great. But he didn't want to push even a better-than-great thing too far.

Even after they were cloistered away inside the lab itself, Joanna knew that she couldn't discuss her suspicions about Morgan with Eric. They'd agreed that until security was again intact, they couldn't take any chances. So, instead of talking, they set to work. The rest of the morning was given over to manufacturing research on the supposedly new project Jen had decided to embark on. Even though it was all decoy material, Joanna found herself fascinated by this unexpected glimpse into the life of a nuclear physicist. While she was completely lost as to theory or technique, she was surprised to find her curiosity sparked.

Eric wasn't the least bit surprised.

"Hey, I think you have a natural aptitude here, Joanna," Eric wrote on his notepad. He smiled as he passed it to Joanna.

She found the compliment pleasing and disquieting at the same time. She found a pencil and wrote her response. "I wonder if Jen's ever thought she had a natural aptitude for modeling?"

A shadow fell across Eric's face. "How about some lunch?"

"Good idea."

Toni was sitting at her desk when they exited the lab.

The secretary glanced nervously at Eric. "I hope you don't think I was in any way to blame for the break-in, Dr. Logan."

"Why would I think that, Toni?" he asked with smooth control.

Bright blotches of pink resurfaced on her cheeks. "In a way...I do blame myself."

"How's that?" he asked.

"Well...I always keep the keys to my desk and the file cabinet in my purse. And I keep that purse with me at all times, Dr. Logan. Only...only yesterday, at the staff meeting, this awful dizzy spell came over me and...and someone had to help me to the ladies' room before I...well, I got sick to my stomach." The pink spots on her cheeks darkened further. "What if...someone swiped the keys then and made a copy?"

"Were the keys in your purse when you came back to the staff meeting?" Joanna asked.

Toni hesitated. "I didn't go back. I was...too sick. Hank drove me home."

Joanna raised a brow. "What about your purse?"

"I...left it behind. Someone dropped it off at my door."

"Who?" Eric asked.

There was a pregnant pause. "Dr. Hauser. It . . . was on her way. I'm not accusing her," Toni rushed on to say. "I mean, anyone could have gotten their hands on the keys while my bag was in the staff room. Anyone."

Eric gave her a reassuring pat on her shoulder. "It's okay, Toni. No one's accusing anyone." He shrugged nonchalantly. "Anyway, whoever's snooping around is wasting his or her time." He cast Joanna a wistful smile. "Just like we, unfortunately, wasted ours for the past ten months, right, Jen?"

Joanna scowled convincingly. "I thought that was a dead and buried topic, darling. Like I said before, no use crying over spilt milk. We have to know when to give up and move on."

Eric acted duly contrite. "Sorry, sweetheart. You're absolutely right." He smiled at Toni. "Hope you're feeling better now."

Clear relief marked Toni's plain but pleasant face. "Oh yes, much better now."

JOANNA POPPED INTO the ladies' room while Eric went on ahead to the mopeds. Just as she was smoothing a few errant brown strands of hair into place, Gerta Hauser walked in. Swept in would be more accurate. Dr. Gerta Hauser radiated an air of self-discipline, and a self-possession that almost slipped into haughtiness.

"So, you're on your feet again, Jennifer." The physicist spoke with a thick Germanic accent.

# PEEK-A-BOO!

# Free Gifts For You!

*Look inside—Right Now!*
*We've got something*
*special just for you!*

U-H-I-11/90

# GIFTS

*There's no cost—
and no obligation
to buy anything!*

We'd like to send you free gifts to
thank you for being a romance
reader, and to introduce you to the
benefits of the Harlequin Reader
Service®: free home delivery of
brand-new Harlequin Intrigue®
novels, and at a savings from the
cover price!

Accepting our free gifts places you
under no obligation to buy anything
ever. You may cancel the Reader
Service at any time, even just after
receiving your free gifts, simply by
writing "cancel" on your statement
or returning a shipment of books to
us at our cost. But if you choose not
to cancel, every other month we'll
send you four more Harlequin
Intrigue® novels, and bill you just
$2.24* apiece—and there's **no** extra
charge for shipping and handling.
There are **no** hidden extras!

## WE EVEN PAY THE POSTAGE!

It costs you nothing to send for your free gifts—we've paid the postage on the attached reply card. And we'll pay the postage on your free gift shipment. We charge nothing for delivery!

SEE WHAT'S FREE!

**BUSINESS REPLY MAIL**
FIRST CLASS MAIL    PERMIT NO. 717    BUFFALO, NY

POSTAGE WILL BE PAID BY ADDRESSEE

**HARLEQUIN READER SERVICE**
3010 WALDEN AVE
PO BOX 1867
BUFFALO NY  14240-9952

NO POSTAGE
NECESSARY
IF MAILED
IN THE
UNITED STATES

"Yes, Gerta," Joanna said with a bland cordiality. "Back to normal." *A touch too breezy?*

"Yes, so I see."

The confirmation brought comfort, but Joanna found the woman herself daunting.

"And how was your weekend jaunt with the good doctor?"

"Fine. Very enjoyable. And your weekend at the conference?" Joanna was pleased at how smoothly she'd been able to respond.

"Dull. Dreadfully dull. I'm sure you wouldn't have wanted to trade places with me. But then, I must admit, I am no longer so eager to change places with you."

"Oh?"

"My dear Dr. Hampleman, surely you must see the writing on the wall."

Joanna forced her defiance to mask the sudden trembling that had taken hold of her. "What is that supposed to mean?"

As response, Gerta just laughed ruefully and murmured, "Ah, for a moment I forgot that you couldn't take a joke."

## Chapter Nine

"Take it easy, Joanna," Eric said, opening the front door.

"I can't," she admitted, as they entered Jen's house. "It could be any of them. Don't you see? Morgan for one. I think there's something going on between him and Toni. An affair, maybe. He could be using her to get to me...to Jen." She pressed her palms to her face. "I can't even tell us apart anymore."

"Joanna..."

She walked into the living room, Eric on her heels. "Toni's not exactly the type a man like Morgan would go for," Joanna said. "And she doesn't seem all that bright. An easy pushover for Morgan's aggressive style."

"It could just as easily be the other way around. Maybe Toni's duping Hank. Maybe she's brighter than she wants people to think."

"Or they could be in cahoots, working together as partners. That's possible, isn't it?"

"Anything's possible," Eric admitted.

"And Gerta said, couldn't I see the writing on the wall? What did she mean by that? I don't buy for an instant that it was a joke."

"No, not a joke—a putdown."

"I don't understand."

"Well, with the failure of your cold fusion work, if you don't come up with something promising in exchange, you'll eventually be booted out of Synergy to make room for a physicist whose work seems more promising."

"She might have meant my days at Synergy were numbered," Joanna said trembling. "But not because I was going to eventually get . . . booted out."

Eric started to put his arms around her, but Joanna pulled abruptly away. "No. Don't. What happened between us this morning . . . was . . . crazy. I'm . . . not even sure . . . it was happening to . . . us." Her voice quivered in confusion and despair. "Was it really me you wanted this morning? Or was it her? Can you even tell us apart? Can I? I want out, Eric. It's too much. It's all too much. Too . . . dangerous."

Eric was sure she was talking about the danger to her heart as well as her life. He was aware of the escalating dangers. He had vowed to guard and protect her without realizing he would be exposing his own heart in the process.

"Damn it, Eric. If you want to have me thrown into jail for diamond smuggling, then do it. If you want to destroy the mind of a poor innocent woman in a sanatorium in Palm Springs, then . . . you're not the man I think you are." She was shouting now and gripping the front of his shirt. "Tell them all I had a . . . a nervous breakdown. Tell them I was so distraught about the failure of my research, I flipped out. Tell them . . . tell them anything, I don't care. I know the work Jen's doing is vital. But I . . . I can't be responsible for her. It's just a . . . freak of nature, some wild twist in the gene pool that turned out two of us. You can't make me go on with it, Eric."

"No," he said quietly, "I can't."

She eyed him with disbelief. "You . . . won't keep me here?"

A myriad of emotions played on Eric's face. "No, Joanna, I won't keep you here. But I'd like one chance to change your mind. If you decide to stay, it'll be your decision." He swallowed all of his emotions. It was the only way he was going to get through the next few minutes.

"Let's take a drive, Joanna. Let's get away from Synergy for a while and talk. We can go down to the beach."

"No, not the beach," she said tightly.

"Okay. I know a place."

"Eric...?" A line of worry cut across her brow. "Whatever you say, I won't change my mind. I'm not going to risk my life for a perfect stranger."

Eric met her gaze, but didn't respond. Her anxiety was palpable, contagious. It was as if she already knew what he had to tell her would alter her life, maybe even shatter it.

Was he doing the right thing? He knew only that he was treating Joanna with a level of candor that every ounce of his training had cautioned him against; indeed, prohibited. While this wouldn't be the first time he'd overstepped his authority, he was well aware that this time his actions would have personal ramifications equal to or exceeding the professional ones.

*Need-to-know* was the operative phrase here. Rule number one: no one was to be told anything if it was not on a need-to-know basis. Would his superiors view this as such? Would they assume his breach was the only way to win Joanna's cooperation? Eric thought so. And, in all honesty, Eric knew he couldn't bear to manipulate her; use her attraction to him, her awakened adventurous spirit, her irrepressible curiosity, or even her sense of duty and loyalty to her country. He had to be able to look himself in the mirror without disgust.

When they left Synergy, Eric drove through the small town of Los Verdes and then headed up a narrow road for the hills. Scrawny desert cottonwoods, bleached by the sun, filled the landscape. The heat was blistering but, as they drove deeper into the hills, a soft breeze stirred.

There was no small talk in the car, no effort to break the strained silence. Eric drove with a race-car driver's grim determination, tearing up and over the hills. Joanna stared out the window, trying to sort out the myriad emotions she'd been experiencing since the start of this incredible escapade. Was she fleeing from her responsibility to her country? Did the fate of the free world really depend upon her charade? That seemed hard to believe.

She shifted in her seat, her gaze moving for a moment from the scenery to the man behind the wheel. Dr. Eric Logan. Didn't he have as much to do with her desire to flee as the sense of physical danger she felt engulfing her?

She watched him skillfully manipulate the car. Hadn't he been equally adept at manipulating her? It was impossible to look at him, think about him, be in the same space with him, without thinking about those moments of passion they'd shared. It was equally impossible to think about that morning without images of Dr. Jennifer Hampleman popping into her head. Who had Eric been making love to? And over the past few days, when he'd called her Jen, was he simply playing out the role of professional agent, or was it wish fulfillment?

Joanna had been only vaguely aware of driving through a clump of trees to stop on a plateau overlooking the blue Pacific. As she stepped out of the car, a cooling breeze from the ocean below rippled her hair. She pulled off her glasses and took out the pins from her chignon so that her hair fell in soft, loose waves around her shoulders.

Eric went to the trunk and removed a plaid blanket. Joanna helped him spread it out on the mossy ground.

"It's beautiful up here," she murmured, her gaze moving from the vista to Eric. *Ah, the secret splendors of Los Verdes.*

He sat down, motioning for her to join him. She hesitated, then sat demurely on the edge of the blanket, at what she hoped was a safe distance.

He smiled faintly at her action, but then his expression became, in turn, brooding and pained.

"Joanna, I never dreamed this would become so...complicated." He was studying his hands, but he forced himself to look at her. "I've dealt with plenty of complications in my line of work, but none like this. None like you. You've come to mean so much to me in a very short time." The words felt as though they were being wrenched from him. He hadn't expected to speak with such passion. It didn't fit his conception of himself, or even with what he'd planned.

Sensing the import of what was yet to come, Joanna could not fully absorb the impact of his admission. "What is it you've been keeping from me, Eric?" Her voice was a bare whisper.

He needed cool, calm objectivity to answer her question, but his control was hampered by his feelings for her.

"Please, Eric." Her eyes fixed on his.

He found her gray-eyed gaze almost hypnotic. *Yes,* he thought, *just tell it as it had unfolded for him. Just tell it all.*

"Sixteen months ago," he began, "when Jen first joined Synergy, she, like everyone else on board, was given a thorough clearance check. In doing that check, we discovered that—" he paused for just a moment, but it was long enough for Joanna to feel all the muscles in her body contract "—Jen had been adopted."

"Adopted?"

He looked at Joanna with intense concentration. "Her natural mother had delivered twins. Two girls. Identical twins."

Joanna attempted a disbelieving smile, but it was unsuccessful, becoming instead a wincing twist of her mouth.

"You're saying Jennifer Hampleman's my twin sister? You're saying that my mother delivered twins and . . . gave one of us away? That's the craziest thing I ever heard. My mother would never do such a thing. She desperately wanted more than one child. She . . . she always talked about wishing I'd had a brother or a sister." She shook her head, the brown curtain of her hair swinging.

*If only it were that simple,* Eric thought.

"Jen's natural mother isn't Alice Clark," he said in a low voice.

She blinked several times, confusion blurring her vision. "What are you saying?"

"Alice Clark isn't Jen's natural mother. Or yours, Joanna. You and Jen were born to Iris Akers, a poor, unwed, nineteen-year-old, who worked for the Hamplemans as a maid."

"Now I know you're crazy, Eric. There is absolutely no doubt that my mother—Alice Clark—delivered me on the night of March seventh, 1963. I've seen my birth certificate. I needed it in order to get my passport." There was a cutting edge to her voice. "Besides, I saw on Jen's ID that she was born on February twelfth. In New York City. I was born in Florida. My parents were on vacation when my mother went into labor. On March seventh. Why are you doing this, Eric? Why fabricate a story that I could see through in an instant? One thing is certain. You haven't the faintest understanding of my mother."

"Do you, Joanna? Do you understand her depression, her inability to cope, her . . ."

"I tell you, she's my mother. I have proof. I've never even heard of this Iris Akers, but whatever she's claimed, it just can't be true."

"You're partly right, Joanna. What Iris Akers claimed isn't true."

She could feel her rage escalating. What was Eric trying to do, drive her to the edge with his confusing, contradictory statements?

Eric went on in an even voice. "On the night of February twelfth, 1963, Iris Akers delivered twins at Mount Cedars Hospital in Manhattan. All along, ever since she'd learned she was pregnant, she'd agreed to give her baby to the Hamplemans for adoption. When she learned that she was carrying twins, the Hamplemans arranged to take both babies."

"But her babies were born almost a month before I was. And two thousand miles away."

"According to the hospital records one of those twins died at birth. That was what Iris Akers was told. It's what she believed until the day she died, five years ago."

"And you're telling me the second baby didn't die? That...the other twin...survived? It doesn't make any sense. Why do it? Why not give the Hamplemans both of the children?" She thought about these two babies as totally separate from herself, intent only on catching Eric in his tangle of lies. For they were lies. *They had to be.*

"The Hamplemans weren't given both babies because someone else desperately wanted that other baby. Your father delivered the twins," he said softly.

"No." Joanna looked away. A wrenching sadness swept over her as she desperately tried to fight not only against Eric's revelations, but what she herself had sensed almost from that first moment she'd studied Jen's photo. She and Jen. So much alike. Appearance, tastes, manners, habits, skin, the same shampoo... Falling in love with the same man. Maybe...maybe, the same man falling in love with them both.

"An FBI agent spoke with the nurse who'd been at Iris Akers' delivery. At first she confirmed the death of the twin. But she was edgy about it and the agent began snooping around. He couldn't interview the doctor, because he'd died a few years back. So he sought out Iris's sister, who'd brought her to the hospital. Iris had told her very little about the birth. For some reason which she didn't understand, the doctor had administered an anesthetic to Iris just after delivery. The nurse told her later that one of the babies had not survived. Iris's sister told the agent that she never forgave the doctor for not facing her sister himself. According to Iris's sister, they'd developed quite a nice rapport during her pregnancy. He'd been very solicitous and nurturing, almost paternal. And then afterwards, he couldn't even face her."

"Maybe he was too distraught. Maybe he felt terrible about what had happened..."

"I believe he did feel terrible. I believe he was distraught," Eric said quietly. "But not because the baby had died, Joanna. Because he had stolen her."

Joanna's gaze hardened. "This is getting crazier and crazier."

"The nurse I was telling you about called the agent who'd first interviewed her. She told him she finally had to get something off her conscience.

"She revealed to the agent a bizarre plot hatched by Iris Akers' obstetrician... Dr. Donald Clark."

Joanna felt numb.

He moved quickly in the recounting now, his words as painful for him to tell as he knew they were for her to hear. "According to the nurse's account, Clark's wife had been disconsolate about being infertile. She'd wanted a baby desperately, but had refused the idea of adoption over and over again. It seems she was paranoid that the natural mother would change her mind at the last minute and reclaim the baby. In addition, she was neurotic about friends and relatives knowing she was incapable of having children of her own."

·"How would this nurse know so much about my mother?" Joanna asked tersely. *My mother?*

"Kathleen Russo—that's the nurse's name—" Eric stopped abruptly as he saw Joanna pale. "You know Kathleen?"

Joanna nodded slowly. "She used to visit...my family when I was small. And then...she stopped coming around."

"Kathleen privately attended to your mother after...a suicide attempt." Eric went on gently. "It occurred shortly after Iris Akers began seeing Donald Clark for prenatal care. When he discovered Iris was going to have twins and that she planned to give them up to her employer for adoption, he hatched a plan that he confided only to Kathleen and to his wife."

"A plan to steal one of Iris Akers' babies? No, never. And why would Kathleen ever go along with anything so...unethical?" *Criminal* she was going to say, but she couldn't.

"Kathleen was in love with Donald Clark. She admitted that she would have done anything for him." He paused. "She did."

"She helped him forge a phony death certificate?"

"She helped him do more than that. She transported the baby down to Florida. Palm Springs, Florida. Where Alice Clark was waiting for the baby. Months earlier, before leaving for her winter hiatus in Florida she'd told friends and relatives that she was pregnant. On March seventh, she sent out an announcement that you were born. Supposedly attended by her husband, Dr. Donald Clark, in an emergency delivery at their rented condo. It was all very carefully thought out, very carefully executed."

"My mother couldn't have done it." Joanna's voice lacked conviction.

"She's paid the price, Joanna. Many times over. Deceit and guilt ate away at her. You can see that. And then, after her husband died, she had no one there to help ease her conscience. As far as she knows, only she and Kathleen Russo know the truth to this day. But now you know the truth, as well."

"And Jen?" Her low mutter held an edge of hysteria.

"She doesn't know. At least...she hasn't been told." He searched her face. "But, like you, she's had a weird feeling all along about your similarities. She felt an immediate connection when she saw that layout of you in *Harper's*."

The dark gray irises of Joanna's eyes seemed to be dissolving, like spots of ink dropped in water. Eric knew she was trying not to cry, not to lose control. That, too, was like her twin. A need for tight control. A fear of emotions consuming and obliterating safety. But Joanna had let down her guard with him. As he had done with her. Passion and happiness were remembered at a distance. Now grief, hers and his, felt like a tangible substance, weighing them both down, dividing them by a chasm too deep to cross.

She stared at him in horror. "How could you have deceived me this whole time?" Her voice was harsh, almost guttural.

"I'm sorry, Joanna. I've disobeyed strict orders and said far more than I should. But I couldn't keep it from you any longer. The truth has been weighing on my conscience all along, especially after—"

"Conscience?" she spat out. "Is that what you call it? The way I see it, Logan, you had a near-hysterical, terrified woman on your hands, who threatened to upset a carefully laid plan. And so you pulled out the trump card." She laughed hoarsely, but tears streamed down her cheeks. "And what a trump it is." She rose and turned away, unable, now, to look at him.

He came up behind her. She wasn't making a sound, but he could see her shoulders heave in sorrow. His mouth twisted in self-disgust. "I would never intentionally hurt you, Joanna. But there was no way of revealing the truth without hurting you. And you had the right to know. I doubt you'll believe this, but I didn't tell you simply to keep you here. I told you because I felt I owed it to you…and to Jen…'' He expelled a heavy breath. "But, yes, to be brutally honest I also thought, once you knew the truth, you would feel compelled to stay. To help Jen. To protect her. Even hating me, you would stay.''

Yes, he was right. She would stay. Hating him, betrayed by him, manipulated by him. Still, she would stay. For Jen. For her sister, the twin she never knew existed. Until now.

Eric stared down at the sea. The sun played on the water, its hard, uncompromising light blurring the edges of the horizon. If he'd hoped the pain inside him would recede after he told her, he'd been wrong. It bit into him like a vise.

His hands reached out for her. She didn't fight him off as he drew her against him. Instead she leaned heavily as if, in absorbing it all, the fight had been knocked out of her.

She began to cry again, leaning against Eric, but thinking, not of him, not even of Jen, but of her parents. Her mother and father, or at least the people she had always thought of as her mother and father. They had each betrayed her, deceived her, raised her to live a lie, deprived her of her own flesh and blood. She thought of her father, so aloof and withdrawn, so controlling and yet protective. Had his personality been shaped by his dreadful actions or had it been the other way around? As for her mother, Joanna had no doubt that the deceit had weighed heavily on her already fragile mind.

Did she hate them, too? Didn't their actions deserve far more hatred than Eric's?

But they had done it out of desperation. They hadn't meant to hurt anyone. She was certain her father had rationalized his doubts away. Why should Mrs. Hampleman have two children and his poor wife have none? In giving his beloved wife a child, hadn't he saved her from another suicide attempt? Hadn't he done it out of abiding love?

Those thoughts brought her back to Eric. Had his actions, too, been guided by love? But love for whom? Her, or her twin sister?

"I want to see Jen. She has the right to know the truth. And I want to be the one to tell her."

"It's not possible right now. Later—"

"Then let me speak to her on the phone. And Kathleen, too. Damn it," her voice cracked. "You owe me that much."

He couldn't argue that. "All right. I'll arrange both calls."

"We better get back." She smiled faintly and wiped her eyes.

He made no move.

"If you're worried about raising eyebrows back at Synergy because of my red eyes, we can stop at a service station in town and I can run into the ladies' room and wash my face."

Eric frowned. He was more disconcerted by her suddenly cool, controlled manner than he had been by her burst of tears. Her grim expression, rife with disillusionment, was almost brittle.

Eric hurriedly gathered up the blanket and tossed it in the trunk. When he slid behind the wheel, Joanna was already in the front passenger seat, hands tidily folded in her lap.

He felt her gaze on him as he stuck the key in the ignition. He looked over at her. There was a questioning expression on her face. He waited.

"Did you ever plan to tell Jen the truth?"

He placed both hands on the steering wheel. "I wasn't sure," he admitted. "Until now."

"I want to see her, Eric. I want . . . to tell her myself."

"Yes, I understand."

"When?"

"As soon as it's safe."

She nodded.

"Joanna..."

"No." She stared out the window, her expression impassive. "Don't apologize. I am glad I know the truth."

They drove to Los Verdes in silence. Eric stopped at a service station at the far end of town and Joanna went into the ladies' room to wash her face, comb her hair and put it back into a chignon. She exited wearing her glasses, looking amazingly cool, calm and collected.

Eric wasn't fooled. Joanna's successful career was based, in part, on her ability to convey emotions she didn't necessarily feel. She was a pro. Just as he was.

When she slipped into the car again, Eric muttered a low curse under his breath. For a moment she thought it was directed at her and was about to counter with a few choice words of her own. Then she saw Lou, the security guard from Synergy snub out his cigarette and trot over to Eric's side of the car.

Lou had exchanged his Synergy uniform for a pair of white duck slacks and a pineapple-colored polyester shirt open halfway to his navel. A thick gold chain sparkled against his tan chest, a flashy ring on one finger. He wore white loafers on his bare feet. Joanna couldn't help but see him as an aging gigolo gone to seed.

"Hey, folks, could I ask a favor? My car's on the fritz and I need a lift back to Synergy. You wouldn't be heading that way by any chance?"

"Why...uh...sure, Lou. Hop in," Eric said after a quick glance at Joanna. She didn't look happy to have the additional company, but then neither was he. Still, it was so deadly quiet and tense in the car. Maybe the affable, loquacious guard would ease the tension. Lou could generally be relied upon for a few laughs and a bit of gossip. Some of that gossip, idly and often raunchily given, had come in handy for Eric on a few occasions.

"So, how are you two doing?" Lou settled his broad, paunchy frame into the center of the back seat.

"Fine," Eric said off-handedly, pulling out of the station.

"Good. Glad to hear it. Of course, I heard about that gas leak over at your place. Terrible scare you must have had, Dr. Hampleman."

"Yes, it was scary," Joanna said softly. She'd hoped she'd have a little longer to pull herself together before having to reassume the charade, a charade that had now taken on far greater significance. She was no longer just masquerading as a scientist who was a perfect stranger to her. She was masquerading as her twin sister.

"They say most accidents happen around the house," Lou mused philosophically. "I'll tell you both something, though. This schnoz of mine," he tapped his rather generous nose, "can smell something rotten brewin' down on the farm."

Joanna turned in her seat and gave the security guard a scrutinizing look. "What do you mean?"

"Well, for one, that gas leak."

"That was an accident," Eric said quietly.

"Maybe." Lou leaned forward a little. "But what about all the break-ins? Morgan's beside himself. Looks bad for the head security honcho when first the old man's house gets robbed, then your place, and then your offices. Morgan's been on my case. Like I'd let someone in just for the hell of it. I tell you, no one's gotten in or out of Synergy who doesn't belong there."

Joanna felt her stomach churning. "Then you think these break-ins are inside jobs."

"Sure, they're inside jobs. And if I were the kind of guy that flapped my tongue a lot I'd make a few educated guesses as to who it was."

Of course, Lou *was* just that sort of guy. Eric knew that for a fact. So he just waited quietly for Lou's *educated guess* to surface.

"I'll tell you one thing, Docs. I've always prided myself on being able to read people. Don't ask me how, but I can just tell when they're on the up and up, if you know what I mean?"

Joanna shot Eric a fleeting glance. He swallowed hard.

"Not that I would ever go around accusing someone on appearances alone. 'Cause I also know appearances can be deceiving." There was a slight pause before Lou continued. "Take Dr. Hauser for one."

"What about Dr. Hauser?" Joanna jumped in a little too quickly with the question.

Lou gave her a knowing smile. "Yeah, I know there's no love lost between you two. Well, make that ditto for me. I've never cottoned to Reds. Hauser probably saw the handwriting on the wall back there in Poland and got out before the Commie regime toppled. But don't tell me they're gonna sit on their duffs and just let a bunch of capitalists walk all over them, take away all their power."

Lou's remark gave Joanna a jolt, shaking her out of her shock and temporarily pushing Eric's revelation into a back corner of her mind. Now she was thinking about Dr. Gerta Hauser. If Hauser was still a Communist, and was able to get her hands on Jen's formula for cold fusion, a formula that would mean unlimited, cheap energy, it could be a whole new ball game in the Eastern bloc. Joanna's mind shifted into high gear. Did Gerta Hauser really defect or was she a mole? Bringing the cold fusion formula back to her homeland would not only aid the cause of the Communist ruling class, but Gerta Hauser would be hailed a hero, a savior. Hauser would certainly claim the breakthrough as her own. And she'd probably end up with a Nobel Prize into the bargain. A prize that rightly belonged to Joanna's twin.

"What makes you think Dr. Hauser's a Communist?" Eric asked, keeping his tone low key.

"She's been holding secret meetings with one I know for a fact is KGB, that's why." Lou gave a wide, self-satisfied smile.

Joanna stared at him. "You sound very certain of that."

"Sure, I'm certain. You know I didn't spend my whole life in a guard house outside a research compound." His chest puffed out a little. "I put in some time with the CIA. Fact is, I gave the Company the best years of my life."

"CIA?" Eric mused.

"Yeah, well, I wasn't exactly an agent, mind you. You gotta have a college degree and whatnot for that. Nevertheless, you could say I had my finger in the pie. Clerked for a key man in the bureau. Name of Lawrence Melton. But that's neither here nor there. What's important is that I did some filing of records on some active KGB boys that were known to surface in the States now and then. Well, a few weeks ago, when I was in town, I spotted one of the bastards." He paused for effect. "Spotted him in the Mill End Restaurant sitting with Dr. Hauser. As soon as I got back to the compound I reported it to Morgan. And let me tell you, Docs, those two were chummy as all get out." He rested one hand on Eric's shoulder, one hand on Joanna's. "Now, you tell me what you think those two Reds were powwowing about?"

Eric glanced surreptitiously at Joanna. He didn't have to answer Lou's question, but he was certainly going to check Lou's story out with his contacts.

# Chapter Ten

It was a bad night. Joanna, still dressed, paced in her room.
There was no point in getting into her nightgown and
crawling into bed as she was unable to even hope for sleep.
Over and over, Eric's revelations of the afternoon repeated
themselves: Jen, her twin sister; a woman by the name of
Iris Akers, her natural mother; Alice and Donald Clark, the
parents she had known and loved, co-conspirators in a hei-
nous crime. It was all true. Eric had kept his word and she'd
spoken on the phone to Kathleen. It had been an over-
whelming conversation for both of them.

Joanna tried to will her mind to blankness. When that
didn't work she sat down on her bed and picked up a magazine on the bedside table. Immediately her eyes fell on the
now empty spot where she'd placed the framed photo of Jen
and Eric. She could picture the eight-by-ten glossy in her
mind. The image was haunting because it revealed so much
and yet so little. What was the relationship between Eric and
her twin? And where did she, Joanna, fit in?

She tried to recapture the hatred she'd felt toward Eric
that afternoon. Not only didn't she succeed, she wasn't even
certain why she'd hated him with such force. Was it really
because he had kept the truth from her, or was it because he
had finally revealed it? One thing was certain. His revelation had locked her into this charade. She was responsible

now for the life of the twin sister she yearned to meet and know.

She checked the time. Nearly midnight. For a few minutes she skimmed through the pages of the magazine, but she couldn't concentrate on any of it. Finally she decided to go down to the kitchen and get herself a cup of hot milk. When she was little her mother had always brought her warm milk when she couldn't sleep. That pleasant, comforting memory abruptly engulfed Joanna in grief. Would she ever again be able to remember her past without sorrow? To have had so much and yet to have lost so much seemed impossible to reconcile.

She stepped into the hallway. Eric's door was closed, and there was no sliver of light showing at the bottom. She hoped he was asleep, and she moved stealthily so as not to awaken him. She needed solitude.

She was at the sink, rinsing out her cup when she saw the bedroom light blink on across the way. The curtains were drawn, but Joanna could make out the shadow of a woman passing by the window. Gerta Hauser. So she couldn't sleep, either.

Joanna shut off the tap and watched Gerta's house with growing curiosity. After about three minutes the light went out again. Joanna sighed feeling oddly deflated. Gerta must have gone back to bed.

But a minute later the light came on in Gerta's kitchen. Here, only a café curtain trimmed the window, allowing easy viewing of the scientist's actions. Joanna, who hadn't bothered to turn on her kitchen light, remained where she was, knowing Gerta couldn't see her.

Gerta walked over to the wall phone beside the refrigerator. She dialed. A brief conversation ensued, and then the scientist hung up. She stood for a moment in profile and Joanna was able to make out the self-satisfied smile on her lips.

Joanna's mind kicked into overdrive. Had Gerta been speaking to the KGB agent Lou had mentioned on the drive back to Synergy? Or was she talking to someone right here on the grounds—a cohort?

Joanna's breath caught as she saw Gerta cross the kitchen and head for her back door. Twelve o'clock and the scientist was going out. A midnight stroll? Not very likely, Joanna thought. A rendezvous with the person she'd just spoken to? Oh yes, that certainly seemed a good bet. The light went out in Gerta's kitchen and the back door opened.

There was no hesitation in Joanna's decision or movements as she flew to her own back door. She was determined to follow Gerta Hauser and see for herself who the scientist was going to meet.

She knew Eric wouldn't be happy about it. She knew he'd want her to waken him and let him handle the situation. He was, after all, the pro. But she couldn't be entirely sure it wasn't Eric that Gerta was meeting, and the intrigue at Synergy was different now. It had become a fiercely personal matter.

Joanna carefully closed the door and waited in the shadows as she watched Gerta head straight for her moped.

She doubted that the scientist would leave the grounds, since that would mean having to go past security where her departure at such a late hour would certainly be questioned. If Gerta had gone on foot, Joanna might have thought it possible that the scientist was planning to sneak away from Synergy—perhaps via a secret, carefully concealed escape route.

Instead of starting up the bike, Gerta chose to push her moped down the driveway and some distance along the road. Joanna surmised that the scientist wasn't keen on waking up the whole neighborhood and announcing her departure.

Giving Gerta a good head start, Joanna followed suit pushing Jen's moped. There was only a sliver of a moon, just enough to make out shadowy shapes in the night. Joanna tried to keep far enough back from Gerta so that if the scientist happened to turn around she wouldn't spot her stalker. But Joanna wasn't too worried about that happening. Gerta was pushing her moped along at a fast clip, practically running with it. A woman with her eye on her destination.

About a quarter of a mile from the housing complex, at a fork in the road, Gerta swung onto her bike, revved it, flicked on her low beams and took the right fork.

The laboratories, Joanna concluded, that was where that road led. She, too, revved her moped, praying Gerta wouldn't be able to distinguish the sound over the low roar of her own engine.

The labs were a little under a mile from the fork in the road. Joanna was forced to keep more of a distance now, since she, too, had to switch on her low beams in order to make her way along the many sharp bends in the road. When she got to the labs she spotted a lone moped in the parking lot. There were no other vehicles in sight.

Joanna ditched her moped behind some bushes on the far side of the parking lot, so that it wouldn't be noticed. Running across the lot, she dug into the pocket of her jeans for her ring of keys, one of which would gain her admittance to the labs.

The door clicked open and gave easily without so much as a squeak. Only the green emergency lights were on in the hallway, bathing the corridor in a pasty, eerie glow.

This main hallway led to a maze of corridors leading to labs, offices, conference rooms and the cafeteria. Joanna listened hard for the sound of Gerta's footsteps, her tension building. She heard nothing. Like her, Gerta was probably wearing sneakers.

She tried to picture the schematic map of the labs that Eric had shown her on her arrival. Where was Gerta's office and lab? Wasn't that the most likely place for her to go?

Joanna started down the hall. Her own lab, Jen's that was, was off to the north, and she remembered that Gerta's space was almost at the opposite end of the complex. Somewhere off to the left then. But there were several offshoots along the corridor she'd chosen. As she threaded through the labyrinth of gloomy green-shadowed spaces, pausing to listen at closed doors for a sign of activity, her tension rose.

It was a piece of pure luck that she spotted the sign, Dr. Gerta Hauser, tacked onto a closed door. She was pressing her ear against the door when, instead of sounds from inside the office, she picked up the faint thump of footsteps behind her.

Joanna's legs started shaking and she could feel the blood surge in her veins. In panic she froze at the door for a moment, but then she pulled herself together and took flight. If the footsteps belonged to Gerta's comrade, they'd likely stop at the scientist's office. Once the two were inside, Joanna could stealthily make her way back and try to hear the conversation behind the closed door.

Joanna dashed around the next corner and flattened herself against the wall. The sound of the footsteps behind her remained muted. Someone was either not heavy footed or trying his or her best not to make noise. Joanna squeezed her eyes shut, waiting for the footsteps to stop, waiting for the sound of an office door to open and close.

But the footsteps didn't stop at Gerta Hauser's door. Any minute the person those feet belonged to would round the corner and spot her.

Joanna wasn't about to stand around and wait. She broke into a lightning sprint and raced for the next corridor and the next, looking now only for an exit. The footsteps behind her grew more distinct, the pace quicker, close to matching her own. Joanna tried to run even faster, no longer thinking about Gerta and her mysterious friend, intent on getting away somehow. With no exit sign in sight, she began pausing for an instant at each door to test it, praying that, despite security regulations, one had been left open and she could duck inside to hide.

Miracle of miracles, a door gave way and Joanna lurched through. She found herself in a large, well-lit, cherry-wood-paneled office. And she wasn't alone there.

Joanna swallowed back her gasp of surprise so that it stuck in her throat like a bone. The two occupants of the room broke off their conversation and turned startled and sharply inquisitive eyes on Joanna.

"Jen, what in heaven's name are you doing here at this hour?"

Joanna stared into the cool blue eyes of Martin Matthias as he waited impatiently for a response. Even given her awkward and possibly dangerous predicament, her curiosity was piqued. Gerta and Marty? Cohorts in a plot to steal Jen's cold fusion discoveries? She'd been suspicious of them both from the start, but she'd never pictured them in it together. What else could it be? They certainly didn't look as if romance was on their minds. Nor did they look too pleased with Joanna's silence.

"I . . . was working late," she muttered. "And when I walked by your office, I . . . heard voices."

"And so you barged in?" Gerta glared at her with haughty disdain.

For all her fear, Joanna felt a surge of indignation. The nerve of this woman trying to put her on the defensive when she was the one . . .

"There've been so many break-ins around the compound, I was worried about intruders. I didn't realize the two of you were in here. Working late as well?"

Marty was observing her more carefully. "It was rather foolhardy to barge in, Jen, if you'd been right."

"What?" Joanna'd been waiting for an answer to her question.

"What ever would you have done if there had been a couple of thugs in here?" Matthias's voice and expression reflected concerned exasperation, but his cool blue eyes looked nervous.

Joanna felt her cheeks warm. "Why, I . . . I suppose I would have screamed, turned heel and rushed to set off the alarm."

That brought a dry laugh from Marty and a predatory grin from Gerta.

"My, my, Jennifer, you're certainly full of adventure and daring lately," Gerta said in a cold, low voice.

A flash of terror whipped through Joanna. Had she just been dumb enough to give the entire ruse away?

"I think Marty was more accurate, Gerta," she said with far more calm than she was feeling. "Foolhardy. It happens to the best of us at times."

Joanna hoped her remark was the sort her twin would have made. She knew that she ought to beat a hasty retreat, before she ended up making a remark that would really tip her hand. But there was still the matter of the unknown stalker cruising the halls. Maybe it was one of Gerta's and Marty's watchdogs. Joanna cringed. Her options were looking all too bleak. And as Gerta took an advancing step toward her, Joanna feared that the worst was yet to come.

"What I don't understand, Jennifer," Gerta said in typical clenched-teeth fashion, "is what you were doing all the way over here in the first place? Your lab is in the north quadrant and there's an exit right down the hall from you."

It was a very good question. Unfortunately Joanna didn't have a good answer at the ready. So, she took a pointer from the two pros in the room and decided on an evasive and offensive strategy. "What I don't understand, Gerta, is what you and Marty are doing here in the middle of the night?"

Her attack worked on the head administrator. Tiny specks of pink sprouted on his cheeks and he cast Gerta an uneasy look before glancing at Joanna, but not, Joanna noted, meeting her inquiring gaze directly. "Gerta was...struggling with a problem. A work problem. You know how it is, Jen. Something weighs on your mind and you can't sleep. Gerta phoned me. I was awake, going over some papers. And so I agreed to...meet her over here for a brief powwow, go over her...problem...and then we could both go home and get a good night's sleep."

If Marty was satisfied with his answer, it left Joanna knowing very little more now than before, and it left Gerta Hauser teetering on the fine edge of self-control. She was clearly not happy with her accomplice's rather lengthy explanation. And she cast Joanna a look that said she would never have fallen for such an obvious maneuver. More to Joanna's dismay, Gerta's look also conveyed mounting suspicion. The question was, would Gerta be foolhardy enough to press the issue? But hadn't Joanna just finished saying even the wise could be foolhardy on occasion? And, as far as Joanna knew, Gerta Hauser was pretty wise. Pretty slick, too. Sticking around here much longer would definitely make Joanna tops in foolhardiness. She was just about to bid a hasty good-night, make a quick exit and take her chances with the lurking corridor prowler when there was a knock on Matthias's door. They all jumped: Joanna, Gerta and Marty.

The door opened.

"There you are, Jen. When you left the lab, you forgot the papers you needed to leave off here for Marty." Eric Logan's eyes revealed just a touch of surprise as he looked over at Gerta and Marty.

"It looks like we've all been burning the midnight oil," Eric said lightly. He stretched his arms up to the ceiling. "But I for one am ready to call it a night." He tossed a small sheaf of papers on Matthias's tidy desk. "Just some requisition papers, Marty. No big hurry. We're just getting underway with the new project." He smiled at Jen with a touch of seductiveness apparent to all. "Ready to hit the hay, darling?"

Whatever the jumble of emotions Eric had dragged her through up to now, at the moment she was filled with nothing but pure gratitude. "Definitely," she murmured. She started for the door where Eric was waiting, but spun around to face the rival physicist one last time. "Oh Gerta, I do hope you resolve your little problem. I certainly wouldn't want you to start seeing any writing on the wall." Joanna winked. "Just kidding."

Gerta gave her a cold smile. *Talk about not being able to take a joke!*

"WHAT DO YOU MEAN, it wasn't you?" Joanna said as soon as they had gotten back to Jen's place.

"Joanna, come on, why would I be chasing you around the halls? I told you, I really had no idea where you were. I went into your room to check on you, saw you were gone and started searching everywhere. I went to the health club first, thinking maybe you went for a swim. Then I checked with the night guard at the gate on the chance you'd gone into town. When I came up empty-handed I swung by the labs. That was my last guess. I probably would never have even gone inside if I hadn't spotted the lights on in Marty's office."

"Do you do that every night?" Joanna asked in a low voice.

Eric threw her a baffled look. "Do what?"

"Check on me?"

"I thought we were discussing what you were doing down at the labs."

"We were," she said with a faint smile.

Eric hesitated. "How could I check on you every night? You usually lock your door."

"You test it to make sure?"

"I can hear the click of your lock from my room," he said tightly.

"Then what made you test it tonight?"

"After everything that happened today I was . . . worried about you. So, I went and knocked on your door, to find out if you were okay. You didn't answer." He paused. "The door was unlocked. I walked in."

"I am okay," she said softly.

He stared hard at her for longer than she liked. "No you're not," he said finally. "You're crazy."

"What?"

"Crazy to be going off in the middle of the night tracking suspected spies."

"Suspected? Look, Eric . . ."

"I am looking." He was looking at the way her eyes shone with excitement and fire. He gave her an odd, disconcerted smile, all at once remembering the way she'd looked at him that afternoon. So much pain, agony, shock and hatred had radiated from her eyes then. And while he knew it hadn't all been directed at him, he'd received more than his share. He was relieved now, to see her looking so alive, so vibrant— even though her actions worried him.

He wasn't even aware he was reaching out for her until he heard her strained voice.

"No. Don't."

Immediately he let his arms drop, his hands slapping against his sides. The warmth of his ragged sigh flowed over her face. "Sorry."

For a moment the living room was very still. Joanna sensed a danger in the restless silence.

"How about some...warm milk?" There was an odd catch in her voice. "My mother always used to make me warm milk when I was worked up over something—a hard test, a spat with a friend. It...helped." *There. Not so bad.* She didn't have to deny herself the good memories, whatever else was true. Alice Clark had been a loving, caring, tender mother. She had tried her very best. Joanna loved her. Even now she loved her and wanted to go on protecting her.

Some of the brooding tension left Eric's face. "Yes. Warm milk." But he doubted any beverage, warm or otherwise, would calm what he was worked up over.

They walked together into the kitchen. Joanna got the milk from the fridge and Eric retrieved a small pot from the cupboard.

"Does Jen drink warm milk when she's...worked up?" Joanna asked in a hesitant voice.

Eric turned on the stove and caught her gaze before answering. "Sometimes."

Joanna nodded reflectively. "It is strange, Logan. It's all so very strange."

He leaned against the counter, and they both watched the milk heat up.

"What are we going to do about Gerta and Marty?" she asked after the silent watching took on too much weight.

"*We* aren't going to do anything, darling," Eric said resolutely.

Joanna poured steaming milk into two mugs. "I have some ideas."

"Joanna..."

"Jen. Remember, darling?"

Eric smiled ruefully. "Oh, if only models really were dumb blondes."

Joanna laughed. She was surprised to find herself laughing. After this afternoon, she'd begun to think laughter would be a long time coming.

Eric, too, was thrilled to hear Joanna laugh again after all she'd been through. She did have a wonderful and enticing laugh. Not at all like her twin. There were some very definite differences between the two of them.

"HI, LINDA."

"Jen. What are you doing here?" There was clear surprise in Linda Matthias's expression as she greeted Joanna at her door. But there was delight as well.

"I took the day off. I thought, maybe, we could spend a few hours in town together."

"Shopping?"

Joanna smiled. She knew from Eric that Jen wasn't one to make the rounds of the shops in town. "Actually, I thought we could visit that gallery where you bought the Navaho rug. I was thinking of buying Eric one for his birthday."

"Oh, that's a thought. It would make a wonderful gift. And Eric was crazy about it. When's his birthday?"

"Not until November." She'd done a spot check on his ID this morning. It noted his birthdate as November fourth, 1958. "But I imagine a rug like that would cost a pretty penny and I'll have to save up."

"It was rather... expensive," Linda said awkwardly.

Joanna grinned amiably. "Actually, I was hoping they'd have some others to choose from that are a little smaller and a little cheaper." She shrugged. "If not, we can at least splurge on a fancy lunch in town. What do you say?"

"Just let me grab my purse," Linda said with cheery enthusiasm.

Five minutes later they drove out past the gates of Synergy, both women waving gaily at Lou who looked quite envious.

Joanna chuckled softly to herself.

Linda glanced over at her. "What's so funny?"

"I always feel this little rush of adrenaline when I leave the compound. Almost like a criminal on parole."

"Do you really?"

Joanna tensed. She had decided to wing it, given the fact that she knew from Eric that Linda and Jen hadn't really spent much time together. She'd trust to their genetic similarities.

"We've never really gotten to know each other in all this time," Joanna said wistfully. "Typical scientist, I get so absorbed in my work..."

"And in Eric," Linda added with an impish smile.

"Yes," Joanna said, her voice dropping a notch. "And in Eric."

"Is something wrong between you and Eric, Jen?"

"Oh, we got into a little spat last night. Over at the labs." She allowed a brief pause. "By the way, did Marty tell you how I barged into his office around midnight? I don't know who was more surprised, him or me."

"Or Gerta." Linda gave a little laugh. It was clearly forced.

"Marty said Gerta had called him about a problem she was having."

Linda didn't say anything, but when Joanna gave her a quick look she saw that the young woman's features were taut and her hands were no longer folded together in her lap. They were clenched.

So, Joanna thought, I am on the right track. Linda knows or at least senses that something is going on between her husband and the Polish physicist. Did Linda think it was romance? Was that why she was suddenly so tense? Or had she chanced to overhear something between the two that gave her very different worries?

"People take advantage of him," Linda mumbled long after Joanna had given up any hope of her making a response.

"No offense intended, Linda, but Marty impresses me as a man who gives as good as he takes."

Surprisingly, Linda smiled. It wasn't an altogether warm smile. "Yes, he can be a bit . . . assertive at times. But that's why he's so successful, isn't it?"

"Is it?"

"I know what all of you think. Marty's very strong-willed and opinionated. And once he makes his mind up about something, he absolutely can't be swayed."

"I would think," Joanna said softly, "it might be hard to live with someone like that."

Linda laughed. "Oh no. It's really quite easy. And quite pleasant."

Joanna did a double take. Linda was full of surprises.

"It's all a question of what you measure your present life against," Linda went on philosophically. "Compared to what my life was like growing up, living with Marty is a dream come true. Whatever his faults, I wouldn't consider anyone else. I love him very much."

Joanna had heard a distinct emphasis on Linda's *"whatever."* Was she saying she'd love him and want him even if she knew he was a traitor? Or had Linda simply deluded herself into believing her husband would never do anything really despicable and evil?

Joanna couldn't share that naive presumption. She now knew the evil that men could do. Men who were loved and trusted, respected by wives . . . and daughters.

ERIC AND JOANNA drove toward downtown Los Verdes, ostensibly to have a nice, romantic dinner at a little French restaurant. But a couple of miles from Synergy, Eric pulled the car up by a public telephone booth beside the road.

He turned to Joanna. "You can talk to Jen from this phone. I'll dial the number for you."

Joanna experienced a rush of anxiety and anticipation.

Eric smiled sympathetically. "I doubt she'll be surprised when you tell her the truth." He hesitated. "You should keep it brief. We don't want to stick around here too long."

Joanna nodded. She couldn't imagine it would be a long conversation, at this point anyway.

A few moments later Joanna was gripping the receiver as if it was her lifeline. "Hello Jen. This is Joanna . . ."

## Chapter Eleven

The pair paused on the narrow trail. Below them the brackish water of Los Verdes' upper bay slapped at the rocks.

"I tell you she's changed."

"Yes, I think you are right."

"And you are the thinker." Thin lips curved into a wry smirk.

"Don't be smug. It isn't at all becoming."

The smirk gave way to pensiveness. "It's as if she has become a different person. Now why do you suppose that is?"

"They say love can change someone's whole personality."

"Or success."

"Yes. Success can do that, too."

"She must have found the solution. Somehow, since she's been back, she must have figured out some way to secretly continue her work."

"Yes, it's as though they're both gloating, our lovebirds."

A harsh laugh. "I'm not so sure Logan's all that keen on his lady love's success. A man like that doesn't enjoy taking a back seat. He does a good job of concealing it with his lovey-dovey smiles, but I'd lay odds there's a storm brewing in paradise."

"WHERE ARE YOU GOING?" Eric followed Joanna to the door of her bedroom.

"For a swim."

"There's a storm coming."

"I won't be swimming outside. I'll use the lap pool. Do a bit of a workout. Take a sauna."

"Alone?"

Joanna made a production of collecting swim suit, towel and a change of clothes.

Her lack of response told Eric enough. "Your new chum, Linda, again. I don't like this one bit. You're way out of line here, especially if you're right. If Marty and Gerta are the ones, you're playing with fire." The lines at the corners of his eyes deepened. "I know why you're doing it . . ."

"Then give it up, Logan."

He frowned. For the past five days, ever since he'd told Joanna the truth, she'd been cool and distant toward him, and solely intent on her own pursuit of Gerta Hauser and Martin Matthias. Her plan, and Eric begrudgingly had to admit it was not a bad one but for the risk, was to get to Matthias by using her relationship with Linda. And Joanna was counting on Marty not being the sort to take the rap alone. She'd leave it to him to implicate his buddy Gerta.

Eric also had to admit that, so far, Joanna's plan had been working. Linda was hungry for a friend and confidant. And the more Linda confided in Joanna, the more Joanna was convinced Linda had more than an inkling about her husband's traitorous activities. The problem was that Linda, desperate to be loved and taken care of, seemed willing to overlook just about anything her husband did, as long as he continued to treat her as a treasured possession.

Joanna was subtly working on the pliant young woman, encouraging her to be a little more independent, a bit more assertive. She was hoping that if Linda pushed, Marty might expose his true colors, and then Linda might begin to feel differently about her adoring hubby.

Eric watched Joanna pluck a plain gray sweatsuit from Jen's closet. "Don't you realize that if Marty gets wind of your little plan, it might push his hand?"

"All the better," she retorted.

He narrowed his eyes. "Not if he wrings your neck because of it."

Joanna tilted her head up, gave Eric a long look and smiled tightly. "I thought it was your job to see that that doesn't happen."

He left the doorway and walked over to her. "Joanna." He raised a hand to stop her as she opened her mouth to speak. "I know. I know. I should call you Jen. But we've got to stop playing games, Joanna." He said her real name with deliberate emphasis.

"I'm not playing any games, Logan. Are you?"

"So why am I Logan all of a sudden?"

She made an uncharacteristically helpless gesture with her hands. "I'm just trying . . . to keep the charade in perspective."

"What is your perspective?"

"My perspective is that for a week, maybe two more, I've got to make sure that my twin sister's life and work . . ."

"What's your perspective on me?" he broke in.

She clutched her sweatsuit, turning away from his intense gaze. "This isn't the time. Linda's . . . waiting for me. At the club."

"You think any of this is easy for me, Joanna?"

She shook her head and, despite all her efforts, tears welled up in her eyes, causing them to lose focus.

He stroked her cheek. His touch was warm, familiar, wonderful. Her hand covered his, rubbing gently.

She drew his hand away from her face, and then released her own hold on him. But as she stepped back, Eric caught her wrist, wrapping his large, strong fingers firmly around it.

"Eric..."

He smiled because this time she didn't call him Logan. He could feel the pulse in her wrist beating wildly.

"Give Linda a call and tell her you can't make it." His voice was deep and urgent.

Joanna would have to be a liar to tell herself she wasn't tempted. She *was* tempted. But she also knew that temptation could be a dangerous thing. Temptation had a way of blurring priorities, shading harsh reality with pastel colors, turning ordinary men into heroes. And the fact that Joanna didn't see Eric Logan as one bit ordinary to begin with, made temptation all the more risky and the price too great to pay.

Her gray eyes took on a hard, defensive look. "No, Logan. Let's leave it as it is. For...all our sakes."

"All?"

"Yours, mine, and...Jen's."

LINDA WAS ALREADY at poolside, her slender, willowy body clad in a silver bikini, stretched gracefully out on a blue-and-white striped plastic lounge chair.

She looked tense and agitated, but as soon as she spotted Joanna her demeanor changed in a flash. All at once she was perky and animated.

"Hi, I was worried you'd changed your mind," Linda said, swinging herself up to a sitting position.

"Why would I do that?" Joanna asked. She was already wearing a simple black one-piece bathing suit and moved to drop her towel and sweatsuit on the empty lounge chair beside Linda's.

"Oh, the storm. Or...maybe you had something better to do."

Joanna felt her cheeks grow warm. "Oh no. Nothing better."

"Eric's working, too, then?"

Joanna nodded. She really hated lying to Linda. But then she hated the fact she was living a lie with everyone here. Even with Eric there were some things she kept to herself.

"Lately Marty seems so preoccupied with his work, sometimes I wonder if he even remembers we share a house." Linda toyed with a corner of her towel as she spoke.

Joanna noticed an edge in Linda's voice and was about to pursue the topic of Martin Matthias's preoccupation with work, but Linda looked immediately regretful about having been critical of her adored spouse. She put on a bright smile.

"I'm so glad you came, Jen. I really look forward to our get-togethers. I've never had a real friend. Until Marty came along, men were only interested in . . . hitting on me. And most women thought I was either too dull, too poor and unsophisticated, or too ordinary to bother with. Your friendship . . . means a lot to me."

Joanna's smile was tinged with guilt and sympathy. She didn't like her ulterior motives for instigating this "friendship." And she knew that, under normal circumstances, it was unlikely that she and Linda would have been friends. Not for the reasons Linda gave, though. For Joanna, it had more to do with Linda's passivity, her willingness to accept whatever she was handed in life.

But Joanna did feel sorry for the shy young woman, especially after Linda had confided in her that she'd been abandoned as a small child and raised in a series of foster homes. Linda had told her that she'd always felt unloved and never felt that she belonged, until Marty Matthias had swept her off her feet and given her everything she'd ever dreamed of—love and all the creature comforts to go with it, too. And if in return Linda had to remain subservient, pliant and ingratiating, well, in Linda's eyes, it seemed a small price to pay.

"Do you want to swim first or work out?" Linda asked.

"I should work out." Joanna knew she needed to get in shape for her Paris shoot, now less than three weeks away. But, of course, she couldn't explain that to Linda. Well, maybe one day when this was all over... Joanna felt a wave of guilt. What would become of Linda if Matthias was fingered? Here she'd been accusing Eric of being manipulative and deceptive. Was she any better?

"You don't look like a woman who wants to work out, Jen," Linda said with a little laugh. "How about a swim and a sauna, instead?"

Joanna smiled. "Sounds great."

For all her seeming frailness, Linda was a strong swimmer and, surprisingly, strongly competitive.

Climbing out of the pool, Joanna gave Linda an assessing look. "You really do have a lot of spunk. You shouldn't hide it, Linda."

Linda drew a deep breath and let it out in a sigh. "It would be nice not to be afraid to be—" she hesitated and gave a little laugh "—my real self, whatever that is."

They headed for the showers and then made their way to the sauna.

"It's so quiet here today," Joanna commented, climbing up on one of the planked benches while Linda threw a small wooden pitcher of water on the hot rocks so that a thick steam sizzled up toward the cedar ceiling.

"The storm, probably." Linda stretched out on a low bench. "Or, more likely, everyone's busy working on their projects."

"What's Marty working on?"

There was a distinctly pregnant pause. "Oh, something with...Hauser."

"You don't like Gerta very much, do you?"

Linda laughed uncomfortably. "Do you?"

"No," Joanna said frankly. "I think she's a very ruthless woman."

"Ruthless?" Linda echoed. "Yes, maybe. You think Marty's ruthless too, don't you, Jen?"

"Don't you, Linda?" Joanna asked softly, her body tensing as she waited for Linda's response.

There was no answer. Joanna leaned her head over the edge of the bench and looked down at Linda who seemed on the verge of tears.

"I'm sorry, Linda. That was a very tactless question."

"No, no. I want you to be able to ask me anything, tell me anything." Linda smiled weakly. "Not about your work, of course. I know that's off limits. But . . . about anything personal. I want you to see me as someone you can . . . trust."

Joanna swung her legs over the bench and jumped down, taking a seat beside Linda. "I do trust you, Linda. The question is, do you really trust me?"

"What do you mean?"

"I think you've been very upset about something lately. To do with Marty. And Gerta Hauser, too."

"I know they're not having an affair," Linda said with a firm assurance in her voice. "A woman can tell those things. Feel them. Marty and I have a . . . great relationship . . . in bed. Lately, it's been better than ever. Which is why—" She stopped abruptly.

Joanna didn't pounce. Instead, she leaned back against the hot cedar wall and waited. Linda wanted to confide in her. Joanna was sure of it.

"Oh Jen, I don't know what to do."

"About Marty and Gerta?"

Linda swallowed hard, wiping sweat from her face with the edge of her towel. "And about . . . you."

Joanna knew that they wouldn't be able to stay in there much longer, but she was afraid Linda would clam up if she suggested finishing the conversation in a cooler spot.

"What do you mean, Linda? Where do I fit into the picture?"

Linda faltered, looked close to tears, then pulled herself together as best she could, looking at Joanna with clouded eyes.

"I... overheard them... talking. Gerta and Marty."

"About me?"

"I... think so."

"What did you overhear?"

Linda shrugged. "Not much. I wasn't... close enough. But... something about you... seeming different... lately."

"Different?" Joanna hoped Linda hadn't heard the catch in her voice.

"You are different lately, Jen."

"I suppose I am," Joanna said slowly. She forced a little smile. "I guess that's what humility does to a scientist."

"What do you mean?"

"I've never really failed at anything before," Joanna said evenly. "And it's doubly hard when you get so close...only to run smack dab into a stone wall."

Linda gripped Joanna's wrist hard. "Oh Jen, is that really true? Have you truly given up on your project?"

"What makes you think I'd lie about something like that?"

"It's not what I think," Linda said, desperation in her voice. "It's what... they think. They think... you've succeeded. That... that you've found the secret to the cold fusion theory."

"You overheard them say that."

"Yes. Yes, they both believe it. And . . . and what's driving me crazy is . . ." Again, she couldn't finish. She shut her eyes tightly.

"You think they want to get their hands on my work and use it for their own purposes."

Linda shook her head violently, her hair flying every which way. "No, no, no. They couldn't. They wouldn't." She was still gripping Joanna's wrist. "Oh Jen, if they were absolutely sure you had failed, then it . . . wouldn't matter. Marty . . . would begin to . . . see reason. It's Gerta. She's so . . . awful. I hate her. I hate her!"

Joanna had to work hard not to allow Linda to slip over into hysteria. The frantic, betrayed young woman was right on the brink. She extracted her wrist from Linda's tight grip and gave her a little shake.

"Did they say what they planned to do, Linda? How are they going to decide whether they're right?"

"I . . . don't . . . know."

"You didn't overhear them say anything about their plans?"

"I was scared they'd see me. I didn't hear anything more." Her eyes widened. "Jen, listen to me. I really care about you so much. I wouldn't want anything . . . to happen to you. If you have . . . succeeded, then your life . . . is in danger. I'd help you . . . if I could. But there's no way . . . without—"

"Without betraying Marty?"

She dropped her hands in her palms and sobbed. "Yes. Yes!"

Joanna put a comforting arm around the distraught woman. "I understand, Linda. Really, I do. Come on. Let's get out of here before we start frying like eggs."

Linda forced down her sobs and looked over at Joanna. She stared at her intently for several moments, not a muscle moving. And then she let out a low, heaving sigh. "Oh

God, they're right, aren't they? You have found the solution. Or...you're close.''

"Linda..."

She shook her head despondently, as though all was lost. "It's all right. You don't have to say anything." Her voice sounded hollow. "Just be careful."

Joanna helped Linda to her feet and guided her to the door.

When Joanna shoved the thick cedar door with her palm, it didn't budge.

"The wood must have swelled," Linda said dully.

Joanna pushed harder. "That's weird. It won't budge."

Linda, still lost in her own worries, gave a half-hearted push of her own.

Joanna gave Linda's shoulder a little shake. "It's really jammed, Linda. Let's push together. Give it all you've got. At the count of three. One, two, three..."

Nothing.

A rush of panic swept across Linda's face. "It won't...open. Jen...I'm scared." She started pushing and banging on the door in an increasingly frantic effort to force it open. "Oh no! What if Gerta followed you here, Jen? She may have decided to act on her own because Marty wouldn't do anything...drastic. What if she means to sweat the truth out of you?"

"That doesn't make any sense," Joanna argued, but her own panic was mounting.

Linda clutched at Joanna's arm. "We can't last in this heat too long. What if...we pass out? Maybe that's what Gerta's waiting for. Then she can unlock the door, grab you and take you off somewhere, make you talk, and I...I won't be able to even prove it was her. But I know...I know..." She started pounding furiously on the door again.

"Wait," Joanna said, trying to contain her own escalating panic, realizing that Linda's theory made frightening sense. "You're going to use up all your energy that way and you really will pass out. Take it slower. Again, I'll count to three. One, two, three..."

Both women shoved the door, but it still didn't budge. Joanna's eyes shot to the thermometer on the wall.

Then she felt certain. The door hadn't jammed. Someone—if Linda was right, Gerta—had fixed it shut. And the same someone or that someone's partner had turned up the thermostat just outside the sauna.

A bubble of hysteria slid up Joanna's throat, a spasm of terror jerking inside her chest. In the escalating heat it was increasingly difficult to breathe. Her chest burned fiercely, but she tried to hold back her panic, especially as she knew her companion was close to the breaking point.

Linda had sunk to the floor and was curled up in a fetal position. Joanna joined her, trying to soothe her.

"It'll be okay, Linda. Eric will worry that I'm not back. He knows we're here. He'll come looking for us soon."

It was a fraction cooler on the floor. Joanna flattened herself out on the ground.

"She's out there. Waiting..." Linda gasped. "We've got to hold on. We mustn't pass out. Oh, I can't breathe. I feel...so dizzy."

Joanna felt weak and dizzy, too. At least Linda had stopped for a drink of water before she went into the sauna. But Joanna clung desperately to consciousness. Gathering all of her strength, she grabbed the empty water bucket on the floor, dragged herself to her feet and began pounding at the door with it. She was determined to keep it up until the door gave way.

"HOLD A SEC, Eric. I've got another call on the line."

"Damn it! Do not put me on hold."

"Okay, okay. Calm down. What's the problem?"

"What's the problem? I've got a ticking time bomb on my hands, and you're asking me what's the problem?"

"Our gal's doing great. Just great."

"Great? She's playing junior G-man. The joint is jumping here. The deal was for her to sit quietly in her lab and play physicist, not secret agent. She keeps this up and she's going to be a sitting duck. And I can't guarantee I can beat out the hunters."

"Hauser and Matthias?"

"So she thinks."

"The question is, do you think she's right?"

Eric let out a blast of breath. "Maybe. I haven't written the others off my list, though. Not yet. So far she's working strictly on intuition and speculation. I'm not ready to point any fingers until I have something more tangible."

"Well, if she keeps up the good work, that junior G-man of ours might just get it for you. You just stick close to your little lady, Eric, and be there when the time bomb goes off."

Eric's features darkened, his voice taking on an icy edge. "You bastard. That was the game plan all along. Wasn't it? You set her up.... No, you let *me* set her up. Not as a temporary fill-in—as a decoy. You wanted her here to bring on the heat, force some hands."

"Now, now, Eric..."

"You told me we wouldn't move in for the kill until after she was safe, sound and primping for the cameras in Paris. But that was never your plan."

"We're playing for high stakes here, Eric. Look at the big picture. We have a dual responsibility. One is to see to it that Hampleman's work is not compromised. And the other is to purify Synergy."

"That's the bottom line, isn't it? The little people themselves don't count. And when they're no longer of value to your plan, they're expendable."

"You're overstating things."

Eric expelled a hard breath.

"You're doing an excellent job, Eric. Everybody is pleased with the way you've handled yourself up to now. Just don't put this on a personal level, my boy. That's when people get into trouble."

"I am in trouble," Eric said in a low voice. "I'm in love with her."

"You've got to keep a cool head, Eric. There are lives at risk. And if you really care, you've got to..."

"I've got to do something about it. And I intend to." Eric hung up the phone.

The "clean" phone he had used was less than a mile from Synergy. It didn't take him long to get back to the house. He parked the car in the driveway, noting with irritation that Joanna's moped was still gone. The roads would be slick.

He checked his watch. She'd been gone more than a half hour. His features hardened. *"Everybody's pleased with the way you've handled yourself...up to now."*

Eric drew a sustained, angry breath. Yeah, they were all pleased as long as he played by their rules, accepted their values. But they'd never really understood him, never knew what drove him. They saw the scientist in him—detached, precise, logical, intuitive, meticulously attentive to detail. And they'd very successfully zeroed in on the part of him that quested for that unique high, the thrill that came from living on the edge. He was clever, wily, even ruthless when necessary. And he was gung ho enough to put himself on the line if it counted. But he was not willing to put someone else's life on the line. Especially not someone he'd promised to keep safe from harm. Eric Logan was a man who kept his promises. Whatever it took. And the way he saw it this time, it was going to take getting Joanna Clark on an earlier-than-expected flight to Paris.

A moment later he was back in his car heading over to the clubhouse.

## Chapter Twelve

"Jen? Jen? Can you hear me?"

Joanna stirred, more from the change in the texture and temperature of the air than from the voice that still seemed part of a dark, suffocating dream. But it wasn't a dream. Vaguely she recalled the splintering sound of wood as the sauna door finally gave way from her pounding at it.

Her vision was blurry, but as it came into focus, she let out a sharp cry of terror.

"Jen, it's okay. Everything's okay."

The man she was staring at in horror—Martin Matthias—wasn't the man speaking to her. A warm, tender, familiar hand smoothed her damp hair away from her flushed cheek. She turned her head to look at him.

"Here, drink this." Eric cupped her head, lifting it slightly.

"It's water," he said as she protested weakly. "Come on. It'll help make you feel better. You're so dehydrated. Just a little at a time. That's it. Good." Eric's tone was soft and coaxing.

"Linda . . . ?" she croaked anxiously.

Martin Matthias came closer to Joanna and kneeled down. Now that she knew Eric was so close, she was able to control some of her fear.

"Linda's fine, Jen," Matthias said, his voice heavy with concern. "She came to, a few minutes ago, and I insisted she lie down in the lounge. Dr. MacIntyre is coming right over. Linda asked me to come see how you were. What happened exactly?"

"You tell me," Joanna said accusingly.

"All I know is what Linda told me," Matthias said. "That the door to the sauna jammed."

"Morgan was checking it out while I looked after you and Linda," Eric said, urging Joanna to take another few sips of the water.

*So Morgan was here*, Joanna thought. He could be in on this, too. It was too risky for Gerta, so she and Marty sent him over to do the dirty work.

"When did you get here?" she asked Matthias wearily, sitting up fully, grateful for Eric's comforting arm around her.

"I was practically on Eric's heels," Matthias said. Something flickered in the administrator's eyes. Fear? Yes, it was fear, Joanna thought. And now he was bumbling through an explanation. "I came over to see if Linda wanted to go into town for lunch. We haven't had lunch together in weeks. I've been . . . preoccupied."

*Preoccupied*. Linda's word for Marty. Had the passive Linda actually shown some spunk with her husband and accused him of being preoccupied? Joanna wondered.

Marty was rushing ahead with his tale. "When I got here I found Eric dragging you and Linda out of the sauna. Both of you were unconscious. I went to call Dr. MacIntyre."

"The door didn't jam," Joanna said in a low voice, her eyes fixed on Matthias.

"Yes, Eric just said . . ."

"Someone deliberately locked us in there."

Matthias's eyes hardened. "Really Jen, that's hard to believe. Hank Morgan was here when we arrived. When

Linda told us what happened, he went and checked the sauna door. He said he didn't see any sign of physical tampering. But, since Linda thought maybe something had gone haywire with the thermostat I sent Morgan to get an electrician over here.''

Joanna stopped listening. *Linda's covering up for Marty. She knows he locked us in there.* Joanna was certain that if Eric hadn't shown up, just beating Matthias out by seconds, Matthias would have— What would he have done? What was he planning? To kill her? No, that didn't make any sense. How would he ever hope to get the cold fusion process then? No, he must have meant to kidnap her. The sauna was just a prelude for what was to come.

Only Joanna couldn't reveal the process, because she wasn't Jen. And even once that became clear to Matthias, it wouldn't be over. He and Gerta could hold Joanna for ransom. Twin for twin. Oh, most likely they'd promise that Jen would come to no harm; that they just wanted Jen's cold fusion process; but would they be believed? And even if they were believed, would the United States government ever allow that secret to get into the wrong hands? Joanna wasn't pinning any hopes on it.

"Jen?" Eric stroked her back. "You're trembling." He drew the towel he'd wrapped around her higher up on her shoulders.

"Take me home, Eric," she whispered, a note of urgency in her voice. She had so much to tell him.

"Don't you want to wait for the doctor?"

"No, I'm fine now. The water helped. I just need to rest in a nice air-conditioned bedroom," Joanna insisted.

"I'll wait for MacIntyre and send him over to your place and I'll go tell Linda you're okay," Matthias said quickly. "I know she's worried..." He started off just as Eric was helping Joanna to her feet, but then he stopped and turned back around, anxiety etched in his features. "You won't use the sauna again until the electrician checks everything out?"

Joanna laughed harshly. "You won't catch me in there again, Marty, dead or alive."


"WHY ARE YOU GIVING ME such a hard time?" Joanna exclaimed in exasperation. "I tell you the door was blocked, and that Marty or Gerta were behind it. And they must have sent Morgan in after we were in the sauna, to fix the door. Marty was to finish the job. But you showed up first. You don't really buy his story about wanting to take Linda out for lunch. Oh, he's been preoccupied all right. If what Linda overheard between her husband and Gerta is true . . ."

"All it means is that Gerta's on the rampage as usual about you—I mean Jen—beating her to the glory. She was the one to give up on the cold fusion theory first, convinced it was impossible to achieve. She's not going to be happy to see you prove her wrong."

"But Linda overheard—"

"Joanna, all Linda told you was that she overheard her husband and Gerta talking about you being different lately and thinking you might be covering up your work on the process. She didn't actually hear them plotting anything sinister, did she?"

"No," Joanna said reluctantly. "But her gut feeling . . ." She stopped. Why would Eric buy Linda's gut feelings any more than he was buying her own?

"Okay," she said finally, still refusing to give up. "What about the sauna door? I tell you, it was rigged shut."

"I'll talk to Morgan," he countered.

"If Morgan's involved, he won't tell you the truth. We've got to think of some way to—"

Eric flinched. "*We're* not doing anything. *You're* getting out, Joanna."

She squinted at him. "What do you mean, I'm getting out?"

"Exactly what I said. I've already called the airlines. There's a flight to New York this evening. And a morning flight to Paris. You can wire your agent that you decided to have a brief vacation in gay Paree before your assignment with *Elle* gets rolling. Don't worry, I'll get your passport back for you. I think, under the circumstances, the farther away you are from here, the safer it'll be."

"For me, you mean. What about Jen?"

He folded his hands together tightly, so that his knuckles turned whiter than school paste. "We'll change the game plan," he said quietly.

She stared at him for several long moments. "As simple as that. First one game plan that just happens to turn my entire world topsy-turvy. And then you just push another button, dig up another game plan that throws me around another 360-degree loop. But how much do *I* count in all this? How much does Jen count? We're not really your concern, Logan, just how we can be used. Oh, you'd use the old JFK line—'Ask not what your country can do for you, ask what you can do for your country.' Only I never asked. I didn't exactly volunteer, if you'll remember. Until…until you told me about Jen. Well, it was effective persuasion, Logan. You won me over. I'm volunteering now."

"I wasn't in on the original game plan any more than you were."

Joanna scowled. "What's that supposed to mean?"

"All along, my people meant to set you up. They told me to bring you in as a substitute. No big risk involved as long as you played Jen well enough. Which you've done." He paused to take a breath. "But they never meant you to be just a substitute. You were the bait. If I could keep you alive, fine. But if not, the primary goal was to secure the operation. They were using you, damn it, to get at the people who were after Jen and her breakthrough. And they were using me, too. If I'd figured it out faster, you'd have been out of here that much quicker. You're in way over your head and I'm pulling you out. That's final.'' He fixed her with a hard look.

Joanna braced herself, her expression equally stony. ''Oh no, Eric. No one is pushing any more buttons or changing any plans that affect my life or my sister's. I don't care what role you meant me to play, or what role this mystery organization of yours meant me to play. From now on, I'm playing it my way.''

''You talk pretty cocky.''

''Well, then I'm a better actress than I thought, because I'm scared stiff, Eric. It's just that I'm not going to let that stop me.'' She gave him an elusive and yet alluring smile that would have melted the heart of any man.

Eric's heart was already in a weakened state. He smiled back, marveling at her ability to appear so self-contained.

Joanna was warmed and encouraged by Eric's smile. ''I'm feeling a little better than I was back there at the club-house,'' she said softly.

Eric was glad to hear it. He felt awful.

JOANNA PACED around her room. It was nearly 11:00 p.m., but once again sleep eluded her. She kept thinking about Hank Morgan.

Was Marty paying Morgan off? Was Morgan in on the whole operation? It could have been Morgan who'd chased her around the lab complex the night she'd found Matthias and Hauser having their little tête-à-tête.

Joanna began pacing again, as she explored another new track. Maybe it wasn't Morgan whose footsteps she'd heard pursuing her back at the labs. It could have been Linda chasing after her. Not to catch her, but to scare her off, to protect her husband. Just as she'd protected him this morning when she'd lied about the door not being jammed, making up some absurd story about a faulty thermostat. The only thing wrong with the thermostat was that it, like the door, had been tampered with.

Linda had confessed to Joanna that she'd overheard Gerta and Marty talking about her. She could have learned what she did by eavesdropping outside her husband's office when Gerta and Marty were having that midnight "problem-solving" discussion. Only Linda's plan backfired and she and Joanna had ended up dodging each other in the shadows.

Poor Linda. She seemed intent on protecting her husband at all costs. Joanna wondered if Linda had at first been afraid he was having an affair and so she'd followed him. Instead, she'd found out—

Joanna stopped pacing. She had to talk to Linda and to Hank Morgan.

Joanna decided to deal with Morgan first. If he was covering for Marty, maybe she'd be able to pick it up in his voice or in his mannerisms. Maybe she could force his hand, blow his cover. Evidence of a pay-off would be concrete proof of Matthias's duplicity. Then Morgan might even agree to come forward and point the finger at Marty and Gerta, in exchange for cutting a deal with the government in order to save his own hide. Of course Joanna knew she'd have to play this very cautiously. If Morgan was in cahoots with the deadly duo, she was taking a big risk. But she'd cover herself. Eric could come along with her to Morgan's place. He could post himself outside to make sure nothing went wrong.

The problem was, could she convince Eric to go along with her plan? He was so desperate to keep her out of harm's way. But she was desperate, too. She couldn't simply fly off and leave her sister's destiny in Eric's hands alone. Surely, Eric would understand that. He'd brought her in on this in the first place. He'd wanted her to trust him, and now that she finally did, he wanted to ship her off. Well, she would just have to convince him that they had to see this through together. And as for Morgan, she'd been successful at bluffing up to now.

Hank Morgan lived in one of the town houses that was two streets over from Jen's. While it looked the same as the others on the outside, inside it was divided into four studio apartments. Morgan lived in one. Another was occupied by Jen's secretary, Toni, who'd moved back about a week ago. The reclusive chemist, Andre Hoffman, whom Joanna had only seen once over at the labs, lived in the third unit. And Barry Lester, Matthias's assistant, who'd been away on vacation for the past four days, had the fourth.

Once inside the town house, Joanna passed quietly by Toni's apartment on the first floor. The secretary might think it odd that her boss was paying a late-night call on Morgan. And Toni might possibly be jealous, as well. Whatever Morgan might be feeling toward Toni, Joanna was convinced, after observing Jen's secretary for nearly two weeks, Toni was wildly in love with Hank Morgan.

His apartment was at the top of the stairs. Joanna lifted her hand to knock on the door, only to realize it wasn't fully shut. Her heartbeat quickened. She knocked anyway. Probably Morgan had gone out and forgotten to shut his door. Although that wasn't too likely for a man who was supposed to be an ace at security. Maybe he was there and expecting someone. Like Toni.

After she knocked, the door swung open a little more. She knocked again, and it opened fully.

Hank Morgan was in. And it was doubtful that he'd forgotten to shut his door. Even if he had, it was too late to worry about it now. Hank Morgan was through having worries of any kind. He was stretched out on the floor in a pool of blood, beside his half-opened sofa bed. He must have been in the process of opening it when someone had murdered him. A faint scent of gunpowder still hung in the air. At least, it was what Joanna imagined gun powder smelled like. She'd never actually smelled gun powder. She'd never seen a dead body, either.

Her knees felt soft, sourness slid up her throat, and the color bled from her face as she shrank back in horror, her back pressed against the wall.

Just as she was forcing herself to get out of the apartment and go get Eric, she heard footsteps on the stairs. The sound raised the hairs on the back of her neck.

The footsteps were stopping outside Morgan's door. When Joanna had entered the apartment she'd shut the door behind her.

There was a soft rap on the door. For an instant she thought it might be Eric who hadn't been too thrilled to stay posted outside as backup.

"Hank? Are you still up?"

It was Toni Conners. Joanna froze. Maybe Toni would simply think Morgan was sleeping when she got no answer, and she'd go back to her own apartment.

Joanna's breath held.

Another rap; this one louder. "Please, Hank. Let me in. I can see under the door that you've got your light on." She knocked again.

Joanna stared in horror as the doorknob jiggled. *Oh no. The bolt wasn't drawn. All Toni had to do was push the door open.*

Joanna looked frantically around the one-room apartment for a place to hide. The bathroom. That was the only choice. She made it in just as the apartment door swung open. There was a heartbeat of silence and then she heard Toni's shrill scream of horror followed by a hard, dull thud. Joanna concluded that Toni must have passed out from the shock.

Toni's scream brought the reclusive scientist, Andre Hoffman, out of his apartment across the hall. Joanna heard him mutter sharply and the next thing she knew Hoffman was opening the bathroom door....

JOANNA SAT on her bed, still dazed. Eric sat down beside her.

The local police had been notified. But, since Morgan's death had occurred on a United States Government installation, the Los Verdes Police Department had no authority. Special government agents were being sent in to conduct an investigation of the security chief's murder.

Dr. Andrew MacIntyre had examined the body and declared that, as rigor mortis had already set in, the murder must have taken place some time before noon. Probably very shortly after Morgan had completed his check of the sauna door.

Joanna was cleared, since she'd lacked both opportunity and motive. Going over and over the case in her mind, Joanna realized she'd been wrong. Morgan hadn't been opening the sofa to bed down for the night, he'd been closing it up to make the apartment tidy for the day ahead. Only the day ahead never came.

"What a day," Eric muttered somberly.

It was such an incredible understatement, Joanna started to laugh. The laughter just burst from her, unstoppable. She was laughing so hard, her sides hurt, her head pounded, her throat throbbed. Only it wasn't really laughter, she realized. It was closer to sobbing. Soon she was sobbing in earnest and trembling.

Eric held her tight, easing her onto the bed, drawing her against him.

Finally there were no more tears left. Drained and exhausted, Joanna lay next to Eric and they looked at each other, both of them absolutely still. Even when she closed her eyes, she could feel his eyes on her, never leaving her. She didn't want him to leave her.

"I'm so sorry all of this happened to you, Joanna. It's my fault. I should have—"

She put a finger to his lips. Her hand wasn't trembling anymore. "I should have trusted you," she whispered. "We need to trust each other." She sighed. "Neither of us is very good at trusting."

"We can try to improve."

"Yes...maybe..."

He caressed her hair, her neck, her shoulder. *Trust us together,* his touch whispered. Gently, ever so gently, he kissed her lips and she gasped at the erotic pull.

When he slowly began to undress her, her body stiffened, tightening like a bow. But Eric could hear her whispered yes. Her breathing was shallow. Her nipples hardened at his barest touch. Her eyes were deep liquid pools, welcoming him.

He slipped out of his clothes after undressing her. Joanna curved against him. His body was warm, nurturing, shaped just perfectly to match hers. He stroked her slowly, not in passion yet, but in comfort. Yes, he wanted to comfort her first.

She needed the comfort he offered. And yet she was frightened by it, afraid it would be too hard to walk away from when the time came. And she knew the time would come. The time for her to say goodbye and go on with her own life. Time for Jen to return. *Jen and Eric...*

But he was whispering her name. "Joanna, Joanna, my beautiful Joanna..."

Her breasts felt wonderfully warm and soft against his chest. She was trembling still, but so was Eric. He ran his fingers through her hair, his lips cruising up the side of her neck to capture an earlobe. His warm breath seemed to reverberate through her entire body. Her trembling increased, but it had nothing to do with fear now. It had to do only with want. She wanted Eric. If only for now. *Tomorrow I'll be strong again.*

She was smiling. Her smile filled Eric with joy. He could look at that smile for the rest of his life.

Where he'd sensed fear and hesitation earlier, he now sensed her open desire. His mouth covered hers, his tongue slipping through her parted lips. Her own tongue received him, welcomed him. Just as her body did.

## Chapter Thirteen

Sunlight slanted through the angled blinds of the shabby motel room, catching motes of spinning dust. There was a single chair in the sparsely furnished room. One of the occupants sat in it, the other took the bed, the springs giving a raspy twang under the weight.

"We need a more secure plan. We have to tread carefully. For one thing, Logan's going to be on his girlfriend like glue...."

"He's still just a chemist, not a guardian angel. I can eliminate him." She gave a brittle little laugh, tinkling with malice.

"Oh, I see you'd like that. First Morgan and now Logan. And I always thought murder wasn't your style."

"I'm flexible. Another of my fine traits." Her voice was flat, cold and without sympathy. "Anyway, we wouldn't necessarily have to take care of Logan so permanently. Maybe we could send him on a wild goose chase and you could see to Hampleman. Take her off someplace for a quiet, private chat. We may still be wrong about Hampleman's success, you know."

"Well, if the good doctor hasn't succeeded we'll deposit her back home, bide our time and wait for new developments. As long as she remains in the dark about us I don't think we have much to worry about."

Eric Logan had taught himself, over the years, to tune out his personal feelings and to steer clear of close relationships. In truth, intimacy had never come easily to him. He believed he functioned best alone. Unfortunately his life was not entirely his own. The Internal Research Bureau, a self-contained and secretly sanctioned arm of the FBI that enlisted and trained an elite corp of scientists, owned a fair share of him.

"The time has come to end your solo act," his chief at the IRB had told him one bright, crisp September day, nearly seventeen months ago. He'd just come in from having weeded out a mole at a government-sponsored chemical plant outside of Chicago.

The new assignment his chief was handing him didn't sit well with Eric. He had nothing against being a chemist at Synergy and keeping watch for a suspected mole or two at the compound. What he objected to was playing nurse-maid, and worse still, housemate, to one of the physicists at Synergy.

But he couldn't deny Dr. Jennifer Hampleman was onto something hot. *Cold* was probably a more apt word. And Eric was there to see to it that if she was truly on the right track, no one threw up any road blocks in her way.

Dr. Jennifer Hampleman had been no more thrilled than Eric about the arrangement. Other than her immediate family, Jen had never felt really close to anyone. And she liked it that way. Her work was her life. An intimate relationship with Eric Logan, even a fabricated one created for her own protection, not only displeased her, it made her very nervous.

They did well enough in public, but in private they felt as if they were in an armed camp. At least for the first few months. It was a toss-up which of them had been more surprised that their shared feelings about the inconvenience of their forced intimacy was what made it possible for them to become friends. They saw life in much the same way. They started to relax. There were still some tense moments, some definite adjustments along the way, on both their parts. But all in all, their relationship, in fact as well as in fancy, had really worked out quite well.

Eric couldn't say the same thing on this mid-August morning. While he saw his relationship with Jen as unambiguous, his relationship with Jen's twin was twisted with complexities. In the light of day, when he woke up in bed with Joanna, those complexities seemed insurmountable.

Joanna's eyelids fluttered open. She smiled tentatively as she saw that he was awake. She also saw the look of strain in his hazel eyes. She chose to ignore it.

"What a night," she whispered.

Her remark brought a smile to his lips and a kiss to hers. "A great night."

*If only this could last.* Her smile faded. Strain was contagious.

"Have you heard from Jen recently?"

"Not directly."

"Indirectly what do you hear?"

"She's at the final and most crucial stage of her experimentation."

"Will she succeed?"

"I don't know for certain. I hope so."

"Yes, it would be awful if this had all been for nothing."

He touched her cheek. "It's a chance that had to be taken."

"I suppose so." There was a shadow in her smoky gray eyes, a shift to sorrow that was masked by her forced smile.

His fingers toyed idly with a strand of her hair. "I'm sorry about the dye job. Your natural color is so lovely."

A thought struck Joanna. "Jen's hair must be blond, too. Why does she dye it?"

"I told you once, she's always done whatever she could to play down her looks. She's totally invested in being taken seriously." He laughed softly. "Isn't it true blondes have more fun?"

Joanna merely shrugged. "I wouldn't describe my life as fun. Exciting at times, rewarding..." She stopped, her lips curving down at the corners. "I keep wondering what my life might have been if I'd been adopted by the Hamplemans as Iris Akers had planned." She couldn't bring herself to refer to the woman she'd never met, much less known of before last week, as her mother.

"Was it bad being raised by the Clarks?" he asked gently.

Joanna gave his question intense consideration. "I loved them. My mother was gentle and kind. And even though she was overprotective, my father saw to it that I had the breathing room I needed. He fostered my independence and my self-reliance." She paused. "Oh, my father wasn't an easy man to love. He was stern, controlling, distant. Maybe a guilty conscience for the terrible thing he'd done kept him from getting close to me. I wonder if he ever regretted what he had done?" Her eyes filled with sudden tears. "But, I know he loved me in his own way. And I know my mother loves me."

"Will you tell her you know the truth?"

"At first...I was so angry and distraught, I wanted to confront her, scream at her, hurt her, like I was hurt." She wiped at the tears trickling down her cheeks. "Poor Mom. I've suffered with knowing the truth for a week. She's suffered with it for twenty-seven years. And paid the price." She grew silent for several moments. "No, I won't tell her I know the truth," she said finally.

He nodded. She saw in his eyes that he approved of her decision, respected her for it.

"But I do want to see Jen before...before I leave for Paris."

Again Eric nodded. "I'll see that it's arranged. Back in New York. Whether she succeeds or not, Jen won't be returning to Synergy."

"Because of Matthias and Hauser? But surely we'll smoke them out before too long. They've already committed murder. There are Federal agents investigating right at this moment. Between us and them..."

He took firm hold of her shoulders. "Let them handle it. There are to be no more stunts, Joanna. Mutual trust, remember? Let me trust you to sit tight and you trust me to see that you're taken care of."

"But I have to speak to Linda again. She's our best hope, Eric. After the sauna incident..."

"She's not here."

"What?"

"Marty sent her off to one of those posh health spas near San Diego."

"Oh no. But how did he manage it? Didn't the agents sent here to investigate Hank Morgan's murder insist that everyone stay put until the crime was solved?"

"Linda was already cleared of suspicion. She wasn't even at Synergy when Morgan was killed."

"Where was she?"

"She left the health club and drove directly into town. Dr. MacIntyre says she and Matthias left the club at 10:45. They each got into their own cars. The doc says Matthias told him he was heading over to his office, and he saw Linda head for the main gate. Lou was on duty. He says he checked her out at 10:50 a.m. He didn't check her back in again until 2:15. I guess the sauna incident really shook her up. She made some comment to Lou about giving herself a parole."

Joanna sat up in bed. "So, Marty didn't take Linda to lunch."

"Maybe he lost his appetite."

"Maybe Linda lost hers. Maybe she's starting to see the light. And just maybe Marty's realizing his loving wife might crack. So, he's gotten rid of her."

"Joanna..."

"Oh, I don't mean he killed her, Eric. I mean, sent her off to the spa where she'd be out of his way." She gave him a sharp look. "Which one? There are a half dozen spas in and around San Diego."

Eric shrugged and decided to level with her. His people were checking into Linda's whereabouts. Joanna had done a good job with Linda. He agreed with her that Matthias's wife just might crack under pressure. Unlike Joanna, though, he wasn't absolutely convinced it would happen. Sometimes women like Linda Matthias proved to be tougher to crack than they appeared.

TONI CONNERS wasn't at work that day. She was in mourning. Hank Morgan's body had been shipped home to Dallas, Texas, and Toni wouldn't be going to the funeral. She was holding a silent and private vigil back in her apartment, where she vowed to stay until her lover's murderer was found.

In the windowless confines of the lab, Joanna felt restless. Where was Linda? Eric would know soon, but she was afraid he wasn't going to tell her about it.

She stared across a long metal table to where Eric was quietly mixing some chemicals in a test tube. She marveled at his calm. He really was a pro. She had no doubt his track record for his agency was excellent.

He felt her looking at him and met her gaze with a smile. "Hungry?"

She shrugged. "I suppose."

"Two more minutes and we'll head over to the cafeteria."

"Maybe we can share a table with dear, sweet Gerta."

Eric smiled wryly. "Think you'll spot blood stains on Lady MacBeth's hands?"

"I doubt she does the dirty work—probably leaves that for Marty. I'll lay you odds he went directly from the club-house to Morgan's apartment. Our pair wouldn't take any chances with Morgan changing his story about the sauna door." She eyed him curiously. "You didn't get a chance to check the door yourself, did you?"

"Matthias had a maintenance man replace it."

Joanna gave a rueful laugh. "Always one step ahead, our Marty."

"Let's hope not always."

Joanna thought about Matthias's wife and felt a chill of alarm. "I'm worried, Eric. If they killed Morgan to prevent him from changing his story, can we really bank on them not harming Linda?"

In truth, he wasn't banking on anything. But he didn't want Joanna to worry more than she already was, so he said with manufactured confidence, "Marty is too crazy about his wife to let anything happen to her. She's played along all this time. As long as he keeps her out of the picture he'll figure she's no real threat."

"But you intend to put her back in the picture, don't you, Eric?"

He sighed wearily. "If we have to."

"She trusts me, Eric. If she opens up to anyone, it's going to be me."

"I can be pretty persuasive," he countered. Joanna couldn't argue the point. "Besides," he went on, "she's al-ways liked me. Other than Marty, I was the only one she ever seemed to relax around. The other scientists intimi-dated her, including Jen, until 'she' made this sudden ef-fort to befriend her."

A brief, quirky smile came and went on Joanna's lips. "Is Jen all that intimidating?"

He began to clean up. "No. Not once you get to know her."

"I wonder if I will. I mean, really get to know her. We travel in rather different circles. All we truly have in common besides blood, is . . . you."

THE ONLY OTHER PERSON in the cafeteria besides Joanna and Eric was Dr. Hoffman. The eminent biochemist was making one of his rare appearances. He almost always ate lunch in his lab. Or, Joanna guessed, often skipped it. He was exceedingly thin, but surprisingly spry for a man in his early sixties.

"I should invite him over to join us," Eric said, watching the scientist carry his tray over to an empty table.

After her brief, mortifying face-off with Hoffman in Morgan's bathroom the night before, Joanna wasn't keen on another encounter. "Why push it? He might put me on the spot with some scientific question."

Eric disagreed. "Hoffman's not the sort."

"How would you know? I thought he hardly ever surfaced."

"Trust me." He rose from the table, walked over to Hoffman, exchanged a few words and brought him back to their table.

"Doctor Hampleman," he greeted her formally, taking a seat across from her at the table. Then slowly, meticulously, he removed from his tray a plastic-wrapped sandwich, carton of milk and a clear plastic container of chocolate pudding. "I hope I'm not imposing."

"No. No, of course not," Joanna said quickly.

Dr. Hoffman's brown eyebrows were thick and streaked with gray. They rose into little arcs. "And how are you feeling today, Dr. Hampleman?"

"Better."

They ate in silence, Eric taking large bites of his turkey sandwich and washing it down with milk. He was the only one at the table who ate with gusto. Hoffman nibbled delicately on ham and cheese on whole wheat. Joanna sipped her tea, leaving her sandwich untouched. Her thoughts kept drifting to Linda Matthias, and she found herself with no appetite at all.

"Aren't you hungry, Jen?" Eric asked.

"No, not really."

Dr. Hoffman shook his head disapprovingly. "You should eat, Dr. Hampleman. You're looking pale. But, then, finding Mr. Morgan like that must have been a terrible shock."

"Yes. Terrible," she muttered.

Hoffman smiled suddenly, revealing a couple of gold-capped teeth. "I have something to show you that might cheer you up." He looked over at Eric. "Might I borrow the doctor for a short while?"

Joanna's heart lurched. *Get me out of this, Eric.*

Eric had no trouble predicting Joanna's response. "Well, we are right in the middle of something..."

"Yes, yes, but this will only take about a half hour."

Joanna's eyes were burning into Eric.

"Surely you can manage without her for that long. I've been experimenting with a new VLSI chip for the nuclear resonance imager that I'm sure will fascinate Dr. Hampleman." Hoffman turned to her. "That's an area you've done some fine work in yourself, Doctor."

"That...was a while ago. If you're asking for advice..."

"Oh no, no. Nothing like that. I am not at the stage of needing advice. I simply want to show you my progress. You don't have to feel in any way imposed upon, I assure you."

Eric wadded up the plastic wrap from his sandwich and gathered the rest of his trash onto his tray. Then he reached for Joanna's untouched roast beef sandwich. "Dr. Hoffman is right, Jen. I can wait. I know you'd never want to turn down a golden opportunity to see something like that. I'll bring your sandwich back to the lab for you. You might get hungry later."

She stared blankly at him. What was he saying? What was he doing? A half-hour with Hoffman and his VLSI chip? Maybe Jen would have never turned down the offer. But *she* didn't even have the faintest idea what VLSI stood for. Eric was taking this charade one step too far.

Not surprisingly it turned out to be the longest half hour Joanna had ever spent—the longest, the most tense and the most mind boggling. She did leave Hoffman's lab knowing that his VLSI chip, when perfected, would reduce electrical consumption by half, as well as making a big dent in the cost of production. However, she still had no idea what VLSI stood for. Or any idea what a nuclear resonance imager was, for that matter.

But she was quite proud of the way she'd handled herself. She was sure Hoffman hadn't had the least suspicion she wasn't Jen. She'd played it like the cool, observant, but contained scientist she guessed her twin to be. Jen would have been proud of her. Eric was going to be proud of her.

When she got back to the lab and found it empty, she realized Eric's stamp of approval wasn't going to be immediately forthcoming. Eric wasn't in the lab, although her wrapped sandwich was, sitting on the metal table on top of a hastily scribbled note.

"I had to drive into town to pick up some supplies. See you back at the house later tonight. Sit tight and wait for me. Love, Eric."

Joanna crumpled up the note and tossed it across the lab. He must've gotten word on Linda's spa and he'd gone off to see her on his own. She knew Eric wasn't deliberately intending to keep her in the dark. He must have figured while she was safely in Hoffman's care, he could go check on Linda. He couldn't afford to wait around and possibly lose Linda again.

Maybe it wasn't too late to follow. She left the lab, only to bump into Hoffman again in the corridor. For a man who was a recluse, he was certainly managing to be plenty visible all of a sudden.

"Ah, Dr. Hampleman. I meant to give you these notes. I thought you might be interested . . ."

She grabbed them up. "Thanks, Dr. Hoffman." She started for the exit.

"But where are you going? I thought Dr. Logan said you were in the middle of a project." He caught up with her at the exit.

"It seems our project is on hold. He's taking a *short* break."

"Well, that's good news for me, then," Hoffman announced almost gaily, taking her arm. "Why don't we go back to my lab and . . ."

"I can't, Dr. Hoffman. I really can't just now."

But Hoffman refused to release his grip on her arm. "Please calm yourself, Dr. Hampleman. You mustn't get so worked up. I know. Let me drive you back to your home and you can rest for a while."

She forced herself to appear calmer. "I suppose you're right. I need to rest. The strain and all. I think I will go home."

"Good. And you'll let me drive you."

"There's no need. I've got my moped just outside. The ride in the fresh air will do me good."

He eyed her with open concern. "You will go straight back home."

She nodded. "There's no point in doing anything else."

"I tell you what I'll do. You didn't eat any lunch and surely that can't help how you're feeling. I have some excellent vegetable soup at home. I made it myself. I'll go home, pack you up a container and bring it over for you.''

"Oh, I wouldn't put you to so much trouble, Doctor."

"No trouble at all. I feel a bit responsible for your upset."

"You do?"

"Yes." His cheeks reddened. "I shouldn't have barged into Mr. Morgan's bathroom last night the way I did. I never enter bathrooms without knocking first, under ordinary circumstances."

Joanna had to smile. "Well, last night wasn't exactly an ordinary circumstance."

"Ah, true enough. And I didn't really know Mr. Morgan well."

"Well, I'll be heading home then," Joanna said, cutting him off. "And if the soup really isn't any trouble..."

"Oh, no trouble at all. Really, none at all. In five minutes I will be—'' he gave an impish smile ''—knocking on your door."

Joanna hurried out to her moped. When Hoffman came knocking at her door in five minutes she hoped to be well off the compound. He'd already stalled her by a good three minutes. But if Eric had left within the last ten minutes or so, she still might be able to catch up with him.

When she started off on her moped she saw Hoffman pulling out of his parking space. He gave a little beep of his horn and followed right behind her. Joanna was forced to head back to the town house. When she pulled into her driveway, Hoffman drove by. He gave another friendly toot of his horn and she waved. As soon as he turned the bend, she pulled back out of the driveway and headed for the gate.

When she got there, Lou and another gate guard came over. Lou gave her a bright smile. Ever since the day she and Eric had given him a ride back to the compound from town, he'd become her buddy.

After the guard on duty had checked her ID and returned to his post, Lou, who was off duty, started chatting.

"Hi there, Doc. Where's the fire?"

"Lou, did Dr. Logan just pass through?"

"Well...not just. About twenty minutes ago."

"Twenty minutes," she echoed despondently.

"Hey, don't tell me you two had a lovers' quarrel?"

"You could call it that. I was hoping I could catch up with him and...make up."

"Well, if it helps any, he mentioned something about a drive down the coast road."

Joanna brightened. She'd take the same route and stop at every spa along the way until she found Eric.

Joanna was tempted to give Lou a big hug, but she was sure it would have been out of character for Jen. Instead she gave him a winning smile and took off for the coast road. The last thing she heard was Lou shouting, "Good luck."

Good luck wasn't in the cards for Joanna. Less than five miles down the road a car came speeding up behind her. As it passed her Joanna swerved to keep from being sideswiped and ended up in a ditch. Fortunately, she wasn't hurt.

"Oh great," she muttered dragging the bike back onto the road. No matter how many times she tried to start it, she couldn't get more than a weak cough out of the engine.

Hot and sweaty, she wheeled the bike well over to the side of the road and started praying for a car to come along. There was no option but to leave the bike and try to hitch a ride back to the compound and get Eric's moped. He'd taken the car.

Within a couple of minutes she spotted a blue sedan coming down the road, traveling in the same direction as she'd been going. Oh well, maybe she could convince the driver to take a quick detour. She squinted into the sun, waving the car down, thrilled to see it slow and finally pull to a stop about ten feet in front of her.

As Joanna ran over, the driver leaned across the front seat and opened the passenger door. "Trouble?"

As soon as Joanna bent down to tell the driver her dilemma she knew *trouble* had been an understatement.

The driver of the car was wearing a black full-face mask and he grabbed her wrist so fast that Joanna had no time to even scream, much less make a run for it. Another masked figure, sitting in the back of the car, helped pull her inside. Her legs were still dangling out of the car with the passenger door crashing into her thighs, when the driver stepped on the gas and took off. Once she was pulled the rest of the way in, the second person reached for the front door and slammed it shut.

Joanna opened her mouth to cry out as the side of her head banged against the dashboard. The scream never materialized. It was stopped by a vile-smelling cloth clamped down over her face.

## Chapter Fourteen

"Jen? Jen, come on now. Wake up."

"She's out cold. Can't you see that?"

"Wake up, Jen. You've got to wake up now."

"I told you not to give her that shot in the car after she was already out."

"Did you want her waking up along the way?"

"What difference would it have made? We were wearing masks and we had her blindfolded. Sometimes you take caution a little too far."

"Oh, do I? We have her, don't we?"

"She may never wake up, but we have her, all right."

"You're just sore because we didn't get Logan, too. But this plan worked out far better. We're sitting pretty, and Logan's off on his wild-goose chase. And the farther away Logan is, the safer it is for us."

"Oh, I feel real safe. If dear Jen doesn't come to, we score a big fat zero. Then how will your comrades in exile feel about our brilliant plan?"

"*Our* comrades. Don't forget that. Sometimes I worry that your memory is too short, that you've lost sight of the big picture here."

"That picture changed, didn't it? Suddenly Communism's out of vogue."

"Look at history, my dear. It always repeats itself. Our time will come again. And just think. You and I almost single-handedly will bring about the rebirth."

"You and I can't do it alone. Unfortunately. We need Dr. Jennifer Hampleman."

"We have her. And in a short time we'll have the benefit of her brilliant mind and her nearly seventeen months of work perfecting the cold fusion process."

"We hope . . . Comrade."

"Have faith, my dear. We've watched and waited, planned and schemed. We're not about to blow it now. I promise you that. At the very least she knows enough to give us an excellent head start. If she needs more time, more money, more of anything, she'll get it. All that will change is the source of her support."

"Do you really think she can be turned?"

He laughed sharply. "What choice does she have?" He looked down at the unconscious figure on the bed, her hair fanned out on the pillow. He stared at her for several moments and then, his expression perfectly blank, he swung his hand and slapped her hard across the face.

Joanna groaned.

He slapped her again.

"No . . ." she moaned.

He looked back up at his partner. "See, I told you she'd come around."


"WHAT DO YOU MEAN the Matthias woman isn't at La Costa?" the voice on the telephone asked.

Eric leaned his shoulder against the wall of the phone booth. "She was registered. She just never arrived."

"Maybe she stopped somewhere along the way."

Eric let out a sharp laugh. "Sure. A little pit stop." He shut his eyes. Why'd he have to use the word, *pit*? It evoked a gruesome image.

"This is our day for lousy luck."

"What does that mean?" Eric straightened up, his body stiffening. "Joanna? What happened to her? Where is she? What . . . ?"

"She went off looking for you."

"No. No, damn it. She couldn't have."

"I tried, Eric. I thought I had things under control."

"When did she take off?"

"About forty minutes ago."

"And you didn't follow her?" Eric cursed under his breath. "She's probably hitting every spa from Los Verdes to San Diego. Damn, she could be anywhere. Something could have happened to her."

There was a disquieting pause before Eric's chief responded.

"Eric, is there any chance Joanna might know Jen's whereabouts? Any chance at all?"

The reality of what his chief was hinting at sank in fast. "You think they have her? You think they kidnapped Joanna?" He was afraid he already knew the answers to those questions. His expression turned grim and desperate, even the rage was wiped out.

"I found her moped at the side of the coast road about five miles south of Synergy. There were some fresh tire marks on the road. Looks like a wide-body car came to a stop and then burned rubber pulling out again. I must have missed it all by two minutes or less."

Eric let his head fall back against the phone booth off the lobby of the La Costa Spa. "No, no, no." The words erupted from him like tears.

"You're sure Jen's location hasn't been compromised, Eric? It's vital—"

Eric gripped the phone hard. "Jen isn't the one at risk here, damn it. It's Joanna. What's going to happen when the bastards discover she's not the one they want?"

There was another lengthy silence. "I'm sorry, Eric. Truly, I am. But there can be no deals, no exchanges. There are times..."

Eric slammed the receiver into the cradle.

A middle-aged woman rapped on the glass. "Are you finished with the phone?"

He made no move. He didn't hear the question. Tears came to his eyes. He felt empty, impotent, defeated.

"Excuse me. Sir? Sir, I need to make a call."

Eric blinked several times. Then he pulled himself together and opened the door. "Sorry. I've got another important call to make. I'm sure there are other phone booths around."

"Well, thanks a lot," the woman in her baby-blue designer running suit said acidly as she stomped off.

Eric held the receiver for several moments before dialing. *No deals.* As if he needed to be told. As if he could ever live with himself if he, singlehandedly, put the free world in jeopardy. The question was, how was he to live with himself if he left Joanna to her own fate? He felt like a drowning man clutching at straws.

He stared at the phone. He would have to call Jen. For one thing, he'd promised to keep her informed about Joanna. For another, Joanna's capture meant Jen would be compromised. He would have to step up all precautions for her safety. He dreaded making the call, knowing that Jen's pain would be a measure of his own. But he owed her the truth. As he'd owed Joanna. As he owed her now.

Eric shut his eyes, trying to shut out the pain. But that pain had become a part of him. God, how he wanted to reach out to Joanna, take her in his arms so that nothing or no one could hurt her. Somehow, some way, he had to save her. Slowly, resolutely, he dialed Jen's secret number.

"Hello, Jen. Listen..."

"Oh Eric, what perfect timing for your call."

"Jen, something's happened."

"Wait, wait. Let me tell you. That missing link. I found it. It's done. Well, of course, there's endless work ahead. But now we can proceed. We can set the wheels in motion. We..."

"Jen." His voice was sharper than he meant.

"What is it, Eric? What's wrong?" All of the excitement disappeared from Jen's voice. "It's...Joanna, isn't it?" There was a heartwrenching gasp. "She isn't..."

"She's been kidnapped."

"Oh, Eric, no. What will happen to her when her captor realizes he's kidnapped the wrong woman?"

Eric let out a long, low sigh. "I imagine he'll try to...make a deal."

"You mean an exchange. Joanna for me."

"Listen to me, Jen. I'll find her. I'll rescue her. I won't eat, sleep or breathe until I do. You just sit back and hold tight."

"Hold tight? Eric, there's no way..."

"Jen, there's nothing you can do."

"I'm the one that they want, Eric. I'm the one that can save her. I'm not about to sit back and wait while Joanna's life is in danger. The project's finished, Eric. It won't be jeopardized. I'm going to get out of this place and I'm going to find my sister."

"Jen...you can't take this thing on. You're dealing with professionals..."

"You're a professional, Eric. If you don't want me going off half-cocked on my own, then I suggest you get down here pronto and help me."

"It's against orders. You know that, don't you?"

"Yes, I know that."

"And I'm not going to let you take any crazy risks, completed project or not."

"I know that, too."

"Then sit tight. I'm on my way."

ERIC KEPT CHECKING the clock on his dash as he sped down highway 103, praying his chief hadn't already thought to do what he was about to do. If so, he could kiss his plan goodbye. He could kiss Joanna goodbye, too.

His mouth was set in a tight grimace. No way. He wasn't about to kiss her goodbye. He planned to spend a lifetime kissing her.

He took the turnoff a little too fast. The rear end slid and the car almost skidded off the road. Sweat poured down his back as he fought to control the steering wheel. He wasn't even worried about crashing. All he could think about was losing precious minutes. Every minute counted.... He worked his way out of the skid, forcing himself not to floor the gas pedal.

Now he was on a winding country road about ten miles from the Mexican border. He turned onto another dirt road, this time wisely slowing down enough to deal with the deep ruts. He jostled along, nosing the car into a narrow little clearing. He'd go the rest of the way on foot.

Half-hidden in a stand of trees was a low, brown, one-story building. It resembled a miniature warehouse, and from all outward appearances it looked abandoned. Eric kept on praying that it wasn't.

He slipped his hand into his slacks pocket, making sure he had the book of matches he'd picked up in the lobby of the spa. Yes. If she was in there, he'd have to create a diversion in order to get to her. He bent down and started gathering twigs.

Fortunately it hadn't rained in weeks, and Eric got the small brush fire going with the strike of one match. Then, crouching, ducking and dodging, he made his way to the back of the building and peeked in through a window.

The plan worked like a charm. The three guards inside caught sight of the fire from one of the front windows. One of them shouted orders and the other two ran for fire extinguishers and then took off out the front door.

Eric reached in his waistband for his snub-nosed revolver. He aimed the gun at the lock on the door, pulled the trigger, then kicked the door open and entered, gun hand extended.

The young, muscular man in the room had swung around at the sound of the shot, going for his gun as he pivoted. But when he saw who the intruder was, he was thrown completely off guard. His hand never got to his gun.

"Logan? What the hell...?"

"Where is she?"

"Down in her lab. Where she always is. What's going on?"

"We have to move her. Fast. Her position's been compromised."

"But, I didn't get any word..."

"They're on my tail, man. I thought maybe they'd gotten here before me. When I saw the fire..."

"Damn..."

"Get her," he barked. "Show some hustle."

The young man hesitated, but Eric's entrance had him thoroughly confused. He was used to following procedure, and this was definitely not procedure. If the other two agents had been in the place, they'd probably have taken it slower, given themselves time to get suspicious, check things out. Eric was banking on the element of surprise. He was in luck. The agent's hesitation lasted a couple of moments at the most, then he went downstairs for the scientist.

He came back up with her a minute later. Jen, good old Jen, was a study in calm.

"Eric." She greeted him with a businesslike nod.

"We gotta move, Jen."

"What about all her papers, notes?" the agent asked anxiously.

He gave the agent a nod. "I'll take her, you and your boys see to her papers. Get everything out and leave fast."

"Where are you taking her?" As soon as the agent asked, he flushed. He must have realized it was a dumb question. Logan couldn't tell him where he was taking Hampleman. Not if enemy agents were on her tail. The agent would know from training that if they got to him there were plenty of ingenious ways to make a person talk. Even if you could withstand torture, there were all kinds of drugs.

Eric already had Jen at the door. "Just report back to headquarters once everything's secured."

He took Jen's arm, gave her a quick smile and led her out the back door.

So far, so good.

SHE HEARD THE SCRAPE of a key in the lock. The door swung open. Footsteps. Heavy footsteps. Matthias.

Joanna lay unmoving on the bed. There was a faint breeze. He must have left the door open. Forcing the terror from her mind, she tried to think of some way to make her escape.

"I know you're awake, Jen."

Joanna, still blindfolded, was confused. The man speaking to her had a thick southern drawl. It didn't sound familiar; didn't sound like Marty Matthias. Of course, she was still woozy, and the accent could be put on. There was something vaguely familiar about the pitch and texture of the voice, but oddly enough it didn't bring Marty to mind. Then who? If only she could think straight.

"I'm going to untie your wrists, Jen. I brought you something to eat and something to drink. You must be thirsty."

She was desperately thirsty, but that wasn't what she was focusing on. He'd agreed to untie her wrists. There was her chance. If she caught him by surprise, maybe...just maybe, she could make a break for it.

She shivered despite the heat as he untied her wrists. The very touch of his skin on hers repulsed her. Her heart raced as she rubbed her wrists. She forced herself to stay calm. She'd have to act fast. He wouldn't keep her untied for long.

"Here now, drink up. It's nice, refreshing mint tea. Cool and thirst quenching."

Even though her hands were free, she pretended to be too weak to hold the glass. Her captor held it to her lips.

She forced herself to take a swallow of the sickly sweet, chilled, minty brew even though it made her sick to her stomach.

"That's it. Take some more," he drawled.

She tried to picture his position in her mind. When she struck out she'd have to make it count. She clenched her right hand into a tight fist and shot it out with all her strength into what seemed to be his solar plexus.

Her captor let out a surprised groan, the glass falling from his hand and crashing to the floor. A much needed shot of adrenaline allowed her to shove him away and then get off the cot. Her hand was ripping away at her blindfold, but before she managed it she felt her captor's arm circling her neck, the ring on his finger scraping against her cheek. Moments later she was back on the cot, her wrists tied more tightly together.

"I'm going to be sick," she muttered.

"Just take a few deep breaths."

"I can't breathe in here. I'm...suffocating."

"Now, now, Jen. You're tougher than that." He gave an insidious laugh.

*Jen.* What was going to happen to her when he found out the truth? How tough was she?

"Air. I need . . . some air. I'm so sick . . ." Her only hope was to play for time. And pray that somehow Eric would track her down. But time seemed such an elusive element now. She had no idea how long she'd been here. She was unsure, even, whether it was still the same day.

"Bring in that fan," he called out suddenly. "Our scientist needs some cooling off."

After a minute, Joanna heard new footsteps approaching, these lighter. Was it Gerta? Gerta who hated her. No, no. Gerta hated Jen. Oh, but once she knew, she'd hate Joanna, too.

Joanna felt a slight breeze. It was warm but it did help a little. Over the drone of the fan, she heard the light footsteps departing.

"Now listen to me, Jen." Again the Southern drawl, now a little more strained, impatient. Joanna still couldn't pin down whom it sounded like, but it almost had to be Marty.

"Some more...tea, please." She knew it would make her dreadfully sick, but convincing him she was sick might force him to put off his questions for a while. Every minute she could delay him was a minute more Eric had to find her.

"Not so fast," he muttered. She managed to hold the glass now and began gulping down the tea. "Not so much. You said just a minute ago it made you sick . . ."

She retched all over his shoes.

He cursed and slapped her hard across the face.

Despite the pain, the stench and the heat, she smiled as she heard him storm out of the room, slamming the door behind him.


JEN LOOKED ACROSS at Eric, who was a study in concentration behind the wheel. She studied him in turn. "I think you'd better tell me all about it," she said slowly.

He gave her a quick, hooded glance. "You mean my plan?"

She smiled faintly. "That, too."

He nodded, but kept his eyes straight ahead on the road. It was suddenly hard to look at Jen; not so much because of the similarities to Joanna, which were uncanny, but for the subtle differences.

THE DOOR OPENED and Joanna noticed a scent of tobacco smoke mingling with the rancid air of the room.

"Wake up, Jen. Let's start all over again."

"Damn you. How many times do I have to tell you. I gave up on the project just like I said . . ."

"Now, now, that's becoming a very worn record, Jen."

"Will you cut out that phony Southern drawl. You think because you've blindfolded me, I don't know the truth, Marty. You think I haven't been on to you for . . . weeks? Why isn't your partner asking any of the questions? Because it's too hard to mask that thick accent of hers? Or is she back at Synergy, covering up, leaving the dirty work to you? And what about Linda? If you've done anything to that poor girl. . . ."

She could hear him take in a deep drag of his cigarette and then exhale.

"If I were you, Jen, I'd be far more concerned with what's going to be done to you if you don't start cooperating. Now, where are you precisely in your work? My guess is, you've finally done exactly what you originally set out to do. Isn't that right, Jen?"

She heard him make a scraping sound with his shoe and imagined he was putting out his cigarette. "What do I have to do to convince you . . . ?"

He gripped her shoulders hard, very close to her neck, his ring cutting into her skin. It brought tears of pain to her eyes, dampening her thick blindfold. She struck out with her legs, making contact with his shin. He let out a sharp cry, but it only made him tighten his grip.

"Foolish of you, Jen. Now we'll simply have to tie up your legs as well." He struck a match and once again Joanna smelled cigarette smoke.

"Please, please, stop this insanity. I'm telling you the truth, Marty." Suddenly something struck her and she stopped talking. Her captor was smoking. Yet, all the time she'd been around Marty Matthias she'd never once seen him smoke. Not a cigarette, a cigar, not even a pipe. But if her captor wasn't Matthias, then who...

"Well, my dear, the time has come to test that out."

Joanna shivered. *Test it out?*

"Now listen to me, Jen. I'm going to give you something to help you relax."

She struggled wildly against his grip. "No, no..."

"You'll be quite pleased with the results." He laughed dryly. There was no Southern accent in the laugh. It was low, guttural, ugly. "In fact, I think we're all going to be pleased with the results."

Oh God, she thought with utter despair as she felt the sharp stab of the hypodermic in her arm. Now all was lost....

"ERIC, I'M VERY disappointed in you."

"I guess we all have our disappointments," Eric replied sardonically into the phone.

"Where are you?"

"Don't you mean, where is Jen?"

"Yes, that's what I mean."

"She's perfectly safe."

"For how long?"

"You don't really care about her. Just about her work. Well, you've got all her findings, all her papers. Nothing is going to happen to her. Nothing is going to happen to either of them. Not as long as I'm running the show."

"You're not making any sense, Eric. Okay, let's say they find out the truth and want to make a swap. That's what you're assuming, isn't it?"

"That's what I'm depending on."

"Well, how do they reach you?"

"I've left a message on Matthias's phone machine. What I want to know is how he got away from Synergy. I thought the Federal agents investigating Morgan's death were keeping all suspects on the grounds."

"Matthias stopped being a suspect about five minutes after you took off for La Costa."

"What?"

"The murder weapon was found...in Toni Connors' trash."

"It's a set-up."

"Her fingerprints were on the gun, Eric. Maybe Morgan's death was just coincidental. A lovers' quarrel or something."

"You don't buy that. How does she explain the fingerprints?"

"She can't."

"Well, I can. Either Marty or Gerta could have gone over to her place to offer condolences, made her a cup of tea or something, slipped a few sleeping pills in it and once she was out cold, they put the gun in her hand and dumped the weapon into her trash."

"Eric, that's a nice little tale, but we have no proof."

"Where are Hauser and Matthias now?"

A long pause. "Hauser's around. She spends most of her time holed up in her lab."

"And Marty?"

"According to Lou, Matthias took off about ten minutes before Joanna."

"And pulled his car over to wait for his prey to come along."

"Eric, don't showboat this deal. You're part of a team. Nobody wants to see either of the women get hurt. Nobody wants to see you get hurt, either."

"Thanks, Hoff. I'll hold that thought," Eric said sardonically, dropping the receiver back into its cradle.

IT FELT LIKE an eternity until the phone rang. Eric grabbed for it, his eyes resting quietly on Jen, who sat on a chair by the window of the motel room.

"Very, very clever, Logan." The voice at the other end of the line was low and muffled. It sounded like the mouth of the receiver was covered with plastic wrap.

Eric wondered why Matthias was bothering to mask his voice. Could he really still hope to get away with this treachery? "Is she all right, Marty?"

"What a tale she wove, Logan. Quite unbelievable, but, of course, under the circumstances, I have to accept it as the gospel truth."

"Damn it, is she okay? If you've hurt her in any way, Marty..."

"Be quiet, Logan. This is my dime. So you just listen. Now here's the deal..."

"ARE YOU SCARED, Jen?"

Jennifer Hampleman's gray eyes were on his face. "Yes, I'm scared. But I trust you."

He smiled. "You're quite a woman, Jen."

"She must be, too."

"She is."

He wore a strained expression as he gave her one last assessing look.

"Will I do?" she asked anxiously.

He swallowed hard, nodding slowly.

She turned and walked over to the mirror. For several long moments she stared at herself.

"It's amazing, really," she said in a low voice. "This color blonde is my natural hair color. I remember the first time I dyed it brown, my mother was quite distraught. She thought I was beautiful as a blonde."

"You are," he said coming up behind her. He smiled at her reflection. Yes, it was amazing to see Jen transformed into Joanna's image. The butterscotch-colored hair, the subtle makeup that added a special luster to her complexion.

"Do you know what scares me most about this little adventure of ours, Eric?"

"What?"

"Coming face to face with her. With Joanna."

He placed his hands lightly on her shoulders. "It's definitely going to feel strange. It did for me."

She turned and looked at him. "But it was different for you."

He touched her cheek lightly. "You'd better finish getting ready. We have to leave in ten minutes."

"WELL, JOANNA, we're going for a little drive. Won't that be a nice change?"

It was weird to hear him call her by her real name now. He knew it all, even the bizarre twist of fate that had separated her at birth from her twin sister. Under the influence of that drug it had been impossible to keep anything from him.

"Where are you taking me?" she asked weakly, still woozy from the drug.

"Why, I'm taking you to meet the real Jen. Now, doesn't that perk up your spirits? You must be simply dying to meet her after all these years. Identical twins reunited at last. I feel privileged to be responsible for creating such a moving occasion."

"What are you going to do to her? After... after you get her to tell you what you want to know, what are you going to do to her?" Joanna's voice was strained with fear.

"Now, that depends on Jen. So, are you ready for the two of us to take that ride?"

"Where's Gerta?" Despite her confusion over the smoking, Joanna's best guess still was that Marty must be her captor, and Gerta his accomplice.

"Why, she's hard at work in her lab, of course. Gerta is a fine physicist. Not as fine as your twin. But then, Jen is exceptional. You should be very proud of her."

"And Linda? Where is she?"

"Your concern for her is quite touching, Joanna. And all this time I thought you were just using her."

"And all this time I thought you loved her."

"Oh, but I do. I love her deeply. I'll always look after her."

"Then... then she's all right?"

"Come on, Joanna. Smile now," he drawled cheerily. "It won't be long before the big reunion. Personally, I just can't wait."

# Chapter Fifteen

Jen made a few final adjustments as she sat beside Eric in the car.

Eric gave her a quick glance. "That's it. You look just right."

Her hand moved from her hair to her purse. She flicked the snap closure open and shut a couple of times. Not out of nervousness. Just to practice. Just to make sure, when the time came, she would do everything with precision.

Eric smiled faintly to himself. Yes, she looked perfect and she'd carry this off without one false move. Jen was sharp, clear thinking and determined. She and Joanna were twins, all right.

They were on a two-lane road when they passed a sign that read Pala, Two Miles. He checked automatically to see if anyone was following him, but they seemed to be the only car on the road. His hands tightened on the wheel. He could feel his pulse pounding close to his skin. A bead of sweat broke out across his upper lip like a mustache. What had become of his reputation for being cool under fire? When had the fire ever been this hot?

"One quarter of a mile from here, and then we turn off onto an unmarked road on the right. Are you ready, Jen?" He could barely keep the tremor out of his voice.

She adjusted her glasses more firmly, then reached over and squeezed his arm. "Don't worry," she said softly.

JOANNA RODE in the front seat beside her captor. She was still blindfolded, her hands bound together behind her back.

"Listen, Marty, it isn't too late. Even now. You can still get out of it. Is it that Gerta's holding something over your head? She must be. Otherwise, why isn't she here now? Why is she letting you do all the dirty work?"

The car made another sharp left and she fell against him. "Why, sugar," he drawled, placing his hand on her thigh, "I don't find this dirty work."

She kicked at him, despite her bound ankles. "You disgusting beast," she hissed. As she felt his warm breath close against her face, she spat at him. He merely laughed.

"You think as long as I can't identify you, you'll get away with it all, don't you, Marty? But you won't. What is it you think you're going to do? Hand over Jen's process to your pals then sit back behind your desk at Synergy and wait for the next brilliant scientist to come along so that you can sell your country out again? It's not going to happen, Marty. You won't get away with it."

"Are you trying to tell me that treason doesn't pay?"

"That's exactly what I'm telling you."

"Oh, that's where you're wrong, Joanna. It does pay. Very nicely."

"But you've got plenty of money already, Marty. Eric says . . ." She stopped abruptly.

"What does Eric say, Joanna?"

"He says you've got it all," she said tightly.

A raspy laugh. "Ah, yes, Eric. I'd say he doesn't have it so bad, either. He's figured out how to 'double the pleasure, double the fun' for himself."

"You're disgusting," she said acidly.

"Now don't feel bad, Joanna. Once Jen's out of the picture you can have Eric all to yourself. Of course, you and Eric don't have as much in common as he does with Jen, but I'm sure you've found some mutual interests during the past few weeks. And it should comfort you to know that he's actually chosen you over Jen. After all, he has agreed to our fair exchange."

But there was nothing fair about it. And Joanna knew Eric would never put either Jen or her work into jeopardy. He had to have a plan in mind. Because if it really did come down to a choice...

"We're almost there, sugar." He reached behind her back.

Joanna froze.

"Relax. I'm just going to untie you. But you're not to remove your blindfold until you step out of the car and walk ten paces forward. Is that understood?"

She was rubbing her freed wrists, trying to bring back the circulation.

"Is that understood, Joanna?" he repeated, this time jamming the barrel of a gun into her side for emphasis.

"Yes! Yes," she gasped. "It's understood."

She tried to steady her nerves, but her fear kept getting the best of her. *Eric has to have a plan. And it's got to work. It's got to. Because this is definitely not the kind of reunion with my twin I was planning on.*

The car came to a halt.

"Okay, Joanna. This is where we part company."

She couldn't move. As desperately as she wanted to escape that car, she was terrified to leave. What if he was planning to shoot her in the back as she started for Eric's car? Why not? She didn't serve any purpose now. In fact, she was a liability.

He reached across her, grabbed the door handle and pushed the door open.

Still, Joanna made no move. "Are...are they here?" she asked anxiously.

"They're here. Get out, but don't move until I give you the go-ahead. Then, remember, ten steps before you take off the blindfold. And don't turn around, Joanna. If you don't follow my exact instructions... well, I think you can figure out what will happen. Even if you're only a model, you've got brains enough to add two and two."

*I have brains enough, you bastard, to have fooled you for weeks into believing I was Jennifer Hampleman.*

He gave her a rough shove so that instead of stepping out of the car, she stumbled out. The push, combined with being blindfolded, didn't exactly help her equilibrium. It took her a couple of moments to steady herself.

She heard the driver's door open. Her captor was exiting the car as well.

"Okay, Logan," he called out. "Let's see her."

THE NONDESCRIPT BLUE SEDAN was parked thirty feet from Eric's car. His heart lurched when he saw Joanna, blindfolded, stumble out of the car, drop to her knees and then slowly pull herself up. His features turned to stone as he saw the man step out on the driver's side, his body hidden behind the car door, his head covered with a black mask that had slits for the eyes, nose and mouth.

"Let's see Hampleman, Logan. Or Joanna here gets back into my car."

Eric almost lost it for a moment. The sight of Joanna in that awful condition made his mind turn in frantic circles like a rat lost in a laboratory maze. He wanted nothing more at that moment than to leap from his car and shoot the bastard and watch him drop.

But he couldn't do that. Joanna'd be at too great a risk. No, he had to stick to his plan. He took a deep breath and from somewhere far away he heard his own voice saying, "It's time, Jen."

Without a word, without hesitation, she opened the car door and stepped out.

So did Eric.

"Uh-uh, Logan. Get back behind the wheel. We don't want anyone getting hurt, now do we?" the masked man drawled.

"I'm just going to stand here and watch." Eric held up his hands, palms facing out to show he wasn't holding a gun.

"Okay, okay. Just make sure you keep your hands right up there, Logan. When I give the count of three, both women start walking forward. And remember, no funny business."

"How about you show your hands, then, too?" Logan called out.

For a reply, he got a cold, dry laugh. And then the count. "One, two...three. Move, Joanna."

Her legs felt like lead. She held her hands out to keep her balance. And she began counting...one, two, three, four five...

Jen was counting, too, her eyes shifting back and forth between her double and the man behind the car door. Her gait was slow and measured, keeping pace with Joanna's.

Eric was counting, too.

At the tenth pace, Joanna came to an abrupt stop. Immediately, Jen did, too.

"Ten steps. I'm taking off the blindfold," Joanna shouted.

The light hurt her eyes and her vision was very blurry.

"Keep moving."

Joanna heard the order from behind her. She rubbed her eyes, blinked several times, and then, at last, her gaze fell on her twin, no more than ten feet away from her. She let out a little gasp, tears immediately erupting. "Jen," she said plaintively, staring at last into the face that was so like her own.

Jen had thought she was prepared for this. Eric had emphasized that the likeness between them was uncanny. But seeing Joanna took Jen's breath away, and for one desperate moment she lost count of her steps, lost sight of the plan. But she pulled herself together quickly, especially after the barking order, "Keep coming toward me, Dr. Hampleman."

Jen smiled at Joanna. "It'll be okay," she murmured without moving her lips. Joanna smiled back tremulously and dried her eyes. Somehow, she believed her twin.

Again the two women started walking, each taking strength and courage from the other. *One, two, three...*

Just two more steps and they'd cross paths. Every muscle in Jen's body tensed. *Four...five... Now!*

Jen's left hand shot out for Joanna's arm and she yanked hard so that she fell forward, flat on the ground. In the same instant, the timing being absolutely crucial, Jen pulled off her glasses and tore off the brown wig that had been first meant for Joanna. Her newly dyed butterscotch-colored hair fell loosely about her shoulders.

"You bastard, Logan. You tricked me. It's not her. It's not Hampleman..." And as the hooded figure was staring at the blond woman, stunned and furious at what he was certain was a decoy, Eric dropped his hands.

Jen dove to the ground, sprawling beside Joanna. She waited, letting Eric take the first shots. He'd taught her to use the weapon, but she was to use it now only if necessary. Back-up.

Eric fired, the burst smashing into the blue sedan car door. The hooded man behind it stumbled backward and for a moment Eric thought he'd hit his mark. Instead, a burst of return fire sprayed back, one bullet catching Eric in the shoulder. He let out a sharp groan of pain. As Jen began firing, Joanna, seeing that Eric had been shot, went racing toward him, ignoring Jen's panicked cry for her to stay put.

"Are you crazy?" Eric muttered, through teeth clenched in pain, as Joanna got to him.

"Is it bad?"

He shook his head. "My gun..."

He'd dropped it when he'd been hit. Joanna grabbed it. But, instead of handing it back to him, she took aim. She'd learned how to shoot at a self-defense course in Manhattan. When she fired at the hooded man, nearly hitting her mark, Jen glanced back and gave her a quick grin.

The hooded man let off one last volley of shots and then leapt to safety behind the wheel of his car, revved the engine, and raced away in reverse.

Joanna was helping Eric to his feet, despite his protest that he was fine and could manage on his own. Jen raced over to help get him up. "That doesn't look good, Eric."

"It's nothing."

Joanna tried to get a better look at the damage to his shoulder but Eric waved her off. "Not now. That bastard'll be back soon. We don't want him on our tail."

"Jen, you drive," Joanna said, as they all hurried to Eric's car. "I'll see what I can do about stopping the bleeding..."

Eric climbed into the back seat with Joanna and Jen pulled out. They hadn't gone five feet before they heard the sound of a car behind them.

"Step on it," Eric barked.

Jen drove very fast, but under control, while Joanna tended Eric's wound. "It's okay. It's okay," he kept telling her as she tore off the sleeve of his shirt and made it into a bandage. As she tied it tight around his arm, he kept on shouting directions to Jen and twisting his head around so he could keep watch on the advancing blue sedan.

"Turn here," he told Jen.

"Where are we going?" Joanna asked.

"Back to Synergy," he said.

"Synergy?" Jen gave him a quick look over her shoulder.

"Once he realizes where we're heading he'll back off. It's our safest bet. We'll have to stop before the guardpost to hide you in the trunk to get you safely inside the compound. There's somebody there eagerly waiting for you, Jen. I'm sure he's got a nice, new, quiet spot picked out for you."

Joanna gave Eric an anxious look. "Jen won't have to go immediately, will she?" However bad the timing, Joanna needed a little while to spend with Jen.

"Eric, you've got to give me and Joanna a little while to talk," Jen said, echoing Joanna's thoughts. The twins shared a nervous but tender smile.

"I'd like to, but you know Hoff. He'd have my head."

"Hoff? You mean Hoffman? Dr. Hoffman?" Joanna broke in. "So, he is one of you. I wondered after he made such an effort to keep me from leaving Synergy and going off after you." Her eyes narrowed. "He was the one who told you where to find Linda, wasn't he? When you walked over to him in the cafeteria. And that's why you felt safe leaving me with him."

"Hoffman's my chief," Eric admitted. "He's supposed to take a back seat and . . . sort of . . . oversee things. And he isn't very happy with either you or me at the moment. First you get away from him and then I take Jen along on the rescue."

Joanna had to smile as she stared at the back of the blond head of her twin, then at Eric. "You're really a master at transformations. First you turn me into Jen and then you turn Jen into me."

"Brilliant, isn't he?" Jen said from up front.

Joanna could hear the clear affection and pride in her twin's voice. *Pride of ownership?*

"Yes, brilliant," Joanna answered wistfully. "Your stunt took Marty completely by surprise, Eric. He never expected a double switch."

"What was with his Southern accent?" Eric asked.

"I'm not sure," Joanna admitted. "Eric, does Marty smoke?"

"No, I don't think so," Eric said. "Wait, I think he used to smoke. He once mentioned how tough it had been to quit. Why?"

"My captor smoked like a chimney," Joanna said, frowning. "I suppose, with all the tension, he could have taken it up again. If not . . ."

"He's really gaining," Eric muttered.

"In all this madness I never asked. Did you find Linda at the spa?" Joanna regarded him anxiously. "Is she all right?"

Eric frowned. "She wasn't at the spa."

"Oh no," Joanna murmured.

"The spa may just have been a ploy to get rid of me, send me on a wild-goose chase, so he could get to you. And keep me from questioning Linda. He must have felt the same way we did—that Linda might crack. So he took her off someplace else. My bet is she's safe and sound, wherever she is."

Joanna sighed. "I hope so. I feel sorry for her. She's had such a rough life."

"It sounds like you and Linda got to be friends in a very short time," Jen observed.

"Well, not friends exactly. But she did confide in me about some things," Joanna said, still feeling guilty about having had to deceive Linda. Maybe she'd get the chance to rectify that.

"I never really got to know Linda Matthias myself," Jen reflected. "Or anyone else at Synergy really, except for Eric, of course. You seem to make ties quickly, Joanna. I envy you that ability.''

Joanna wasn't sure how to take Jen's remark. Had Jen picked up on the tie between her and Eric? Was Jen afraid she'd moved right in and stolen him away from her? Joanna had plenty to feel guilty about. But she couldn't do that to Jen. And she wouldn't allow Eric to come between her and her twin. Jen loved Eric, and Joanna could guess that her twin did not fall in love very often. Whatever Eric's feelings were for Jen, they had to sort that out on their own. Joanna refused to be the cause of any heartbreak for her newfound sister.

They all rode in silence until they came to the turnoff for Synergy. Eric's assumption that the car chasing them would pull back proved true. As soon as they turned off to the right, the dark sedan behind them slowed and kept on going straight.

"Shouldn't we follow him, though?" Joanna asked anxiously.

"No," Eric said in a low voice. "We can't risk it."

Joanna knew he meant he couldn't risk Jen. But that was fine. She didn't want to take that risk, either. She didn't want to do anything that might hurt her twin sister, physically, or emotionally.

ERIC DID MANAGE to get Joanna ten minutes alone with Jen. She wanted to do something to alleviate any anxiety Jen might be having about her relationship with Eric.

"I guess now that Marty knows I'm an imposter," Joanna said, "I'll be leaving, too. It's been . . . quite an experience, but I can't say I'll be sorry to get my life back in order."

"I owe you so much, Joanna. I don't know what to say. I guess I'm still dazed."

"You didn't look dazed back there at the shoot-out. The way you handled that gun..."

"I mean dazed at discovering how much like me you really look. Eric had shown me that layout in *Harper's Bazaar*, but even though the resemblance was remarkable, I never dreamed, in real life, it would be this extraordinary."

"Yes," Joanna said softly. "I felt the same way. It...takes some getting used to."

Jen sighed. "And we don't have much time."

"Maybe...before I leave for Paris we'll have a chance to get together again and...really talk."

"Paris? How exciting."

"Not really. Work. Well, modeling."

"My guess is modeling is very hard work," Jen said matter-of-factly.

Joanna smiled. "I wouldn't think most physicists would make that guess."

Jen stared wonderingly at Joanna. "You even have my smile. And our eyes are exactly the same color."

"But you wear glasses."

"Well, don't tell anyone, but I don't truly need them."

"Oh, I see."

They shared a small laugh, but then Jen's expression grew serious once more. "It's odd. I feel...like I know you, Joanna."

A faint blush blossomed in Joanna's cheeks. "I probably know you better than you'd like. I've been living in your home, wearing your clothes, using your soap and shampoo, learning how to...pass as you."

"You've obviously done a great job. Eric swore it would work. Remind me never to doubt that man again."

"I'm sure he'll remind you himself," Joanna said, unable to meet Jen's steady gaze.

"I wonder," Jen mused.

"What do you mean?"

"Well, we're both nearly completed assignments for Eric. You're leaving for Paris, and I'm going back into hibernation till things are wrapped up here. The work's done, it's the waiting that's hard."

Joanna could see the excitement in Jen's features. "I'm so glad." She smiled. "Not just for the whole free world. For you."

Jen squeezed Joanna's hand. They both felt a special power in the touch.

"What will you do afterward?" Joanna asked awkwardly.

"Oh, there's still endless amounts to be done in actually putting the process into operation on any kind of grand scale," Jen said enthusiastically. "There's years of work ahead of me."

"And Eric?" Joanna did her best to keep her voice bland.

Jen's features took on an unreadable look. "I don't know what he'll do."

The door to Jen's bedroom opened. Hoffman, the grim-faced elder scientist cum secret agent, nodded at Jen. "It's time."

Joanna felt a tightness in her chest as her eyes met Jen's. Jen merely smiled gently. "We'll meet again, Joanna. It's clearly fated."

"Yes," Joanna murmured. "Fate." And Eric Logan's helping hand.

"ARE YOU OKAY?" Eric asked softly.

Joanna was standing at the bedroom window watching Hoffman's car pull out of the drive; watching her twin being taken away from her, again.

"Yes," she said quietly. And then, "She's wonderful." Joanna kept looking out the window even after Hoffman's car rounded the bend and was out of sight.

"You're wonderful, too, Joanna."

Slowly she turned around. Eric was sitting on the bed, his hands folded. His face was a study in pain.

"Is your shoulder bad?" she asked anxiously.

His eyes lifted to hers. "Did he...hurt you, Joanna?"

She felt a wrench as she realized his pain was for her. She ran to the bed, dropping to her knees in front of him, her hands on his thighs. "No. No, he didn't hurt me. He didn't...touch me."

He pulled her to him, burying his face in her hair. She could feel the tremor in his arms as he held her.

"It's all right," she whispered. "We've all survived. We're okay."

"Well, at least it's over for you. Anytime...you're ready. There's a plane..."

She drew back, her eyes darting to his. "But...it isn't over yet. What about the moles?"

"We can't do much unless you can make a positive ID on either of them. At any time did you see their faces? Any identifying marks?"

Joanna sighed. "They kept me blindfolded the whole time."

"What about where they took you? Did you hear any unusual sounds? A train whistle? The ocean? Horses, cows?"

She kept shaking her head. "Okay, we can't pin kidnapping on them, but there's still Hank Morgan's murder."

"The FBI arrested Toni Conners for Morgan's murder."

"But that's impossible."

"They found the murder weapon in her apartment."

"But..."

"Her fingerprints were all over it."

"She didn't do it. You know she didn't do it," Joanna protested.

"Let's face it, Joanna. We haven't a shred of hard evidence pinning either Marty or Gerta to any crime at all. Not attempted treason, kidnapping, murder. Nothing. For all we know, they're both innocent. You admitted yourself, you've got your doubts about Marty."

"Linda. She's our hard evidence. We've got to find Linda."

Eric came over and put his arms around her. "I'll track her down. Maybe she *will* come through for us. But you've got a plane to catch." He hesitated. "I thought, maybe when this is all over, I could fly out to Paris and we...could talk. I need a vacation anyway."

Joanna turned away from him. "No," she whispered.

"No, I don't need a vacation, or no, you don't want to talk?"

"It can't work for us, Eric."

"Why is that, Joanna?" Gently, he turned her around to face him. He looked searchingly at her.

She felt her throat constrict. How could he not know why? Hadn't he heard the pride in Jen's voice when she'd commented on how brilliant he was? Even if he didn't return them, did he really have no idea of Jen's feelings for him?

"I'm just not interested in getting involved," she said quietly. *Please let my voice sound normal, don't let my feelings show!*

"I thought we were already involved."

She could hear the hurt in his voice which meant he believed her. "We both got swept up in events that weren't really of either of our making, Eric. But you have your life and I have mine. Why don't we just leave it at that?"

He looked at her and a brief quirky smile came and went. "Well, I'll say one thing for you, Joanna. Like your twin, you seem to know exactly what you want."

*Yes,* she thought sadly. *But we can't always have everything we want. Sometimes the price we have to pay is just too high.*

IT WASN'T EASY, leaving this place she'd called home for nearly three weeks. It wasn't easy separating herself from so much that reminded her of Jen—and of Eric. She'd railed so against the charade at first and now she couldn't quite give it up—the excitement, the danger, the passion, the discoveries.... How strange that her life had come to this. How impossible to imagine returning to life as she'd once known it.

And when she did meet Jen again, would she reveal all of her secrets to her twin? Would she tell Jen that she, too, had fallen in love with Eric? No. No. Truths were not equal in her mind. There were truths that healed and truths that served no purpose but to hurt. And Joanna didn't want to hurt Jen. Just as she didn't want to hurt her poor mother who'd already suffered so much. Just as she didn't want to hurt Eric. But she had hurt him. She knew that. That had been unavoidable.

"All set?" Eric's tone was cool and detached now, all professional.

She nodded slowly.

He led the way to the front door.

"Wait."

He swung around. "What is it?" His tone was sharper than he'd meant it to be. But then this was harder than he'd ever dreamed.

She dug her hand into the pocket of her skirt. Jen's skirt. "The key to the house."

"Just leave it on the hall table."

She set it down beside the glass swan, her fingers lightly skimming it. She had to blink back tears.

"Joanna?"

"Coming." Still, she kept her back to him for another moment, trying to compose herself.

He was waiting at the door. She thought suddenly that he was unhappier than she'd ever seen him. And, however she appeared, she felt as miserable as he looked.

The phone rang just as Eric was opening the door for her. She hesitated for a moment, then turned around and ran to answer it before he could protest.

"Hello?"

"Hello, Jen. Oh, thank God you're home. It's me. Linda. I've got to talk to you. Oh Jen, please come. You're the only one I can trust."

"Where are you, Linda?" Joanna asked, her eyes on Eric who'd followed her to the phone in the living room.

"I'm here. At home. Please come right away. Before Marty gets back. Oh Jen, please hurry."

"I'll be right there," Joanna said firmly.

"I'm going with you," Eric said as she hung up the phone.

Joanna wasn't about to argue. If Marty did get home before she'd finished her talk with Linda, she had no desire to face the monster alone.

## Chapter Sixteen

It only took two minutes for Joanna and Eric to get to the Matthias residence. Yet, when they rang the door bell, it wasn't Linda Matthias who answered the door; it was Marty.

Joanna gasped, her heart sinking. Too late. Two lousy minutes and they were too late. She shot Eric a quick, anxious look, but his expression revealed little. Marty Matthias's, on the other hand, could have filled a book—a book with a bad ending.

He looked drawn and ashen, like someone who'd been put through an old-fashioned wringer more than once. The lines at the corners of his eyes and mouth were sharply accented, the gray hair at his temples more defined, as if he'd aged overnight. Or over the last two minutes.

"Linda? Where is she?" Joanna almost choked on the words.

Marty smiled resignedly, adding to his overall appearance of strain and weariness.

"You'd both better come inside," Marty said quietly. He brought his hand out from behind his back. He was holding a gun, which made it one of those invitations you couldn't turn down.

"My den," Marty said as they stepped inside. He closed the door behind them.

As she heard the door shut Joanna felt a flood of emotions: terror, fright, rage and disgust. She glared at Matthias. "So you've decided to come out of the closet, Marty. No more hoods, no more Southern accents..."

"Please, let's just go into my den," Marty said in a flat tone.

"You don't want to do this. Why make it even harder on yourself?" Eric asked softly.

Matthias smiled sadly. "It doesn't get any harder, Eric."

Joanna's terror was palpable. Eric wasn't feeling that great himself, but he could see that Marty was on shaky ground. Maybe, just maybe, Eric hoped, he'd be able to capitalize on that. He put a comforting arm around Joanna as Marty made them lead the way to his den. Joanna prayed Eric had a plan up his sleeve for this one, because she'd about run out of ideas.

Bright early-afternoon sun shone through the windows of Marty's den. This room, like the living room, was done in a sleek but expensive contemporary decor. Lots of glass, chrome and teak. Here and there were artful touches of warmth: cacti plants in bloom in one corner of the room, soft pastel watercolor seascapes on the walls, Indian pottery displayed on Marty's white and gray laminate desk. No amount of warmth, however, could soothe the icy chill in Joanna's gut.

Marty sat down behind his desk and motioned with the gun to the two gray tweed upholstered arm chairs facing the desk. Joanna and Eric had little choice but to sit down across from him.

"I'm truly sorry it's come to this," Marty said quietly, emotion draining from his face. "I thought I could keep a lid on it somehow. But it's spun out of control. I can't stop it now."

"What about Gerta?" Eric asked.

"Gerta?" Marty's face clouded. "It was her fault. It was really all her fault. If she hadn't been so jealous, if she hadn't felt so threatened, I might have prevented this from happening."

Joanna's eyes kept moving from Marty's face to the gun in his hand. While he continued to point the gun at them as he spoke about Gerta, his free hand began to beat a rat-a-tat rhythm on the top of his desk. As if hypnotized, Joanna watched his fingers dance. Long, tapered fingers, graceful, tanned...nervous. Something nagged at her as she stared at his hand, but she couldn't get at what it was.

"I would have done anything for her," Marty was saying in a husky voice, his dancing fingers coming to a slow finale.

"Gerta?" Eric asked.

"Linda," Marty said, smiling at Eric as if he'd made an intentional joke.

At Marty's mention of Linda's name, Joanna's eyes shot to Marty's face. "Where is she, Marty? Where's Linda?" Staring at him, Joanna found it hard to reconcile this morose figure with the surly, cocky man who'd held her captive. Had he had a last confrontation with Linda, and gone, finally, over the edge? He had certainly changed drastically.

"Linda's...gone." Marty gave a sad, wistful smile, but his eyes were like frozen glass.

Joanna shuddered. "What have you done?"

"I did everything I could," Marty said earnestly. "No husband could have done more."

He's deranged, Joanna thought. It was the only possibility. He'd killed Linda, the woman he loved almost obsessively, and it had, indeed, tipped him over the edge.

Marty wore a sickly grimace. "If only she could have trusted me to help her. But she just couldn't let herself trust me. It was always so hard for Linda to trust. I suppose all along I knew our relationship was doomed. She thought I didn't understand her, but I did. I understood her only too well. I suppose I loved her too much. And that is my greatest crime, whatever you might believe.''

"Marty," Eric said softly, "you don't want to go on with this. It's finished. You know that as well as I do."

Beads of sweat poured down Marty's face, starting from his hairline. He wiped a hand over his damp forehead. He wore the look of a man who was tasting defeat, but couldn't quite bring himself to swallow it.

"It isn't finished yet," Marty said in a hoarse, whispery voice.

Joanna saw Marty's fingers tighten around the barrel of the gun. The sun streaming into the room made the black metal gleam ominously. And it cast a brilliant sheen on the thin, gold band on Marty's finger. Joanna thought it obscene, given the circumstances, that he was still wearing his wedding ring. *Till death do us part.*

Then it hit her with so much force, she let out an involuntary gasp. That was it. That was what had been gnawing away at the back of her mind for the past few minutes. It was the wrong ring. Marty was wearing the wrong ring.

In a whoosh of memory it came back to her. Her captor had been wearing a ring, too. But not a wedding ring. He'd worn some kind of a jeweled ring in a raised setting. She had no idea what kind of a jewel since she'd been blindfolded the whole time, but she'd felt that ring scrape across her cheek when she'd struggle to escape from him; she'd felt it against her arm when he'd reached across her in the car to open her door.

Her eyes swept over both of Marty's hands. The only ring he wore was his wedding ring. None of his tanned fingers showed a white strip where another ring might have been worn. And then she realized something else. Marty wasn't smoking. There wasn't even a hint of cigarette smoke in the air. He hadn't taken the habit up again.

"It wasn't you," Joanna gasped, staring into Marty's flat, lifeless eyes. "But then if it wasn't you, why are you—" And then she stopped. She'd had it figured all wrong. But now she understood. Finally she saw it all too clearly. Marty was right. His greatest crime was that he'd loved too well. And far too foolishly.

"Eric, I was wrong this whole time," Joanna muttered. "Marty wasn't the man who kidnapped me. I don't know who it was, but it definitely wasn't Marty. My captor wore a raised ring. And he smoked, remember?"

Eric scowled and then he stared hard at Marty. "Then why are you doing this."

"Don't you see," Joanna said. "He's been covering for Linda. Linda and..." She stopped, her eyes shifting from Eric to Marty. "Linda and who, Marty?"

Marty merely smiled, first at her and then at Eric.

"Make it easier on yourself, Marty. And on Linda, too," Eric added, hoping that would sway Matthias.

"I intend to make it easy on us all," Marty murmured.

The color drained from Joanna's face as she watched Matthias release the safety on the gun. Eric was watching Marty closely, too. He spotted a shadow of indecision pass across the administrator's face, as if he couldn't make up his mind which of them to shoot first. Eric knew he had to take full advantage of that moment. It might be his last. Or Joanna's.

Marty made up his mind quickly. As Joanna gasped in horror, she watched Matthias smile benignly and then turn the barrel of the gun, pointing it at his own head.

Eric had already leaped from his chair and was launching himself across the desk, ready to risk that first bullet, as Marty turned the gun on himself. Eric reached out and grabbed Marty's gun hand just as the shot went off. There

was a sharp cry and a choked gurgle as Marty's chair toppled backward sending both men tumbling into a tangled
heap on the floor.

Joanna raced around the desk. It was impossible to tell
which of them had been struck by the bullet. Then she saw
Eric wrestle the gun from Marty's hand. Marty didn't put
up much of a struggle. Half-dazed, he lay on the floor and
started to cry.

"Are you okay?" Joanna asked Eric anxiously.

"We're both okay," Eric said with relief.

His relief, however, was short-lived. As he rose from the
floor, he saw a figure standing just inside the doorway of the
den. His hand tightened on the gun he'd taken from Marty.
He realized now that when Marty had looked so unsure of
whom to shoot a moment ago, he and Joanna weren't really
in the contest. Marty had had two ways of ending it. He
could kill the woman who'd destroyed his life, or he could
kill himself. Given what Marty'd already done in the name
of love, Eric wasn't surprised at the choice Marty had made.
It had almost worked.

"Put the gun down on the desk, Eric." The order came
from a soft, feminine voice.

Joanna, unaware that more company had arrived until
she heard the woman's voice, spun around to face the
doorway. She wasn't surprised to see Linda Matthias
standing there, gun in hand. The hand holding the gun was
rock steady. Joanna had no doubt it was just the way she'd
held it when she'd shot Hank Morgan in the back.

For all her fear, Joanna couldn't help thinking of the
irony of it all. Here she'd spent all this time patting herself
on the back for playing her role so well, and the whole time
Linda Matthias had been acting rings around her, playing
her own part brilliantly. But Linda was through playing.
Gone was any sign of the meek, submissive young wife

struggling to assert herself. The real Linda Matthias had no trouble being assertive.

Eric was still holding Marty's gun. Linda smiled seductively at him as she spoke. "Don't do anything foolish, Eric," she said pleasantly.

With a resigned grimace, he set the gun down on the desk. Marty was still sobbing quietly on the floor. Linda didn't seem particularly concerned about her husband. She urged Eric to move around to where Joanna was standing.

"You both thought you were so clever." Linda smiled disarmingly. "Well, you did have us going there for a while, I have to admit. Twins. We missed uncovering that angle. It was a good ploy while it lasted. But now it's time for the real Jennifer Hampleman to please come forward."

"Who's *we* Linda? Who's your accomplice?" Joanna demanded.

Linda merely arched a brow. "It really won't help you to know."

Eric saw the color bleed from Joanna's face. She knew as well as he that Linda intended to finish them off. He didn't intend to make it easy.

"Come on, Linda. What do you have to lose by telling us who's pulling the strings?"

Linda gave him a dark glare. "What makes you think I'm not the one pulling them?"

For all her fear, Joanna managed a wry smile. "I'm sure you're clever enough to pull the strings. You've managed quite nicely with Marty."

"And despite it all," Eric sneered, "the poor bastard was still willing to die for you."

Linda's blue eyes took on a harsh glint, her nostrils flared, her mouth became a cruel line. "We all have to die sometime."

By this point Marty had stopped sobbing, and he'd dragged himself up into a chair beside the desk. He looked soulfully at his wife, but her expression held nothing but contempt and disgust as she met his gaze briefly before focusing back on Joanna.

"Marty could never begin to give me what I want. Do either of you really think I'd settle for that driveling, insipid buffoon?"

"So," Joanna persisted, "who did you settle for?"

But Linda didn't seem to hear her. "I was destined for great things. I've been in training for this moment for over fifteen years."

Eric nodded. "Yes, a lost, angry child, abused and abandoned, just like she told you, Joanna. That's how those bastards work. They find kids like Linda, brainwash them, indoctrinate them, turn them into willing pawns."

A chilly smile cracked the cruel line of Linda's lips. "I was being passed around from one lousy foster home to another, until I finally found a place I could call my own and a man I could truly respect."

Joanna laughed dryly. "And I suppose you think he respects you."

"What's that supposed to mean?" Linda asked hotly.

Joanna caught Eric's nervous glance in her direction, but she was determined to try to get Linda agitated. "He sees you as a pawn, just like Eric said. He called you worse than that. He called you a—"

"Shut up. I know what you're trying to do," Linda hissed.

"You must have hated being saddled with Marty, letting him have all the say," Eric mused ruefully. Maybe if they kept it up, even if Linda knew he and Joanna were trying to upset her, they could still manage to throw her off guard.

"I didn't play the poor, put-upon little mouse all the time. Marty might have seemed to be ruling the roost, as it were, but that was only because it was exactly what I wanted him to do. And when that wasn't what I wanted, he was really quite amenable to my...whims. Men." Linda laughed derisively. "I must admit, when I was first given Marty as my assignment, I wasn't very pleased. I detested him. Besides being a pompous, self-righteous bore—physically, Marty reminded me a lot of my father. Needless to say, dear old dad was never very dear to my heart. At first I balked at the order to seduce Marty and get him to marry me. I wanted no part of the man. But, orders are orders. Besides, I've quite enjoyed setting him up as the villain of the piece and watching him fall apart."

"What did he ever do wrong but love you?" Joanna's voice was filled with disgust. "He was so desperate to hold on to you, he was even willing to cover up for you when he realized what you were up to. And he let us believe he and Gerta were the villains."

Linda laughed, a sneering giggle from the back of her throat. "Gerta was forever cornering Marty to talk about Jen and her cold fusion work. If it weren't for Gerta's indiscreet little sessions with Marty, that I overheard, I would never have realized that Jen's project really stood a good chance of succeeding. Gerta started the whole ball rolling."

"It looks like the ball's rolled right up a dead-end street, Linda," Eric said cynically.

"Oh, it will be a dead end for you and your girlfriend, Logan, if you don't produce Hampleman."

"I have no idea where she is."

"He's telling you the truth," Joanna insisted.

"I'm through being patient," Linda said, her expression darkening. "No more stunts."

"You mean like the one you pulled in the sauna," Joanna countered, playing for time. "That was very clever of you, Linda. You pretend you're trapped with me and meanwhile your pal locks the door. I pass out and he whisks me off, and you look like little miss innocent."

Linda glared at Marty who had now dropped his head into his hands. "It would have worked, too. Marty guessed that I was up to something. Of course, he knew what I was after at that point, and he said he wouldn't interfere as long as no one got hurt." Her laugh was sour. "Not very trusting of you, Marty, to come running over to the clubhouse to check up on me."

He looked up for a moment, but his expression was blank. He might as well have shot himself with that gun for all the life left in him now.

"So Marty and I beat your pal to the punch," Eric reflected.

"And so did Hank Morgan," Joanna added somberly.

Linda shrugged. "Hank told Marty the door and the thermostat had been tampered with, and Marty lied about it to protect me."

"So you killed Hank and set Toni up to take the blame," Eric said. "That must be some terrific friend you've got, Linda. He lets you do all the dirty work."

"We share the responsibility. He was the one who had to baby-sit Joanna here while I was working on dear Marty, ensuring his continued cooperation."

"Maybe your friend didn't find baby-sitting Joanna dirty work," Eric said blithely.

Joanna gave Eric a shocked look, but a moment later she realized he was still trying, as she had been, to get Linda worked up. Maybe then she'd get sloppy with her gun and one of them would be able to make a move on her.

Linda almost bit, but then she pulled herself together. She grinned. "Nice try, Logan. But you keep underestimating me." She focused on her husband, who was slumped in his chair. "Snap out of it, darling. Our friends here aren't cooperating. We're going to have to make them see that we mean business."

"Marty's not going to be much help to you in the condition he's in. Where's your good pal when you need him, Linda?" Joanna taunted, following Eric's lead. "Or should I call him your sugar daddy?"

"Shut up, you little bitch," Linda hissed. Then she glared at Eric. "If you don't tell me where to find Jennifer Hampleman, *darling*, I'm afraid your little girlfriend here is going to have to pay the price for your patriotism."

"I don't know where she is," Eric said in a low voice.

Linda's mouth twitched. "If that's true, Eric, than there really is no reason to detain either of you any longer. I'll have to find some other way of finding our missing Dr. Hampleman."

For one fleeting moment, Joanna let herself believe that Linda might actually let them go. But, of course, she couldn't do that. That left only one possibility.

Linda was smiling coyly at her husband. "I've got one last favor to ask you, Marty. I want you to pick up your gun again and shoot these two...intruders."

Marty looked at his wife with a dazed expression.

"You aren't going to let me down after all we've been through?" she murmured.

"Sure, Marty, she wants the murders on your hands. You'll be the one who fries," Eric pointed out. "Don't be a fool. Don't do her dirty work."

"Marty," Linda said sharply.

"No...Linda. No more." Marty's voice was barely audible.

"Don't snivel, Marty. It's so unattractive. How often must I tell you that?"

"I can't...go on with this...any longer," he cried, kneading his hands together in futile anguish.

"But, darling, you have to go on with it. To the bitter end. You're finished here, Marty. You've aided and abetted in murder, kidnapping, treason. Really, darling, what's one more—or two more—little crimes?'' Plainly, she was enjoying his misery and her own mastery. This was her golden moment, and she intended to bask fully in it.

"She's just going to leave you to take the fall, Marty," Eric repeated.

"Hasn't she done enough to you already, Marty?" Joanna added in a low, sympathetic voice.

"Shut up," Linda warned them. "Damn it, Marty, pick up the gun and shoot them. Now."

Joanna thought all was lost when she saw Marty lift the gun from the desk. Eric stepped protectively in front of her, his gaze meeting Marty's. "Don't do it."

Linda kept her gun trained on Joanna and Eric just in case Marty got cold feet in the end. She smiled darkly as she saw him cock the trigger. Almost too late, she realized it wasn't Joanna or Eric he intended to shoot.

Linda just barely managed to dodge the bullet Marty had aimed at her. She ducked behind an arm chair. Foregoing her planned targets, she aimed at Marty, firing back.

The moment Linda started shooting at Marty, Eric shoved Joanna to the ground and took a flying leap toward Linda. Her attention focused on Marty, Linda never saw Eric coming. Joanna, who'd scrambled quickly to her feet, was right on Eric's heels, both of them managing to wrestle Linda to the ground and get the gun away from her.

It wasn't until they'd subdued her, that Joanna and Eric realized Marty had been shot. Blood was oozing from his chest as he sat in his desk chair. He held himself rigid for a moment, then his hand opened and the gun clanked back onto the desk.

Joanna hurried over to Marty. His eyes fluttered open. "I'm . . . sorry," he said weakly and then slumped forward. Joanna quickly felt for a pulse. It was faint, but it was there. She picked up the phone. But as she started to dial the number for security, Eric reminded her, "You'd better call the local police and have them bring along an ambulance. We can't be sure who we can trust on the inside.''

As Joanna phoned for help, Eric dragged Linda into the arm chair and trained the gun on her. ''It's time to come clean, Linda. Maybe it'll go a little easier on you if you cooperate. Who are you working with?''

Linda glared at him defiantly, saying nothing.

Joanna, who was trying to tend to Marty as best she could till help arrived, looked over at Linda. ''We know he smokes. We know he wears some kind of a ring with a raised setting.''

''We'll track him down, Linda,'' Eric said vehemently. ''With or without your help. Why not come clean and save your own neck?''

But Joanna knew why not. Linda Matthias was in love. And, as Joanna knew, a woman in love would take all kinds of crazy risks.

JOANNA AND ERIC were sitting in a coffee shop on Main Street in Los Verdes after handing Linda over into police custody.

''I can't really blame Linda for keeping mum,'' Eric commented. ''The KGB wouldn't take kindly to her revealing the identity of her control.''

''It isn't that,'' Joanna said thoughtfully. ''I think she's protecting him because he's the only man she's ever loved. He took her in, treated her kindly, remained loyal to her through all these years. After all the physical and emotional abuse she'd suffered, it's no wonder she's trying to save him.''

''You sound like you feel sorry for her,'' Eric mused.

''Well, I guess I do identify a little with her,'' Joanna admitted. ''When I was growing up I always longed for my father to make me feel . . . treasured. I was very lonely. I fought it by learning to be tough and self-reliant. Linda led me to believe her abuse had made her weak and submissive. But, really, it made her very tough, too."

"She certainly fooled us. And if she doesn't crack under questioning, we've still got a very resourceful mole on the loose."

"I could try to talk with her again."

"No," Eric said, throwing some bills on the table. "It's really just a matter of time. And we've got to get back to Synergy and pick up your things over at Jen's. You've got a plane waiting to take you off to New York."

When they got to his car, Eric put the key in the ignition, but didn't turn it. Instead, he looked over at Joanna.

"It isn't over yet," he said softly.

"I wish I could stay to help finish it."

"That isn't what I meant. It isn't over between us."

"Eric—"

He pressed his finger to her lips. Then he turned the key in the ignition, flicked on the air conditioning and pulled out.

Lou gave them a friendly wave when Eric's car approached the Synergy gate. Eric rolled down his window and Lou bent low, resting his beefy hands on the door, to do the required ID check.

"Some goings-on. How's Mr. Matthias doing?" Lou asked.

"Hanging in," Eric said, flicking his ID closed.

"Dr. Hauser just left. She said word is out Synergy's gonna close down." Lou bent a little lower to get a better view of Joanna. "What'll the two of you do?"

Eric shrugged. "Right now we're going to pack a few things and have ourselves a few days in the sun."

"Lucky folks. Where to?"

Eric looked over at Joanna and winked. "The first romantic hideaway we come to, right, darling?" His eyes narrowed. Joanna's face looked white as a sheet. It was all finally hitting her, he thought. He gave her a sympathetic smile. But Joanna didn't even seem to see it, much less be comforted by it.

Eric wasn't the only one to notice Joanna's pallor.

"Are you okay, Dr. Hampleman?" Lou asked.

"Jen?" Eric's voice held sharp concern.

"What? Yes . . . fine." She managed a crooked smile, but her heart was beating overtime. She'd just fit the last piece of the puzzle together.

"What was that all about?" Eric asked as he drove out past the gate.

"Stop the car, Eric."

"What?"

"Didn't you see it?"

"What?"

"The ring. The ring on Lou's finger. And, when he bent down by the car, I could smell the cigarette smoke on his breath. I've even seen him with a cigarette before. It just never dawned on me . . ." She gripped Eric's sleeve. "Of course. It all makes sense now. Lou's the one who told us that he'd seen Gerta with a KGB man, remember."

Eric frowned as he turned the bend and pulled the car to the side of the road. "Yes, but my people never found anyone."

"Lou was setting Gerta up. And Linda's job was to get us to suspect that Marty was Gerta's partner in crime. I wouldn't be surprised if Lou really *had* wormed his way into the CIA as a clerk years back.

"Not a clerk. A mole," Eric corrected. He nodded in agreement.

"If you dig into his past, I bet you'll discover he took in foster kids, and Linda was one of them."

Joanna saw it all so clearly now. "The day I took off after you, it was Lou who sent me down the coast road. And then he came after me five minutes later and kidnapped me. Lou and Linda. While you were sent off to search for her at the spa, she was riding shotgun for her foster father in the getaway car. And that explains the phony Southern accent Lou used. He knew that as long as I couldn't recognize his voice I'd jump to the conclusion that he was Marty. As long as I couldn't identify him, he could go on with the pose of jovial security guard until he got at Jen. Eric, don't you see..."

He put his hand over hers and smiled. "Beauty *and* brains. Is it any wonder I've fallen head over heels in love with you?"

"What do we do now?"

"Kiss?"

"Eric, be serious."

"Okay, okay," he said, reaching for the gun hidden in his waistband. "You walk back and tell Lou I'm having some car trouble. Ask him to come over and see if he can help me figure out what's wrong."

Joanna's eyes brightened. "Good plan."

"Joanna," he called to her, as she started off. "Once he gets close to the car, you back off. No more heroics."

Joanna grinned. "Who, me?"

A couple of moments later a cheerful Lou was ambling over to the car. To Eric's consternation, but not to his surprise, he saw Joanna coming up right behind Lou.

As Lou approached Eric, who was standing by the open hood of the car, Joanna stooped down and picked up a large rock. Just to be on the safe side, in case Lou made a fast move for Eric's gun.

"What seems to be the trouble, doc?" Lou asked, bending over the hood.

"That's trouble with a capital T, Lou," Eric said, sticking his gun into Lou's back.

Joanna held onto her rock until the police arrived to pick Lou up.

AN OPAL RING in a fourteen-carat-gold setting and a heavy smoking habit weren't exactly enough evidence to convict Lou Burton. But they did help start the ball rolling, and the investigation picked up momentum along the way.

Lou himself provided the final bounce. When he realized things weren't looking good, he tried to cut a deal with the government, offering to testify against Linda in exchange for a ticket to the Soviet Union. The FBI agent played Linda the tape. And then he started recording. Once she started talking, there was no stopping her.

# Chapter Seventeen

The doorbell rang. Joanna nervously flicked some imaginary dust off the crystal swan which was in its proper spot, smack dab in the center of her hallway table, and then she went to open the door.

"Hi," Jen said softly.

"Hi."

"I see you've gone back to being a blonde again."

Joanna smiled, her hand absently smoothing back her hair. "And you've gone back to being a brunette."

Jen stepped inside. Almost immediately she noticed the glass swan. She gave a small laugh. "I have one that's very similar." She laughed again. "But you must already know that."

Joanna could feel her heart racing. "Yes."

Jen walked into the living room, studying the space with more than casual curiosity.

Joanna came up behind her. "Congratulations, Jen. I've been reading articles about you all week. Everyone says your breakthrough will win you a Nobel Prize."

Jen didn't seem to hear her. "It took me a while," she said softly.

"But you succeeded where no one else could. That's what counts."

Jen turned slowly around to face Joanna. "I mean about us. When Eric showed me that layout of you, I had such a strange feeling. I think I knew then, but I couldn't believe it."

Jen stepped a little closer, as if to get a better look at her newfound twin. "I've always wanted a sister. I remember when my folks told me they were adopting my brother I asked if they couldn't exchange him for a sister." She laughed. "I love him, of course. But a sister...a twin sister...that's something very special." Her warm, lovely gray eyes glistened with tears. "It's much better than a Nobel Prize."

"Oh Jen..."

Joanna rushed over to her twin and threw her arms around her, holding her close. They both cried and laughed and cried some more.

"I'm so happy we found each other, Joanna," Jen said after all their tears had dried.

"Let's try to spend a whole long stretch of time together when I get back from Paris," Joanna said.

Jen tilted her head. "Are you still going?"

"Yes. Why wouldn't I?"

"What about Eric?"

"Eric?" Joanna's throat went suddenly dry and his name came off her lips in a raspy sound.

Jen smiled. "I thought maybe the two of you—"

"No," Joanna said more sharply than she intended. "There's...nothing between me and Eric."

Jen's smile turned rueful. "I am your twin, Joanna. You look just like me when I'm lying."

Joanna felt her cheeks redden. "You love him, too," she blurted out.

Jen laughed. "I do love Eric. And once upon a time I was quite infatuated with him. It was a first for me. Usually my heart only quickens when I prove a theorem."

"Listen to me, Jen. I'd never do anything to hurt you. I'd never..."

"Eric isn't in love with me, Joanna."

"All the more reason..."

"And I'm not in love with him."

"But you said...you said you loved him, that you were infatuated..."

"Infatuation wears off. Mine wore off months ago. And as for love, there's a difference between loving someone...the way you would a friend, or a *sister*...and being in love with a man you want to spend the rest of your life with in passionate bliss."

"Jen, if you're just saying this because—"

"Because you're my twin sister, and I love you. And I want you to be happy."

"I want you to be happy, too."

"Joanna, I've got everything I want in my life—a strong, supportive family, my very own twin sister, a chance to put into operation all that I've worked these long months for, and maybe even a Nobel Prize down the pike. I am happy and fulfilled. Now, you tell me. Without Eric can you say the same?"

They stared at each other in silence for several moments. Finally Joanna's lips curved into a smile. "Finding you has made my life almost perfect. With Eric...my life will be...complete."

Jen hugged her close. "Now that you've confessed to your twin sister, how about confessing the truth to the man himself. The poor guy's probably worn out the carpet in the hallway by now."

"Eric came with you? He's...here?"

Jen laughed. "Go open the door."

Joanna flew to the door. Eric was leaning against the wall just across from her apartment.

His face broke into a sheepish grin. "Hello again."

"Hello."

"How's your twin doing?"

"Great."

"How about you?"

Her beautiful gray eyes sparkled. "I will be great. In another moment."

They met each other halfway across the small space of the hallway.

"This is the moment I've been waiting for," he whispered against her neck as they held each other close.

After a long, lingering kiss, Eric drew back. "I brought your passport."

"Does that mean I've been cleared of suspicion of diamond smuggling?"

He grinned. "Will you ever forgive me for that?"

"Yes," she said in a low, throaty voice, "but you'll have to work at it."

"I brought my passport along, too. And an extra ticket for Paris."

Joanna's arms wound around his neck. "That'll do for starters."

Eric kissed her tenderly. "They say Paris is a great place for honeymoons."

"They do?"

"The line is 'I do.' "

"He's right, Joanna."

She spun around to see her twin sister standing at the open door of the apartment. Joanna smiled shyly. "What do you think, sis? Should I marry him?"

Jen laughed softly and winked. "Well, I would...if *I* were *you*, that is."

**In December,
let Harlequin warm your heart with the
AWARD OF EXCELLENCE title**

*Harlequin Presents...*

# PENNY JORDAN

*AWARD OF EXCELLENCE*

# a rekindled passion

Over twenty years ago, Kate had a holiday
affair with Joss Bennett and found herself
pregnant as a result. Believing that Joss had
abandoned her to return to his wife and child,
Kate had her daughter and made no attempt
to track Joss down.

At her daughter's wedding, Kate suddenly
confronts the past in the shape of the
bridegroom's distant relative—Joss. He quickly
realises that Sophy must be his daughter and
wonders why Kate never contacted him.

Can love be rekindled after twenty years?
Be sure not to miss this AWARD OF EXCELLENCE
title, available wherever Harlequin books
are sold.

HP-KIND-1

# Take 4 bestselling love stories FREE

## Plus get a FREE surprise gift!

# PASSPORT TO ROMANCE
# SWEEPSTAKES RULES

1. **HOW TO ENTER:** To enter, you must be the age of majority and complete the official entry form, or print your name, address, telephone number and age on a plain piece of paper and mail to: Passport to Romance, P.O. Box 9056, Buffalo, NY 14269-9056. No mechanically reproduced entries accepted.

2. All entries must be received by the CONTEST CLOSING DATE, DECEMBER 31, 1990 TO BE ELIGIBLE.

3. **THE PRIZES:** There will be ten (10) Grand Prizes awarded, each consisting of a choice of a trip for two people from the following list:
   i)   London, England (approximate retail value $5,050 U.S.)
   ii)  England, Wales and Scotland (approximate retail value $6,400 U.S.)
   iii) Carribean Cruise (approximate retail value $7,300 U.S.)
   iv)  Hawaii (approximate retail value $9,550 U.S.)
   v)   Greek Island Cruise in the Mediterranean (approximate retail value $12,250 U.S.)
   vi)  France (approximate retail value $7,300 U.S.)

4. Any winner may choose to receive any trip or a cash alternative prize of $5,000.00 U.S. in lieu of the trip.

5. **GENERAL RULES:** Odds of winning depend on number of entries received.

6. A random draw will be made by Nielsen Promotion Services, an independent judging organization, on January 29, 1991, in Buffalo, NY, at 11:30 a.m. from all eligible entries received on or before the Contest Closing Date.

7. Any Canadian entrants who are selected must correctly answer a time-limited, mathematical skill-testing question in order to win.

8. Full contest rules may be obtained by sending a stamped, self-addressed envelope to: "Passport to Romance Rules Request", P.O. Box 9998, Saint John, New Brunswick, Canada E2L 4N4.

9. Quebec residents may submit any litigation respecting the conduct and awarding of a prize in this contest to the Régie des loteries et courses du Québec.

10. Payment of taxes other than air and hotel taxes is the sole responsibility of the winner.

11. Void where prohibited by law.

## COUPON BOOKLET OFFER TERMS

To receive your Free travel-savings coupon booklets, complete the mail-in Offer Certificate on the preceeding page, including the necessary number of proofs-of-purchase, and mail to: Passport to Romance, P.O. Box 9057, Buffalo, NY 14269-9057. The coupon booklets include savings on travel-related products such as car rentals, hotels, cruises, flowers and restaurants. Some restrictions apply. The offer is available in the United States and Canada. Requests must be postmarked by January 25, 1991. Only proofs-of-purchase from specially marked "Passport to Romance" Harlequin® or Silhouette® books will be accepted. The offer certificate must accompany your request and may not be reproduced in any manner. Offer void where prohibited or restricted by law. LIMIT FOUR COUPON BOOKLETS PER NAME, FAMILY, GROUP, ORGANIZATION OR ADDRESS. Please allow up to 8 weeks after receipt of order for shipment. Enter quickly as quantities are limited. Unfulfilled mail-in offer requests will receive free Harlequin® or Silhouette® books (not previously available in retail stores), in quantities equal to the number of proofs-of-purchase required for Levels One to Four, as applicable.

# OFFICIAL SWEEPSTAKES
# ENTRY FORM

Complete and return this Entry Form immediately—the more Entry Forms you submit, the better your chances of winning!
• Entry Forms must be received by **December 31, 1990**
• A random draw will take place on **January 29, 1991**
• Trip must be taken by **December 31, 1991**

3-HI-3-SW

YES, I want to win a PASSPORT TO ROMANCE vacation for two! I understand the prize includes round-trip air fare, accommodation and a daily spending allowance.

Name_____

Address_____

City_____ State_____ Zip_____

Telephone Number_____ Age_____

Return entries to: **PASSPORT TO ROMANCE**, P.O. Box 9056, Buffalo, NY 14269-9056

© 1990 Harlequin Enterprises Limited

# COUPON BOOKLET/OFFER CERTIFICATE

| Item | LEVEL ONE Booklet 1 | LEVEL TWO Booklet 1 & 2 | LEVEL THREE Booklet 1, 2 & 3 | LEVEL FOUR Booklet 1, 2, 3 & 4 |
|---|---|---|---|---|
| Booklet 1 = $100+ | $100+ | $100+ | $100+ | $100+ |
| Booklet 2 = $200+ | | $200+ | $200+ | $200+ |
| Booklet 3 = $300+ | | | $300+ | $300+ |
| Booklet 4 = $400+ | ____ | ____ | ____ | $400+ |
| Approximate Total Value of Savings | $100+ | $300+ | $600+ | $1,000+ |
| # of Proofs of Purchase Required | 4 | 6 | 12 | 18 |
| Check One | ____ | ____ | ____ | ____ |

Name_____

Address_____

City_____ State_____ Zip_____

Return Offer Certificates to: **PASSPORT TO ROMANCE**, P.O. Box 9057, Buffalo, NY 14269-9057

Requests must be postmarked by **January 25, 1991**

- - - - - - - - - - - - - - - - - - - - - - - - - - - - - - ✂ - - -

# ONE PROOF OF PURCHASE

3-HI-3

To collect your free coupon booklet you must include the necessary number of proofs-of-purchase with a properly completed Offer Certificate

© 1990 Harlequin Enterprises Limited

See previous page for details